The

Wedding

Diaries

The
Wedding
Diaries

LINDA FRANCIS LEE

IVY BOOKS • NEW YORK

An Ivy Book
Published by The Random House Publishing Group
Copyright © 2003 by Linda Francis Lee

ISBN 0-7394-3747-X

Manufactured in the United States of America

Acknowledgments

I would like to express my deepest appreciation to my parents, Marilyn and Larry Francis, because they are nothing like Vivi's parents. To my brothers and sister, Rick Francis, Brian Francis and Carilyn Francis Johnson, because I know they would circle the wagons in a heartbeat. To good friends Gloria Dale Skinner and Michele Jaffe for champagne, lunches, and reading everything I sent their way. And of course to the real MBL, who easily could have run in the opposite direction but proposed instead.

My Wedding Diary

THE ORGANIZED BRIDE

My mother says I'm obsessed with being a bride.

Of course she mentioned this in a postcard from India, where she is determined to "find" herself. Had she been here in Texas, she might have seen that what I am actually obsessed with is lists.

I've tried to break the habit. Tried to be freer, to be more spontaneous, to learn to flip my hair over my shoulder like models in shampoo ads.

In fact, being so predictable is high on my list of **Things to Stop Doing** right after Stop Eating Lemon Meringue Pie for Breakfast.

But I rationalize that lists keep me organized and lemon is a fruit. Besides, who can blame me now that I have a wedding to plan?

And my desire to get married?

Based on my parents' marriage or subsequent divorce, tying the knot rightfully should be number one on my list of **Things Not to Do**. But even my parents' very unattractive situation is not outweighed by the dream I've had since I was ten years old . . . of finding a man whose world would stop when he turned around and saw me.

Chapter One

She saw him the minute she walked in the door.

He was beautiful, with dark hair, blue eyes, and chis-eled features. Combined with those amazing looks, there was a raw sensuality rippling through his broad shoulders beneath his starched, white, button-down shirt.

He stood behind his desk, talking into the phone. He had a commanding presence that was at once primal and ruthless. It was a well-known fact that Maxwell Bowden Landry of MBL Holdings went after what he wanted and got it.

Vivienne Stansfield shook the thought away, her long, black-lacquer hair trailing down her back. Her eyes were hidden behind dark glasses, her rosebud lips painted a provocative shade of pink that matched her perfectly manicured nails.

Her skirt was short, her heels were high, her legs long. All in all, she was a beauty with a movie-star shimmer, and anyone seeing her would have sworn she knew it.

As if sensing she was there, he turned and saw her through the office window. His entire body seemed to go still, his eyes darkening. He looked at her with a single-minded intensity that made sensation spin through her,

her breath growing uncomfortably shallow, heat flaring, settling low. He looked at her with something deeper than simple recognition, as if he knew her.

For half a second her world seemed to slow as she tried to remember a previous meeting. But then his face cleared, and he gestured for her to enter, though he was still on the phone.

Regardless, he wasn't the reason she had come to MBL Holdings. The company was one of the largest conglomerates in Texas, handling land development, construction, and real estate. MBL was said to have a lock on any real estate transaction in the Lone Star state. And Vivienne needed a house.

She already knew what she wanted. Despite what everyone assumed she would buy, she was looking for something small, quaint—something that needed fixing up.

She struggled to keep her excitement covered by the reserved facade the newspapers wrote about. Her father would expect nothing less. Though it was all well and good for Jennings Stansfield to act however he wanted, Vivienne Stansfield was expected to be a perfect china doll.

Most of the time she managed to keep the crystalline veneer in place. But sometimes it was hard. If she wasn't concentrating, she laughed too loud, smiled too much. Once she'd been caught doing the Wave at a UTEP basketball game, even though she'd been sitting alone in her father's private box. It had looked like fun—like a fascinating taste of normal.

An assistant led her across the carpeted expanse, phones ringing, people talking, several men stopping what they were doing to stare.

"Is that Vivienne Stansfield?" she heard someone whisper.

Vivienne raised her chin, her expression composed, praying she wouldn't trip on her high heels.

She made it into Max Landry's office, her fuchsia handbag swinging delicately on her wrist, and instantly she knew coming there was a mistake. If she thought he had presence when she saw him across the busy office, when he was only a few feet away she could all but feel the barely contained energy of him charging the room. He exuded power, untamed despite the civilized surroundings of exquisite paintings and fine leather chairs, making her heart beat hard and her knees fuse in a way that she didn't understand.

But that didn't stop her from sitting down and fighting back a blush when she noticed the way he studied her as he listened to what someone was saying to him on the phone. He seemed to strip her naked with his gaze, taking her in. She had the sudden, unexpected image of him in bed, the sheets barely covering his naked hips, as he moved slowly, deeply, his weight supported on his forearms as he watched a woman's passion.

He hung up, bringing her completely inappropriate imaginings to an end. Then he came around the desk and leaned back against the hard edge.

"Miss Stansfield?" A moment of hesitation as if he were testing.

She looked at him curiously. "Have we met?"

He appeared to consider his answer. "No, we've never met. I'm Max Landry."

She shook his hand, feeling the heat of him when his large palm closed around hers. She was sure he was correct. There was no way she would have forgotten this man. "Please, call me Vivi."

Anyone who knew her called her Vivi, though the Living Section of the *El Paso Tribune* seemed set on, "Vivienne Stansfield, the twenty-six-year-old pampered princess of one of the oldest, and more eccentric, families in town."

That was from the newspaper that actually liked her. The rival gossip-filled rag that didn't had called her an "overgroomed show dog who had more shoes than Imelda Marcos."

Vivi fought back a cringe when she remembered. She really did love her shoes.

She glanced at Max, his arms crossed over his chest, the seams of his handmade shirt showing a hint of strain at the broadness of his shoulders, and she wondered if he had read the articles. But then she reminded herself that it was easier to act as if she didn't care.

Besides that, regardless of what people thought of her or her father, she loved Jennings Stansfield. And truth be told, he *was* a bit on the eccentric side. When he played golf, he wore a large-brimmed Stetson like some holdover from the days of *Dallas*, only he mixed it with lime green and bright orange polyester plaid pants, not to mention his personalized golf cart with the longhorn cattle horns attached to the front. No one who met Jennings Stansfield forgot him. He didn't do anything in an ordinary, low-key fashion. If he had a point to make, he made it with grand, larger than life gestures.

Beyond that, Vivi also loved being the fiancé of Grady Pence—steady, kind, perfectly normal Grady with his sandy blond hair and sweet smile. She had no business noticing the notorious Max Landry and his straining shirt seams when she was already engaged to the dearest man in town.

"I'm sorry that Racine didn't get in touch to let you know she couldn't make the appointment. As I understand it, her daughter became ill at school," Max explained. "But she should have called."

He looked at her a second longer, that curious expression resurfacing, laced with an indefinable hardness that she doubted ever completely disappeared. He leaned back and glanced at his schedule that lay open on his desk. Then he stood.

"As long as you're here, I can run you over to see the house now," he offered.

"Me? I mean, you? To see the house?" She coughed delicately into her hand, her ice queen facade trying to melt beneath the idea of going anywhere with him.

"It won't take long."

She told herself to say no. She was engaged to be married. Happily taken. Unavailable.

"I'd like that," she said instead, a tiny sighing breath escaping her lips.

Max called out to his assistant. "Hattie, get me the keys for the Reynolds place."

The woman looked confused. "But you have the staff conference call at three."

"Reschedule. I should be back in an hour."

Vivi felt as surprised as Hattie looked that Maxwell Landry was taking her to see the house. Deep down, she knew it was because her father was too important a man to upset. As a result, MBL himself was showing her the property after one of his salespeople had stood her up. Simple enough. It had nothing to do with her, or the way he had looked when he saw her through the glass.

He pulled on a sports jacket, then guided Vivi down the mirrored and marble elevator to a private parking lot at the back of the building and a sleek black Mercedes sedan. She tried to ignore the feel of his palm resting lightly on the curve of her back, tried to pretend she wasn't aware of him at all.

With a minimum of ceremony, he helped her into the car, then pulled out onto Mesa Street, racing along with one hand on the wheel as he took two phone calls, giving crisp orders as they turned left then right, then left again. Every trace of awareness evaporated as Vivi gave a quick test to her seat belt just when they started to climb the narrow roads that cut along the mountain.

Flipping the cell phone closed, he pulled the car over to the side with smooth efficiency. Max leaned forward and pointed. "Up there," he said. "That's it."

"What?"

Vivi had to crane her neck, but even then all she could see was a centuries-old stone weather station.

Max shrugged. "I know, it's hard to imagine, but they turned it into a house."

"You're kidding."

He glanced over at her with still no hint of a smile, only a dark sensuality that burned through her like the West Texas sun.

"Do I look like the type who'd kid, Vivienne?"

This time she studied him, his use of her full name seeming as intimate as a touch. "I'm not sure what to think, about you or the house," she replied honestly. "But I am sure that my idea of the perfect home isn't a weather tower."

She would have sworn she saw a hint of a smile somewhere deep inside his exacting exterior, like something tightly held had eased just a fraction.

"Come on," he said, his eyes seeming to glimmer, "where's your sense of adventure?"

"I'm saving it up for the drive back." She wrinkled her nose. "I'm more of the turn signal and hands at ten and two type when I drive."

With that he did smile. It was amazing, and did strange things to her pulse.

"Just have a look," he urged. "Then I promise to return you to the office in one piece."

The words came out as a rumbling purr that raced along her senses. When she didn't say no, he shifted into gear, the car sliding back onto the road.

They climbed higher up the winding lane into the startling blue sky, then parked at the curb. She could feel his hand again as he guided her up the walkway to the house, then pushed through a beautifully aged oak-plank front door. Stepping into a Spanish tile foyer, she could see straight through the living room to glass windows that seemed hammered into the thick stone walls. The city spilled out below.

"It's . . ." She hardly knew what to say.

"Different?"

"Yes. But in a powerful way."

"I know," he said with a quiet assurance. "We just got the listing."

She cocked her head. "I'm surprised you show real estate."

"I don't. I haven't shown property in years." He shoved his hands in his pockets, making him look boyish despite the hard line of his jaw.

Somehow standing near this man with his powerful

sensuality made reality fade away, unsettling her, though she didn't feel unsafe.

"Come on," he said, "I'll show you around."

She followed him, her high heels clicking against the tile and wood floors. He showed her the kitchen, gesturing toward the stove, then pulling open the refrigerator, even popping open the trash compactor.

Her facade cracked a bit more, enough that she laughed out loud. "If MBL Holdings goes down the drain, you could get a job on *The Price Is Right*."

He raised a dark brow, his lips crooking at one corner. "I'll leave game shows to Hollywood."

"Who would have guessed that the infamous Max Landry wasn't interested in the spotlight?"

"Me, infamous?"

"Aren't you?"

"Not that I know of."

"Then you should start reading the newspapers. You get written up nearly as often as I do."

He studied her without responding. She felt hot and cold all at once. Feeling awkward and in over her head, she walked to the pantry. Too late she realized she had to step in front of him to get there. She could smell the scent of him, warm and fresh, clean like soap.

"Oh" was all she could manage on a soft exhale of breath, before she gave a nonchalant wave of her hand to cover her nervousness, only to knock an acrylic cup off the counter. The sound of plastic clattering on tiles echoed against the walls, until the cup rolled to a stop at the toes of her high heels.

Max bent down to pick it up, kneeling before her, his hand at her feet, the sleeve of his sports jacket brushing against her shin. Suddenly she was aware of her short skirt, of his head so close that if she reached out just a little she could run her fingers through his hair.

"So, the newspaper is raking me over the coals." A deep ruggedness tinged his voice.

Her throat was dry and parched. "Actually, they go fairly easy on you—"

But her words cut off when he rose slowly, cup in hand, their bodies caught between the counter and the pantry.

Silence surrounded them, the rhythmic tick of the kitchen clock suddenly deafeningly loud, and she was certain he would touch her. Her palms grew damp, and her heart beat so hard she could hear blood rushing through her ears.

His gaze drifted to her lips, then lower to the line of her neck. Her sunglasses were gone, no longer hiding her eyes. She didn't understand the feeling of insanity that swept through her, the sensation of heat and desire. Or the very real wish to damn all else and reach out.

"They go easy on me, do they?" he asked, the words a rumble of sound that slid down her senses.

They were close, too close, and she could feel the startling heat of him. With effort, she tried to bring up the image of sweet, dear Grady, the man she was going to marry. But his soft lines wouldn't take shape.

She reasoned that it was not a surprise that she was unsettled. Given her parents' marriage and subsequent divorce, not to mention her father's long line of brides over the years, she'd be insane not to be a little bit wary of marriage. And this interlude, these wayward, completely inappropriate thoughts, were a direct result of a perfectly understandable spurt of cold feet.

Thankfully, Max stepped away, making it possible for her to breathe.

"Let me show you the garage."

"Tools and car parts. The adventure never ends."

He glanced back at her, his brow lifting, his full, sensual lips pulling into a smile. "I never thought of you as having a sense of humor."

"You've thought of me?" she asked, surprised.

But he had already opened the door and slipped into darkness. A switch clicked, and light flooded the space.

She saw the three-bay garage and made some inane remark before they moved on to the dining room and baths. She saw each one of them without really seeing. No matter how hard she tried to ignore him, she couldn't. She was aware of every accidental brush of his arm, every movement of his hands. She felt mesmerized by his voice, by the way he walked, confident, predatory.

Forcing herself to concentrate on something besides Max, she walked through the next door she came to, only to find herself in the master bedroom. The massive bed, the piles of pillows, the billowing drapery like a woman's sheer nightgown.

Vivi stopped abruptly, her breath catching at what suddenly seemed like an inevitable progress toward this room.

Sharply she turned back. When she did, he was there. Her pulse leaped, her senses shattering with awareness. She felt as if in this disjointed moment she could drown in the tilt of his lips or the startling blue of his eyes.

"What do you think?" he asked quietly.

Her gaze drifted to his lips. "About what?"

"The house."

A second passed. "The house! Of course." She laughed

too loud, then jerked away, looking out the window. "It's nice. Fine. But I was thinking more along the lines of something smaller. Something less . . . perfect. Something I could fix up. I'm really good at fixing things." She groaned. "Though I don't think that is exactly what Grady had in mind."

"Grady?"

Vivi blinked. "Oh, yes! Grady. The man I'm going to marry." She experienced a moment of virtuous relief when her fiancé settled between them.

"You're engaged."

"Yes!" She nearly broke out in a righteous dance.

Silence, then, "Congratulations."

"Thank you," she gushed. "He proposed in June. He's a wonderful man. You might know him. Grady Pence."

"Can't say that I do."

"He's great."

Then why was she noticing this other man if Grady was so perfect for her?

The thought leaped out at her, surprising and uncomfortable.

"Maybe I should show Grady this house after all. Beautiful and perfect can be good." She glanced around the bedroom, thought of the bathrooms with their brass fixtures and a living room with a raised seating area in front of windows with heavy curtains, like a stage carved into granite. She smiled, forgetting herself. "It would be a great place to have fun, play games. A place to pretend."

Max's gaze bore into her, and she was sure he was going to lean forward and run his fingers along her skin.

Run, she told herself. Move away. Leave the house. She looked at his mouth instead.

"If I were your fiancé," he said, "I wouldn't be interested in playing games. I would play for real, for keeps."

The high-ceilinged room grew still and airless. Vivi couldn't say how they had gotten to this place, how a man she had never met before could fill her with such longing. And doubts.

But she was given no chance to find answers when Max stepped away.

"We better start back. I'm sure Racine will have more for you to see tomorrow."

Then he walked out of the bedroom, leaving her alone. Making it possible to breathe.

Good.

Relief washed over her. She didn't want this man. Her life was with Grady. They had made plans, had dreams.

She was going to be a bride on Christmas Eve, and fantasies about this man weren't going to ruin it.

My Wedding Diary

THINGS TO DO

1. Plan intimate dinner for 500
2. Make sure caterer can find Perrier-Jouët La Cuvée Epoque Rosé by the case
3. Send Marcy Green to Velda's Salon for makeover
4. Must make decision about shoes for gown—low heel, stiletto, or Cinderella slipper
5. Forget Max Landry!!

Chapter Two

Vivi sat in a pink and lavender shoe salon in the Sunland Park Mall the following afternoon. She refused to give another thought to Max Landry. She wouldn't think about his sculpted good looks, or the dark hair that was just longer than would be considered standard for an executive of his importance. She turned her mind away from his broad shoulders. His blue eyes were off limits. And she absolutely, positively would not think about how his world had seemed to stop when he turned around and saw her through the glass.

Last night she had dreamed about him. She had tossed and turned, feeling hot and restless and invisibly hinged to a stranger whose eyes made her knees fuse and her breath catch.

This morning she had woken up feeling out of sorts. She wanted to talk to someone, but her mother was still in India. Postcards arrived intermittently with instructions regarding the wedding, as if it were perfectly normal for the mother of the bride to make plans for her only child's marriage by international mail.

Then there was her father, who had suddenly left town with little more than a quick good-bye and no information as to where he was going. That was the way he always traveled, usually with some woman half his age, in his never-ending journey to find his spent youth—or as her mother had explained it in terse, sneering words that didn't match her newfound aura of tranquillity, he had gone off to find the newest plaything to add to his long string of wives.

Not that Vivi had ever been able to talk to her parents. But she might have attempted to talk around the subject of this unsettling attraction to Max Landry because quite frankly, who else was there? Growing up, she had been raised by a series of nannies, had attended private girls' academies, then was shipped off to finishing school in Switzerland, before returning to Texas, where she earned a degree in art history.

"Stand out from the crowd, Vivi," Isabelle Stansfield was fond of saying. "Don't follow the pack."

By virtue of being the eccentric Jennings Stansfield's only child and heir, not to mention having been raised under the enlightened tutelage of Isabelle LeBuc Stansfield, Vivi was automatically different from any other woman she ever met. Hard to follow the sort of female that didn't exist in any followable number.

As a result, instead of calling up a favorite girlfriend and lamenting on the phone about what had nearly transpired with none other than Maxwell Bowden Landry, bachelor extraordinaire, Vivi did what she always did when she was upset. That afternoon she went shopping.

Turning her ankle just so, she looked in the shoe salon mirror and considered the shimmering white silk satin high heel. It was perfect.

For as long as she could remember, Vivi had dreamed of being a Christmas bride, dressed in a flowing white gown with a bouquet of red roses. Christmas holly and candles lining the aisle. Bridesmaids dressed in elegant cranberry satin. Scads of red poinsettias cascading down the steps, and boughs of evergreens gracing the altar and pews.

And now her dreams were coming true. Everything was planned. Dates set, deposits made. The only thing she hadn't been able to find was the shoes. Now even that problem was solved.

"I'll take them."

The saleswoman smiled. "The minute they came in, I knew they were perfect for you."

Vivi touched her hand. "Thank you for thinking of me, Helen."

The woman blushed. "Of course I would. You know how much I appreciate you paying for my Libby's homecoming dress."

Vivi felt embarrassment rush to her cheeks, uncomfortable with the thanks. Buying a teenage girl a dress wasn't any sort of great deed. "It was sweet of you to let me be a part of it."

Again and again, Vivi found herself paying for someone's dress or sending women who were trying to start new lives for makeovers at Velda's Salon. She had even paid a woman's lawyer fees when her ex-husband had tried to take away their children.

According to her father, this was her worse transgression, what he called her very bad habit of throwing herself into other people's problems. It drove him insane. *"Stop trying to fix everything,"* he had demanded more than once. But how could she sit by when someone needed help?

As Vivi went to the register, handing over a credit

card, she made a mental note to check on Bethany and her girls.

Seconds ticked by while Helen processed the charge. Then seconds more, and a line started to form. The sales woman glanced at her, hurriedly swiped the card again, then waited, staring at the machine, as people in line started to grumble. It wasn't until Helen picked up the phone and dialed that Vivi grew concerned.

"Is there a problem?" she asked.

"Ah, well—" But Helen cut herself off and turned away, talking into the receiver. When she turned back, she grimaced. "Do you have another card? This one's been rejected."

By now everyone in line was listening.

"What?" Vivi said, confused.

"You must be over your limit."

Vivi stared, trying to understand. "Please try it again."

"I'm sorry, really—just give me something else."

With her brow furrowed, Vivi pulled out another card. "Here you go," she said with a calm smile, though inside her heart was starting to pound with sheer, unadulterated embarrassment. "Clearly there's been a mistake."

Within seconds, Helen handed that one back to her as well. "This one doesn't work either," she said uncomfortably.

Vivi heard the murmurs from the line of women behind her. When she glanced back, they looked away. Mortified, she tried to laugh. "Could you hold the shoes for me? I'll be right back."

She left the department and went to a cash machine in the mall. But when she tried to withdraw money, her request was denied.

Vivi stared at the screen, embarrassment forgotten as

her heart began to pound in earnest. When asked if she'd like to continue, she asked for a balance.

Stunned, she stared at the very large, very negative figure that sprang up on the screen. This couldn't be happening.

Pressing a few more keys, she requested the balance of her savings account and nearly crumpled onto the floor when it came up empty.

Her heart hammered as she walked as calmly as she could back into the store, then out the other side to the parking lot. After fumbling with the keys, she slipped into her red convertible, pulled out her cell phone, and dialed the bank. But it was after hours. The bank was closed, and the automated teller did little to shed light on what had happened to her money—other than she no longer had any.

With her mind spinning, next she dialed the 800 numbers listed on the credit cards' backs—and confirmed that not only was she over her limit, but her payment checks had been returned for insufficient funds.

Vivi stared blankly, trying to comprehend. A feeling of panic rushed through her. She had never bounced a check in her life. And there was no reason for her checking and savings accounts to be empty. It had to be a mistake.

With both her parents unreachable and fifteen long hours before the bank reopened in the morning, she clutched the steering wheel and drove down the undulating hills to her fiancé's office.

Grady Pence was twenty-eight and on the partner track at Martin, Melby, and Mathers, one of the most prestigious law firms in town. Vivi had met Grady a year ago at an art exhibit. They had talked about a new local painter whose bold colors were vibrant and alive. Then they had gone for coffee. Grady was the first person she had ever met who hadn't asked about her father. They started dating, and four months ago, Grady got down on one knee and proposed.

Racing to her fiancé's office building, Vivi's bracelets jangled on her wrist as she used her blinker again and again to change lanes. It was after six when she arrived, but he always worked late. The door to Martin, Melby, and Mathers was unlocked when she got there. Pushing through, she called out but didn't get an answer.

Her high heels were soundless on the carpeted hallway. When she came around the corner, she stopped. Grady sat at the small table with the new associate they had hired a month ago. Documents were spread out in front of them, cups of coffee at their elbows. They were laughing, leaning close.

It was innocent enough, two colleagues sharing a joke. But Grady rarely laughed. And this associate was a woman who touched his arm possessively, as if she had done it many times before.

Vivi's first instinct was to turn and flee. Which was ridiculous.

"Hey," Vivi said sweetly instead.

The lawyers swiveled to face her.

"Vivi!" Grady said loudly.

"Hello," the woman offered, clearing her throat.

Grady didn't move when Vivi entered the room. When his brain finally kicked in and he stood, he banged into the table, making their coffee slosh.

Vivi came up to the table but he didn't offer her a seat. She wasn't sure why she did it, but something inside her that beat hard and wild made her pull out a chair and sit down anyway.

"Ah, Vivi, you know Sharon, don't you?"

Sharon was short and petite, with blond hair pulled back into a severe bun at the back of her head. Her suit was a circumspect navy, appropriate for a law office. The two women couldn't have been more different. Yet underneath all that severity was a lush figure and a skirt hemmed just long enough to be acceptable but short enough to turn men's heads.

"Working on an important case?" Vivi asked brightly, determined not to be intimidated by this extremely smart and successful woman sitting in front of her.

Grady picked up his tortoiseshell glasses and put them on, then ran his hand awkwardly through his sandy blond hair. "Yes, Vivi, a very important case, with a lot to get done."

"Maybe I could help," she offered.

"Vivi, please, we're really busy," Grady began, clearing his throat.

The woman turned to Vivi. "It's a difficult case," she explained with a fake grin, then patted Vivi's hand in a way that was both condescending and maddening. "Things like land grants and unclear property lines. Boring subjects that would put you to sleep."

It hadn't seemed too boring a second ago.

"It has to be done by morning," Sharon added with a coy smile for Grady. "But I can finish it up myself." She stood, gathering files.

"Sharon," Grady said.

The woman lawyer looked at him. "You don't mind if I present the contracts to Leland Mathers in the morning, do you?"

Awkwardness fled, and Grady's features went tight. "This is my case, Sharon. I hardly think—"

"No, no," Vivi said, feeling ridiculous. "I just need a second, Grady, then I'll be out of your way. Perhaps you could see me out?"

If she could just talk to him for a minute, see him look into her eyes, she was sure she could tamp down the feeling that everything she had worked for was falling apart. First her behavior in the weather tower, then the debacle with her credit cards, and now this.

"What's up?" he asked, as he walked her to the front foyer.

Vivi hesitated, looking into his eyes. Standing there with her parents out of town and that woman only a few offices away, she felt the all too familiar feeling of loneliness. For years she had wanted someone to talk to, someone she could share her concerns with. She had believed she had found that in Grady. "Are we okay?"

Grady sighed, then leaned forward with one of his kind smiles and kissed her on the forehead. "Of course we're okay."

"If you're sure."

"I'm sure. Now, what do you want to talk about?"

She started to say she'd had a problem today—buying a pair of shoes. But before she said the words, she realized how it would sound. Frivolous and irresponsible, certainly not the kind of issues that a woman like Sharon Willis must deal with on a day-to-day basis.

"It's nothing," she said finally.

"Then go on home and flip through wedding magazines so I can finish up. I'll call you tomorrow."

She wanted to feel the reassuring pressure of his lips on hers. If he would just put his arms around her, she was certain everything would go back to how it was before. But when she would have leaned into him, he moved away, directing her out of the offices of Martin, Melby, and Mathers. And no matter how hard she tried, she couldn't ignore the sound of the bolt sliding home as he locked the door behind her.

Chapter Three

"I'll have another, please. And, oh well, while you're at it, you might as well double the cocktail part."

Max heard the voice the second he walked into Bobby's Place and immediately knew who it was before he saw her.

The sweet, twangy sound of western music dipped and swayed through the brass-accented and football-memorabilia-filled expanse as Max found Vivienne Stansfield sitting at the bar. The sight of everything from her dark hair that shimmered in dim overhead light to her stiletto-heeled legs crossed delicately at the ankles ran along his senses. Yet again, she was a contrast. Provocative mixed with demure. Elegance tangling with sultry.

Yesterday, when his assistant had told him that an important client had been stood up by one of his agents, he had said to bring the customer to his office and he would take care of things. He had planned to explain why it was worthwhile to wait until Racine returned. He was even willing to placate the client with the offer of another agent if the person really had to see the property that day. But he couldn't have been more surprised when it turned out to be Vivienne Stansfield.

When he had seen her across the office, he had known instantly who she was. His reaction to her had been hot and intense, the desire to pull her close and touch her. He had nearly hung up on the attorney general of Texas, who had personally called about a land deal Max was handling.

But the molasses-slow heat was followed quickly by much the same feeling he had now. None of it good. Vivienne Stansfield was a spoiled rich girl who was beautiful and knew it.

She had grown up on the west side of town on a prestigious estate in the Upper Valley, he on the south side in a rough ghetto of dirt roads and no running water. She was rich. He was poor. Or he had been.

Since those days, he had worked hard, earning every penny he had made. He was proud of what he had accomplished. But it was more than wealth he had achieved. He sat on bank boards and planning committees. There wasn't a business leader or government official in Texas who didn't ask for his advice. Max Landry had come a long way from the wrong side of town.

Over the years, his friends and acquaintances had suggested he ask out the woman that everyone in El Paso liked to talk about. He had always said no thanks.

But something had shifted inside him when he saw her yesterday afternoon. All good sense had fled.

He still couldn't believe how he had reacted at the sight of her. His body had grown hard, heat rushing through him. His notorious self-control had felt like a thick hemp rope slipping through his grasp.

Taking her through the weather tower house had been an even bigger mistake. The innocent expression of surprise mixing with the sensuality of her body when he had kneeled at her feet nearly undid him. He had never seen such legs, long with narrow ankles. All he could think about was lifting her foot to his knee and running his palm along her skin to the juncture between her thighs. When they had ended up in the master bedroom, it was all he could do not to sweep her into his arms and take her on the bearskin rug.

His thoughts cemented at the thought. Despite his body's reaction, he and Vivienne Stansfield weren't going to happen.

He started to turn away, to head for Bobby McIntyre's office. But before he could move, Vivienne glanced back as if she was hoping someone had arrived. At the sight of him, her strange gray eyes widened with surprise, then darkened with awareness, quickly followed by a disconcerted embarrassment. She flipped her hand up in a quick, awkward wave, then swiveled away. Clearly he wasn't the person she was hoping for.

After a glance at his watch that told him he was early, he cursed himself, then approached the bar like a tide pulled back to sea.

"Hello," he said when he came up next to her.

"Oh, hello, Mr. Landry."

He could all but feel her cringe.

People had a variety of reactions to him when he entered a room. Excitement, the desire to get closer, intimidation. But he'd never seen anyone cringe.

Refusing to admit that it really ticked him off, he sat down next to her.

He caught a glimpse of her image in the mirrored backsplash of the four-sided bar. The shimmering hair, the sensual mouth. And an unsettling darkness in her pale gray eyes.

"Have a bad day?" he asked.

She blinked, then seemed to focus, as if she hadn't realized he was there. "I've had better."

"Which would explain your need for a double."

"What?"

Just then the bartender came up and set a tall, fluted glass in front of her. "A champagne cocktail for the lady." The man smiled. "With double sugar cubes."

Max nearly laughed out loud. Leave it to a woman like Vivienne Stansfield to order a double and have it turn out to be extra sugar. He should have known.

"I'll put it on your tab," the bartender said.

If Max hadn't been watching, he wouldn't have noticed how she flinched.

"A tab?" She pursed her lips and sighed sharply. "Of course you have a tab, Vivi," she muttered under her breath.

She stared at the bartender for one long second before she grabbed her tiny, glittery purse, then rummaged around in the contents. One by one, she pulled things out and set them on the counter. A lipstick. A compact. The tiniest writing pen he had ever seen. A matchbox-sized silver container of breath mints. Her nose wrinkled, her cheeks stained with embarrassment.

Something was wrong, though Max couldn't imagine how this woman could have any money concerns. "Here, let me get it. Peter, put the lady's drinks on my bill."

Max could tell she almost refused. But then she glanced between her purse and the bartender, and she gave in.

"Thank you," she said, her smile growing bleaker. "I didn't think."

"About paying?" he asked, and even he could hear the disbelief in his tone.

She stared at him for a long second, those strange, penetrating eyes seeming to look into him as if she were searching for something. She almost spoke, he was sure, but at the last minute she held back, her gaze clearing, and she laughed. "I didn't think to bring my wallet. I'll be happy to repay you." Her brow furrowed. "I hope," she added softly, glancing at her watch. "I'll know in twelve hours, thirteen minutes, and forty-five seconds."

He looked at her oddly. "No need. Peter, I'll have a draft."

"Sure thing, Max."

Tilting her head, she lowered her chin to her palm and studied him. "You come here often?"

"Now and again. Bobby Mac is a good friend. We do a lot of business together."

"The quarterback?"

"Yes. Do you know him?"

"I know of him. Who doesn't? Though I heard he quit football and got married."

"To Lacey. She's great. I tell him all the time that she's the best thing that ever happened to him."

Vivienne sighed, tucked her hair behind her ear, took a long sip of her champagne, then took another. "True love. I bet happily married Bobby Mac doesn't work late with women associates."

Max glanced from her glass to the high color on her cheeks. "How many of those have you had?"

"Not enough. I can still feel."

She hiccuped, her eyes going wide as she slapped her free hand over her mouth, then she actually giggled. But the giggle quickly gave way to that same gray-eyed darkness.

His gaze narrowed against a sudden tension he sensed winding through her. He saw how she swallowed hard. "Are you all right?"

That's when it happened, as if the little Dutch boy had pulled his thumb out of the dike. Suddenly Vivienne set her glass down with a thunk, swiveled toward him, and started talking. And talking. He had never seen anything like it.

"My life is falling apart," she blurted, as if a world of worries had been swelling inside of her, just waiting to spill out. "First, I go see that house in the tower and get all hot and bothered by you just standing next to me."

She squeaked the words, and he nearly dropped his beer. But she didn't give him a chance to respond, not that he knew what he possibly would have said, when she hurtled on.

"What is that all about?" she demanded of herself. "I am engaged! I shouldn't be noticing another man, much less wanting to tangle my fingers in his hair."

"You wanted to tangle your fingers in my hair?"

"That's not the point."

Right that second, he didn't care about any other point.

"Then this afternoon, depressed beyond belief, I went shopping."

His jaw muscles ticked. "I hardly think the thought of running your fingers through my hair should depress you," he muttered.

"Of course it should. If I didn't feel depressed by it, I'd have to feel guilty. And I really, really don't like doing guilty."

He tried to follow her logic.

"So I went with depressed, which meant I had to go shopping. Besides, I needed a pair of shoes to go with my wedding dress. And I found them." Her porcelain features turned dreamy. "White satin, with the most elegant beading you've ever seen."

"I'm still not clear on how this relates to my hair."

She shook herself. "It doesn't! The shoes were just the next step in my life spiraling out of control."

"Perfect shoes. Life going out of control. I'm not making the connection."

She took another sip and sighed. "My credit cards were rejected. Can you believe it? Me! Rejected in front of every female shopper in El Paso."

"I can't imagine anyone noticed."

"Everyone notices when someone's credit card gets rejected." She took a drink of her champagne and waved his comment away. "Though that was the least of my concerns after I went to the ATM to get money." Her expression shifted, and her delicate forehead creased. "I'm overdrawn."

"You, overdrawn?"

"My thoughts exactly." She swiveled back and dropped her head into her hands, hiccuping once again. "How can I be overdrawn?"

Truth be told, right that second he didn't want to know. Despite the heat that sliced through him at the sight of her legs, despite her comment about running her fingers through his hair, he wanted to get as far away from her as possible. She was upset, about to cry, and he really wasn't good with women who cried.

He wished he had minded his own damned business and stayed away. Hell, he should have turned around and left the minute he saw her, then called Bobby Mac from his cell phone to tell him they'd meet another time.

Scanning the room, he looked for help. But not a single soul looked his way.

"Hey, Peter," he called out hopefully. "Is Bobby Mac back yet?"

Vivienne jerked upright. "Hello! I'm in pain here."

And to think that yesterday he had thought maybe, just maybe, she wasn't as spoiled as he had heard.

"Something has happened to my money."

Since she was the only child of Jennings Stansfield, it was hard to get too worked up for her. "Shouldn't you be telling your father about this instead of me?"

"He's traveling."

"How about your mother?"

"Also traveling."

"Your fiancé? Surely he can help."

She groaned and dropped her head back into her hands. "He's busy."

"Busy?"

"What is this? Fifty questions?"

His jaw went tight. "My apologies for any show of concern."

Her breath caught and she looked at him with large doe eyes of surprise. "You hate me, too."

"Do you come with an instruction book? A step-by-step guide to your pinball method of all-over-the-board conversation?"

"You really hate me."

This time Max groaned. "I don't hate you."

"You were probably in that line at the shoe salon," she lamented, taking another swallow of champagne. "I could have sworn there was a really big woman at the back with a five o'clock shadow."

His hand went to his jaw.

Vivienne didn't notice. "I bet Sharon from Grady's office has never been rejected in a checkout line."

"Who?"

Her face screwed up and turned red. "Sharon Willis. The new *female* associate at Martin, Melby, and Mathers. She's smart and sexy—that is, if you go for blondes who can make a business suit look like lingerie from a Victoria's Secret catalogue." She looked down at the ruffles on her lavender dress. "She's everything I'm not."

His eyes narrowed and he looked at her. Really looked. "What are you?" he asked, surprising himself but wanting to know.

The question startled her and she blinked. As quickly as it had begun, the flood of emotion stopped. Her shoulders came back. Her face cleared, then she laughed self-consciously, waving her hand, scoffing, and pushing the champagne away. "I'm being ridiculous. I'm fine. Really. Totally fine. So she's beautiful. So she's smart. So she's working late night after night with my fiancé. That doesn't mean Grady's going to fall in love with her and leave me. I have plenty to offer a man."

The hint of red returned to her porcelain white skin, her brow furrowing with vulnerability as she looked at him.

"Don't I?" she asked quietly.

Something washed through him. Something softer than he had felt in ages, something that he had intentionally set aside in the years he'd had to fight and claw to work his way up from being the poor kid from the wrong side of town.

Without thinking, he reached out and touched her chin, just barely, but enough that the heat returned, hard and swift. He wanted nothing to do with this woman. But again and again he found it hard to look away. "Of course. You're very beautiful."

The pale gray of her eyes darkened to pewter, but she wasn't deterred. "I'm not talking about beauty. You think I'm nice, right?"

She asked the question as if being nice was far more important to her than being beautiful.

He dropped his hand away. "Sure. You're great."

"And smart?"

"Real smart."

"You didn't say that like you meant it."

"I don't know you all that well," he replied with an indifferent shrug that he didn't feel as he picked up his beer.

"True." She turned back to the bar.

They sat quietly for a moment, each lost to their own thoughts.

"But what if the money really is gone?" she whispered, as if she had been afraid to put words to the fear, as if somehow that would make it more real.

He studied her reflection in the mirror and realized she truly was worried. He couldn't imagine anything was wrong with Jennings Stansfield or his money—and as a result, he couldn't imagine that anything was wrong with Vivienne Stansfield's situation.

"Bank errors happen all the time," he offered, wanting distance, needing distance.

But she swiveled to face him, her eyes intense. "But what if it's not a mistake?"

He stared at her, his gaze taking in the elegant line of her cheek and the slim column of her neck. "Then you'd do what most people do. You'd get a job."

"A job?"

She said the words as if he had spoken a foreign language.

"You've heard of those, haven't you? That human endeavor where you go out and work for money. Time cards and paychecks."

She shot him a narrow-eyed gaze. "I know what a job is." She bit her lip. "I'm just not sure what I could do."

"Didn't you go to college?"

"Yes. My degree is in art history." She sighed. "I wasn't thinking *job* when I chose my major."

They both stared at the pattern in the fine wood grain of the counter.

"What about working for the art museum?" he tossed out.

"Even I've heard about the cutbacks."

"Then teach art."

"Didn't get a teaching certificate."

"Typing?"

"Never have."

"McDonald's?"

Visibly, she shuddered. "Would I have to wear their uniform?"

His brows slammed together. "Surely you can do something."

"You'd think."

He'd never heard anyone sound so glum.

Max swore, hating that he actually felt sorry for her. But there it was. Sympathy.

"Look," he said with impatience. "Everything is going to be fine. As soon as the bank opens, you'll see it's all a mistake. And if worse comes to worst, there are all kinds of jobs out there. Take me, for instance. I need someone to take care of my sisters. Surely you could do something like that."

"You're offering me a job?"

"Well, that's not what I—"

"That is so great of you." Then she stopped and her expression turned to confusion. "You're responsible for your sisters? How old are they?"

"Fourteen and eleven."

"And you're?"

"Thirty."

Max recognized the all too familiar surprise over the idea that anyone would have children spread out between thirty and eleven. He hated the way his shoulders tightened in response.

"My parents had eight children," he explained, holding any trace of emotion at bay. "I'm the oldest. The year I turned eighteen, my mother got pregnant again. Dad ran off. So when Mom died a year later, I took over." As if it were that simple.

He thought of the last decade, of the confusion, of trying to learn how to become a man and be a father at the same time. It was amazing any of them had survived. "I've had custody since then. But now everyone's on their own except my two youngest sisters."

He saw the distaste that lined her perfect forehead, the wrinkle in her upturned nose. But she surprised him when she spoke.

"How is it possible that there are still men out there who'd rather run off than accept responsibility?" She reached over and placed her hand over his. "It must have been hard for you."

She said the words with genuine emotion. It was ridiculous that he cared. Ridiculous that he appreciated her feelings about his father—all feelings that he had lived with for a lifetime.

"I did what I had to do," he said, pulling away from her hand and the unaccustomed emotion she brought up in him.

"What about your other siblings?" she asked. "Can't they take care of your sisters?"

"They've got lives of their own."

"And you don't?"

He almost smiled at the way her chin rose indignantly. It was an odd sensation to have someone feel protective of him.

"It used to be easier," he explained. "With eight of us, someone was always home. But now with Chris out of the house, Nicki is the oldest. At fourteen, she's technically old enough to baby-sit, but I can't expect her to take care of Lila all the time. I need someone there to drive the girls to school. Take care of the house. Cook. Generally run the place. On top of that, since I have real estate deals and construction projects all over the Southwest, I want an adult in the house full-time."

"And you think I'd be good at that," she stated, amazed.

"Well, again, that wasn't—"

She patted his hand despite the fact that he had already pulled it away once. "You are so sweet," she said.

Sweet? Him? His thoughts cemented.

"I appreciate the vote of confidence," she continued with a lilting laugh. "I feel better already. There *are* things I can do. But I'm sure you're right. By tomorrow, this whole mess will be straightened out and I'll be mortified that I even mentioned it."

She gathered her purse, then climbed off the stool. Out of habit, Max stood.

"No need to see me out. Thank you for paying." She hesitated. "And for listening, too. Good luck with your caretaker search."

He watched her slip away, the heavy door swinging shut behind her, the dark wood closing out her delicate beauty.

He sat down and could no longer hold back the memory that had been trying to push forward since the moment she had walked into his office. The memory of Vivienne Stansfield as a little girl, dressed up in mounds of ruffles and crinolines, wearing a glittering tiara, standing next to her father as they opened a new manufacturing plant in south El Paso. The red ribbon. The snip of scissors. The ends fluttering to the ground. But most of all, he saw Vivienne.

He hadn't lied when he said they had never met. But he had seen her, nearly touched her. A princess to his pauper.

He had been ten, weaving his way through the thick crowd of neighborhood people and dignitaries, wearing his best jeans with only a few holes in them and his Sunday shirt. Max had gotten as close as he could to the low stage. Then even closer.

Her father had spoken to the assembled masses, the people letting up a cheer. It was then that she looked at him, those pale gray eyes locking with his.

"Hello," she had whispered.

"Hey." He wanted to be cool, not show how he shook from the sheer beauty of her.

Letting go of her father's hand, she had taken a step toward him, all shiny black hair and eyes too large for her face. With her white gloved hands she had reached out. To him. His heart hammered in his chest.

But just before she touched him, her father noticed.

"Vivi, come back here," he had demanded, his voice like a king's.

She hesitated for half a second, then sighed. When she returned to her father's side, he shoved something into her hand and pushed her back. If Max hadn't been so caught up in amazement that she was returning to him, he might have realized that she had a strange look in her eyes.

"My father wants you to have this," she whispered, her voice oddly strangled.

Max's young heart beat hard. But when she opened her hand, he saw the dollar. A handout.

Anger, fury, and a biting embarrassment sizzled through Max. Until that moment he had never thought about his family's circumstances. They didn't have much, sure, but neither did anyone else he knew.

In that second, Max had understood who he was to the outside world. A poor kid to be looked down at—or pitied. With a surge, embarrassment turned to burning pride, and he told himself he would not be pitied by anyone.

"Keep your money. I don't need it."

Max had worked a lifetime since then becoming who he was, the task made more difficult when he had to leave college to take care of his brothers and sisters. But he had done it, taking real estate classes at night after getting off from that very same plant in South El Paso where he had gone to work the day after his mother died.

Once he sold his first property, he had quit Stansfield Manufacturing. Soon after, the plant closed for good. He had never looked back.

But now the rich little girl had reappeared in his life. And he wished like hell he didn't care that now she was the one who seemed to need the dollar.

My Wedding Diary

THINGS TO DO

6. Never drink champagne again
7. Better yet, never drink again. No alcohol at all, even if it's rum in rum cake or Kahlúa in chocolate Kahlúa balls.

Could I really have been so indiscreet regarding my personal finances?

Me, Miss Tell No One Anything?

Me, Miss Privacy at All Costs?

What was I thinking?!!!

And the entire display in front of the very available and much sought after founder of MBL Holdings. Wouldn't the gossipmongers love to see that splashed across the papers?

But can you believe it?!!! He offered me a job. Completely dreamy of him. And to think he'd never even met me before I walked through his office door!

Chapter Four

At exactly nine the next morning, Vivi dialed the bank's number and asked for the president.

"Conway Garnett's office."

"This is Vivi Stansfield. Is Mr. Garnett there? It's an emergency."

"Miss Stansfield, I was just going to call you. Conway wants you to come in to see him. There's a problem with your account. I'd put you through now, but he's out of the office until four this afternoon. Can you come in then?"

"I'll be there."

As soon as Vivi hung up, the phone rang, and she all but leaped out of the chair. Snatching up the receiver, she prayed it was her father.

"Miss Stansfield, this is First Commons Visa calling in regard to your credit card bill. I see you spoke to customer service yesterday, but there is no date noted as to when you will be resending a new payment."

"I am terribly sorry for this," she said. "I've only recently learned that something has . . ." What? What could she say? "There has been some sort of error. I will get to the bottom of the situation, and get back to you."

"But—"

Vivi hung up. Within seconds, the phone started

ringing again. This time it was a bill collector for the phone company. Next came El Paso Electric. After that she stopped answering. It wasn't until she heard Grady's voice come over the answering machine that she grabbed up the phone. "Grady, I'm here!"

"So I can tell," he said with a chuckle.

She could hear the springs on his chair squeak as he leaned back in that way he had about him, so sweet and endearing, his light brown eyes brightening. She hated having to tell him about the mess she was in, especially given Sharon Willis. But she would tell him tonight at dinner.

"I miss you, Grady."

"Good, good. Now tell me, how was the house that Racine took you to see?"

"She stood me up," she said.

The chair gave a hard, jarring squeak. "Stood you up?"

Vivi knew that Grady would consider that an insult to him. Which was fine with her, because she no longer had any interest in dealing with anyone at MBL Holdings— Racine or MBL himself. Max unnerved her. At least that's what she told herself to explain how she had acted around him. Twice.

Just the memory of walking through that stone tower, aware of every accidental brush, brought heat surging back in her cheeks.

Not to mention the way she had broken down like a fishwife and told him her personal problems. Stansfields did not discuss anything personal. Ever. Not with each other. And certainly not with a perfect stranger.

"I can't believe it," Grady said.

"It worked out. Max Landry showed me the house instead."

Grady almost choked. "What? Max, as in the president of MBL?"

"Yes."

Grady whistled. "This is an incredible opportunity for me to get a foothold into MBL. Call back and set something up. Bypass Racine. Go directly to Landry."

"I can't do that!"

"Sure you can. He's an important contact. Get on the phone and make another appointment." He hesitated, then softened his tone. "Please, Vivi, for me?"

She knew he was doing what it took to get his way. This wasn't the first time, and she kicked herself for falling for that boyish charm.

"All right," she conceded. "I'll call."

"Good. Listen, I've got to go."

"Grady, wait. We're still meeting for dinner, right?"

The springs squeaked again. "Sorry, Vivi. I can't make it. Got to work late. I'll make it up to you tomorrow. How's that?"

She started to protest, but realized there truly was nothing to say.

"Fine."

Vivi would call Max, ask to see another property, talk about her fiancé right and left. But before that, at four on the dot, she'd go to the bank to find out what had gone wrong with her accounts. If she played her cards right, she thought suddenly, she could have this mess straightened out by the end of the day and Grady would never have to know.

Feeling better, she found the number for the offices of

MBL. But in a knee-jerk reaction, instead of asking for Max, she asked for Racine.

"She's not in the office today. Can I take a message?"

"No." She hesitated, then with no help for it, plunged ahead. "Is Max Landry there?"

"Who's calling, please?"

She told the woman her name and hoped he wasn't in. After a few clicks and beeps, Max picked up the line.

"Vivienne?"

Even the sound of his voice sent a shiver down her spine. So intimate and knowing. Like when his hand was pressed so innocently against her back.

"Hello?"

"Yes, yes. I'm here."

Then another pause.

"I asked for Racine, but she's not in and . . . and I really need to find something sooner rather than later."

She remembered Max picking up the plastic cup at her feet. The brush of his jacket against her shin. The way he had stood, bringing them so close that she could feel the heat of him.

"Actually, Grady,—my fiancé, Grady—wants me to find something ASAP," she added quickly. "He asked me to call to set something up."

Max's chuckle was low, and she imagined him leaning back in his thick leather chair, though there was no squeak of springs. He didn't say a word.

She plunged ahead. "Perhaps you . . . or another of your realtors, could show me something else."

"We just finalized a listing for a place close to down-town. I'm not sure that it's exactly right, but it is smaller than the tower house."

"That's fine. How about tomorrow?"

"Tomorrow I'm booked."

Relief mixed with disappointment, leaving her unsettled.

"But I can meet you there this afternoon."

His words caught in her mind.

"Oh." Her pulse leaped. Foolishly she wanted to see him again, wanted to watch as his blue eyes lit with an unexpected smile.

"At three," he added.

She imagined the way his lips curved wryly.

"At three, then," she answered.

As she hung up the phone, she told herself she was overreacting. She was going to see a piece of property. Raising her chin, she added that she'd meet Max and it would be no big deal. He'd show her the place, she would talk about Grady, then she'd leave. Deed done, and her fiancé would be pleased.

Two hours later, Vivi arrived at the address. It was a little after three, which would force her to hurry through the property in order to get to the bank on time. But when she got there, Max was nowhere to be seen.

Good, she told herself with a nod as she waited at the main entrance of the building.

Even better, she added silently ten minutes later when he still hadn't shown up.

With her heart pounding, feeling the need to escape, she fished her keys out from her handbag, then headed back to her car. But just when she thought she had made it, Max wheeled into the parking lot.

The minute he stepped out, she experienced the same

simmering awareness. His height, his broad shoulders. The power he exuded.

He looked at her, just looked, his eyes dark. There were no smiles, no polite greetings, just a hardness that made her think he didn't understand why he was there.

"Sorry I'm late," he said finally, suddenly every inch the professional. "I got caught up with the principal from the high school."

"Showing another house?"

"No." He glanced off in the distance, then she would have sworn he sighed. "Discussing one of my sisters. But we aren't here to talk about Nicki. Come on, let's have a look upstairs."

The building was beautiful and old, standing on the border between Texas and Mexico, on the banks of the Rio Grande. They took an antique elevator to the fifteenth floor, the carved wooden doors sliding open directly into a two-story entryway. Cathedral windows lined the walls, one facing east, the other facing west.

The space was stunning, quaint but open at the same time. For half a second she forgot about Max and reveled in the beauty as the sun spilled through the tall windows. But then he came up beside her, and the same aggravating awareness slid down her spine.

It was all she could do not to turn into his heat and press close to the hard contours of his body. She didn't understand the attraction, didn't understand how again and again he made her feel like someone she was not.

Yes, he was a sensually handsome man. But just one look left no doubt that he had nothing to do with the white-picket-fence sanity and normalcy she sought in her life.

He was raw energy, and she wanted calm.

He was demanding; she wanted ease.

"I love it up here," he said, completely unaware of what she was feeling.

"Interesting," she said, stepping away.

He seemed to shake himself out of wherever he had been. "It belongs to a friend of mine who's been transferred to Houston. He wants to rent it, but he's willing to sell if the price is right."

"There you go again with the game show theatrics."

He glanced at her, and she would have sworn his tight control slipped just a notch.

"Guilty," he offered. "Come on, let me show you around."

He did, telling her about the square footage, the energy-saving insulation, the double-paned windows. She followed along, forcing herself to listen. She made a point of staying a good yard away from him. When he stopped, she made sure she didn't stand too close. When he continued on, she didn't follow until he had taken at least two steps. At one point, he looked back at her.

"Are you okay?"

"Me?" She scoffed too loudly. "Of course I am. Why would you ask?"

"Last night. At Bobby's Place." He shrugged. "You didn't seem so fine then."

She waved the words away. "That was last night. I was tired. I vented. I'm completely embarrassed today. I made a mountain out of a molehill. It's nothing really."

"You talked to your fiancé?"

"Not yet. I'm going to the bank after I leave here to straighten everything out. I don't need Grady's help. Though . . . though Grady would help if I asked." She remembered her promise to interject mention of her fiancé at every turn. "He's a very smart man and . . . and . . . handsome."

Max looked at her as if she had grown a second head. "Let me show you the rest."

She continued behind him, gabbing away about Grady. Grady this. Grady that. Unlike the first day, today her brain had actually kicked in and reminded her that she was engaged. In the living room, she told Max about Grady's most recent case—which she pretty much had to make up since Grady never talked to her about work no matter how many times she asked.

In the dining room, she told him about her and Grady's favorite restaurant, though in truth the only one they ever went to was one close to Grady's office. She didn't even particularly like it, and Grady rarely commented on the food since he usually spent his time on the cell phone. But she wasn't about to admit that to Max Landry.

In the den, staring at a wall of television and stereo equipment, her enthusiasm for her "perfect" relationship starting to dim, she only managed to mumble something about her and Grady's favorite song.

By then Max was looking at her as if she had lost her mind. And she must have, since she realized she and Grady didn't even have a favorite song. She didn't even know what kind of music he liked. Pop? Rock? Country or blues?

She blinked in surprise at the realization, causing her to lower her guard. And when Max halted in the doorway of the kitchen, she didn't think to stop until she found herself in the Spanish arch with him, leaving her with no protection against the surge of heat that rushed along her skin.

Standing there, she forgot Grady as she stared at Max's chest, at the buttons of his shirt, stared so hard that she could make out the tight weave of the starched white material. Seconds ticked by and neither of them said a word.

Finally, she glanced up, and he looked at her with an expression as vulnerable as she felt. Vulnerable and confused by the intensity that filled the room like an electrical charge.

"This is the kitchen," he said quietly.

"It's beautiful," she stated, though she hadn't bothered to look.

"The appliances are top of the line."

"That's good. I love to cook."

"You do?"

Vivi focused. "Don't sound so surprised. I'm famous for my chicken Kiev, and my veal Cordon Bleu has made grown men melt like butter."

"How are you with burgers?"

She watched the way his lips moved on the words. "What?"

"You know—burgers, fries, hot dogs. Picnic food." He hesitated. "You've been on a picnic, haven't you? Barbecue and beer? Softball?"

"Sure. Of course."

He raised a brow, every trace of vulnerability gone.

"Okay, not really."

"Not your sort of party, I take it."

The sound of his disdain registered through the murkiness in her head and she met his gaze. "I've never been invited to one."

Even his implacable features couldn't hide his surprise. "You don't know what you're missing. They're a lot of fun."

A boyish light brightened his features, and for a second he didn't look like the ruthless man who got whatever he wanted. He seemed less forbidding, approachable.

She felt disoriented by the change in him, and every sane thought she had disappeared. Her palms grew clammy, and her heart raced as his gaze drifted to her lips. But it wasn't heat that she saw in his eyes. The boyish approachability evaporated, replaced by more of the same confusion, as if he didn't understand how he found himself here, again, with her, in this strange dance of awareness.

Flustered, she turned to leave, but his hand slipped around her arm. They both stared at his fingers that curled gently around her flesh, his skin with its light tan looking dark compared to the pale white of hers. Then they glanced up at the same time, their eyes meeting.

His brow furrowed, his gaze growing stormy.

"I'm sorry, but this isn't right," she managed.

"What isn't?"

"The apartment, of course, the apartment."

They stood that way, neither of them moving, her breath caught, his hand on her arm.

"If you change your mind," he said, "I'll be at the office."

Startled, she tugged away, then mumbled something about having to go. Pivoting on her toes, she pressed the elevator call button, then sent up a prayer of thanks when the old wooden doors rattled open. But when she turned back, she caught a glimpse of Max standing there, watching her. For a moment she had the very clear thought that he had started to reach out and would have pulled her back to him if the doors hadn't finally slid closed.

My Wedding Diary

MY MR. RIGHT

Can a man be the right man simply because he is safe (why does safe have to seem boring?!) in a world of larger-than-life fathers and vibrantly alive mothers who travel the world?

Chapter Five

Clutching the steering wheel, Vivi tossed caution to the wind and drove thirty-nine in a thirty-miles-an-hour speed zone.

She was on her way to Grady's office. She was hot, but it was a heat born of guilt. She had wanted to kiss Max. Again. She wished he had pulled her back, had let his lips graze over hers.

Vivi groaned, then jumped when an impatient driver gave her a good blast with his horn, then groaned once more at the thought of how she had totally humiliated herself in front of Max Landry.

Forcefully, she pushed Max from her mind. Which left her with thoughts of Grady.

She needed to see her fiancé. She needed to make up for having such inappropriate thoughts about another man. But there was more to it than that. She needed to ask him what kind of music he liked. Learn his favorite food. Find out his middle name.

How could she not know his middle name?

She pulled into the parking lot of the law firm, slid the car into the first space she came to, then headed for the entrance. As soon as she saw Grady, she'd reassure herself that she was doing the right thing in marrying him.

Her attraction to Max was an aberration. Cold feet. Completely understandable when faced with the long-term commitment of marriage. Who wouldn't be scared?

But she stopped dead in her tracks when she saw Grady in the parking lot. He stood next to an old car that she had never noticed before parked at the far side of the building. When he moved just a bit, she saw he was with a woman.

Vivi froze, unable to call out or look away.

Grady had his arm crooked on the open door, Sharon Willis standing in the V formed by him and the car. Vivi watched, her stomach lodged in her throat. Grady smiled down at Sharon, a warm, loving expression that he had never shown Vivi.

As if she had already seen this play, she knew what was coming next, but still she couldn't move or close her eyes. It wasn't the kiss that felt like a jab to the ribs. It was the tenderness.

Grady gently touched Sharon's chin with his finger-tips, tilting her head ever so slightly, before he leaned down and brushed her lips. Vivi felt like a voyeur watching a secret interlude, witnessing an exchange that left her with a poignant ache.

But on the heels of the yearning came something else. Something inevitable. This was where they had been heading all along. This was why she knew so little about him. They weren't meant to be together.

She had been fooling herself that things were working out between them. But if she was truthful with herself, she knew he didn't love her. Not really. Not enough. And she realized then that she couldn't marry him.

She wouldn't be his bride.

It hit her full in the chest, her sharp intake of breath

like a gasp of relief, but also of disappointment and an understanding of what she had to do next—the only thing that was fair and honorable for everyone.

She must have made a noise, because suddenly the secret lovers broke apart. Instantly they saw her.

Grady blanched. "Vivi!"

The old car door swung closed on Sharon when he stepped away. Vivi had dated him for a year, had been engaged for four months. On the night he proposed, they had made love. Her first time.

Like a fool, she had waited for Mr. Right. She nearly scoffed out loud. That wasn't exactly true. She had waited for the only man she'd ever dated. Strict boarding schools followed by a barrage of unflattering articles only attracted the wrong sort of guy. This man's soft blandness had made him seem right in a world of fathers who drove horned golf carts and mothers who went looking for themselves with bearded gurus who promised happiness.

"Vivi, it's not how it looks."

"Oh, Grady, it's time we stop pretending." She said it as kindly as she knew how.

Red surged into the blank white slate of his face. "What are you talking about?"

"You and I aren't going to work. Deep down we both know it." As she said the words, her conviction grew. This had been coming, but she hadn't wanted to see it.

He hurried over to her, taking her arms. "Of course we're going to work out. We are going to be married in a matter of months. Everything's planned. Everyone knows."

He stared at her for an eternity, pleading and desperate, and she nearly gave in. Maybe she had misunderstood what she'd seen. But then she pushed the thought away. She hadn't been mistaken. Besides, it was far more than a kiss with another woman that had made Vivi open her eyes.

"I don't even know your favorite song," she said with feeling.

"What?"

She tugged her arms away. "Grady, I kept telling myself that you and I were meant to be together," she explained. "But it's time I was truthful with myself."

"Truthful with yourself?" he demanded. "This whole thing has been a lie?"

"Not a lie, Grady. But the fact is you are more interested in your work and a colleague than you are in me."

His expression hardened, but she persevered.

"It's better we accept that fact now rather than later, after we're married and miserable together."

He smiled, and for half a second she was relieved.

"You're right," he said, his harsh tone confusing her. "We really aren't compatible. The truth is, we're too different."

"Meaning?"

"Come on, Vivi. Don't play dumb."

She told herself he was lashing out. She told herself that she should turn around and walk to her car. "Dumb? Why is that, Grady? Because I'm not a lawyer? Because I can't talk about legal briefs and court summations? Explain it to me."

"Because you're a rich daddy's girl."

Her knees locked.

"You *are* the pampered princess they write about in the papers." His voice rose. "In fact, the truth is I can't tell you how many times I have wondered how I would deal with the way you never get messy. The way you always have to be so perfect. You can never do anything wrong. But nobody's perfect, Vivi, and it's like you spend your life trying to be just that."

"You think I'm trying to be perfect?"

He lowered his voice, though there was a fierceness in it that she had never heard before.

"Have you ever done anything wild, Vivi? Hell, you were a twenty-five-year-old virgin when I met you," he said. "I didn't think it was possible that there were still women like you in this day and age."

He's hurting, she told herself. Don't take it personally. She smiled over her pounding heart. "I'm sorry that not sleeping around turned out to be a bad thing."

"I'm not talking about being easy, Vivi. But a man wants a woman who's a match for him in life." He straightened his shoulders defensively. "And in bed. Let's face it, Vivi. You're boring in the sack."

Her breath exhaled with a sharp rush, and the last few days of holding on tumbled in on her. Memories rushed through her head, and before she could think, she snapped. "Maybe I wouldn't have been so boring if you didn't have such a . . . a . . . puny penis."

As soon as she said the words, she gasped. Grady's mouth fell open.

Dear God, what had she just said?

"I've got to go," she squeaked, then practically threw herself into the car.

Counting to ten, then back again, she shifted into reverse, almost running over Grady's toes. Then she sped away, so upset that she didn't even think about turn signals and speed limits.

Puny penis?

What were you thinking?

Clearly she hadn't been thinking, at least not about anything a nice girl from Texas would think, much less say.

She clutched the steering wheel with a deadly grip, holding emotion in check as best as she could. She had been mean. Horribly mean. Not to mention that who was she to judge the merit of his penis? It wasn't as if she had anything to compare it with. For all she knew, they were all that size.

She drove, not using her blinker a single time, until she ended up at the bank only a few minutes before four. She'd think about Grady later. She had more pressing problems.

She flew into First National, her high heels and jangle of bracelets echoing in the marble and granite lobby, then she took the carpeted steps to the executive offices.

Elizabeth took one look at her and opened the president's office door without pause. As soon as he saw her, Conway Garrett grimaced and stood. "Vivi, it's good to see you."

Stepping into the leather and book-lined office, she felt a budding sense of relief start to push away her anxiety. At the sight of the older man's kind face, she was ready for him to tell her this was all an unfortunate mistake.

"Conway, thank you for seeing me."

He smiled like a benevolent grandfather, all but patting her on the head. "Vivi, let's sit down and discuss this."

Alarm rang through her. "What is there to discuss? My accounts are empty and my payment checks are bouncing. I don't feel like sitting. Please just tell me what's wrong."

"All right. If you want it straight . . . Vivienne, your accounts are empty because your money is gone. Your checks are being returned for insufficient funds."

Her head swam. "But I have overdraft coverage."

"Unfortunately, not anymore. Not since your father withdrew your balance just before he left town."

"Withdrew it? How can he withdraw my money?"

But she knew.

"He is a cosignatory on the account, as you well know."

"This doesn't make any sense. Why would he withdraw money from my account when he has his own?"

"Vivi," he said, his voice kind. "Your father's money is gone, too."

She sat down like a piece of lead.

Minutes ticked by, the distant sound of normal, business-day voices and transactions drifting to her. But nothing was normal for Vivi.

"How can that be?" she asked.

Conway sighed. "While I was out of town, he came in and emptied the accounts. By the time I returned, it was already done. That's all I can tell you."

Vivi's mind spun and her stomach reeled. How many times had her father left her? How many weeks and months had she spent alone, waiting for him to return?

"It's all a mistake," she whispered. "He'll come back and explain."

The banker stared at her. "I hope so, Vivi. I truly do. But in the meantime, you have no funds."

Numb, she swallowed hard. "Could you give me a

loan? Just long enough until I can figure something out?"

"Vivi, I'd like to help, but the board won't allow it. You have no collateral."

"Use my father's condominium."

"It's a rental."

Her chest clenched. A rental?

"Then my jewelry. It's here in the safety deposit box." The man flinched.

Vivi gasped. "He took that, too?"

"I'm sorry."

She thought she'd be sick right there on the bank floor. "What's left?"

"Nothing, I'm afraid." He grimaced apologetically.

She sat very still for what felt like an eternity. Somewhere in the back of her mind she realized the voices had faded as the bank closed for the day. Employees would be locking up, going home, their work finished until tomorrow, when they would return, punch their time cards, and count the hours until paychecks arrived.

"Then I'll get a job," she said suddenly, sitting up straight.

"You? A job?"

"Why not?"

"Well, it's just that . . . I never thought of you working."

If he had thought to deter her, his question did the exact opposite.

"That's because you don't really know me. I'll find work."

"Doing what, Vivi?"

She eyed him hopefully. "You could give me a job."

His look of doubt turned to panic. "You don't have any experience in banking."

"My family has kept their money here for years. Surely you can give me something to do. Anything. Just something to carry me through until my father returns and clears up what has to be a mistake."

"Vivienne, the truth is I've been covering your father's overdrafts for months. And now that he's withdrawn everything without so much as a word to me, he's left me with a pile of debt." He cut himself off. "I'm sorry. As you said, I'm sure it's all just a misunderstanding. But I'm really not in a position to give you a job."

Mortification mixed with her shock.

"Vivi, I really am sorry."

She stood. For half a second it seemed that her legs wouldn't hold her. But when Conway hurried around his desk and took her arm, pride surged and she stood on her own. "I'm fine. Not to worry."

Concentrating on putting one foot in front of the other, Vivi made her way back through the bank, stood dazed as the security guard let her out the door, then walked to her car. But when she started the ignition, she noticed the red light flashing on the gas gauge. Suddenly tears burned in her throat.

She felt as if her back was against the wall and she had nowhere to turn. Her father had taken everything.

Why would he do it?

She started to drive, having no idea how far she could get with a red light flashing. A mile? Two? It hardly mattered. Her mind was in shock, her stomach grumbling as she realized she hadn't had anything to eat all day. Just as her car sputtered its last gasping, no-gas breath, she coasted into the parking lot of a busy Taco Bell.

Food. And, for the first time in her life, inexpensive food.

She rummaged through the ashtray in the console for change, just enough for a taco. Then she'd make a plan. She needed to think of a way to make some money to tide her over until her father returned. And he would return, she told herself firmly.

As she walked toward the entrance, a sign taped to the window snagged her attention.

**Help Wanted
Apply Inside**

Vivi felt her heart lurch at the thought that this was something she could do. But then a reflection in the glass caught her eye.

Slowly she turned around and came face-to-face with the glimmering granite building of MBL Holdings across the street. Max Landry would be inside. Max Landry and the way he made her forget. Max Landry with his not-so-simple touch that had the ability to make reality fade away. His smile that somehow made the world seem more manageable.

Still numb, she walked across the street. Her throat was tight and her eyes burned when she made it to the smoked-glass doors. But when she pulled, they were locked.

She stared at the chrome handles, perfect circles with the company logo at the center of each, before she tugged again, hard. The doors rattled, but they wouldn't give.

Finally emotion spilled over, tears streaking down her cheeks, her head falling against the glass. Sobs racked her body, overtaking her so completely that she didn't notice when a door pulled open.

"Vivienne?"

With a start, she looked up and saw Max through her tears, his face lined with concern, his stance warrior-fierce. As if he had known her forever, he cupped her cheeks with his warm, strong palms and wiped her tears away with his thumbs.

"What's wrong?" he demanded.

"You said if I changed my mind, you'd be here," she said on a whispered breath.

It didn't matter that he had been talking about something completely different when he said it. She could feel the heat that flashed through him, followed quickly by a tightly held control.

"Vivienne, you're upset. You should go to your fi-ancé."

She tried for flip. She searched for a wry smile. "Guess what," she managed, before her voice broke. "I don't have a fiancé anymore."

"The engagement is off?"

"Yes."

Then suddenly she was in his arms, as if this was what had been inevitable all along, holding on tight as he pulled her into the building, his mouth finally, and completely, coming down on hers.

Chapter Six

Max gave in to the need he felt for this woman in a way that deep down he knew he'd regret. The desire. The loss of control.

Tangling together, they fell back against the wall. His hands cradled her face to tilt her lips to his. But before he kissed her again, he met her gaze, saw confusion mix with desire in her eyes, reflecting his emotions back to him like a mirror to his soul. She didn't understand this any more than he did.

But in that second he didn't care. He only wanted to press her body to his, discover her contours as he had wanted to since he leaned down and picked up the plastic cup from the floor.

He had wanted her then, wanted her in a way that surprised him, just as he wanted her now. Consequences be damned.

His hands trailed back to her shoulders, then down her spine, molding her to him.

She moaned, the vibration sending sensation sizzling through him. She was hot and pliant as she closed her eyes over her confusion, giving in much like he was.

He kissed her then, his mouth covering hers. Heat flared between them, the heat that was never far away, smoldering, since the day she walked into his office, held in check until he opened the door and found her there.

He lost himself to the feel of her, the billowing silk of her dress brushing against his forearms where he had rolled up his sleeves at the end of the day. It was that time, those few minutes by himself, when he could let down his guard. No ringing phones. No problems to solve. No brothers or sisters who needed answers from him while he struggled to understand the questions.

Then Vivienne had appeared. Vivienne, who made him remember. Vivienne, who made him feel young and vulnerable. But he pushed that away.

Clinging to him, she kissed him back with an innocent wonder that he hadn't experienced since grade school. But that innocence was combined with a primal yearning.

The last of his restraint vanished despite the many reasons he didn't want her there. In that second, better sense was replaced by desire. He didn't want to talk, or to understand. He brushed his thumb over her lips, touched her body, savored her taste.

After one long second she melted completely with a groan. He bent down to kiss her again, sucking her lower lip in his mouth, his teeth nipping, before he slid his hands into her perfect hair. Gently he pulled her head back to expose the swan's arch of her neck. And when she reached up and wrapped her arms around his shoulders, he felt as if he had been waiting for this forever.

The intensity grew, his fingers moving along the lines of her body.

"Vivienne," he murmured in a ragged voice.

With infinite care, he kissed her again, the sound of a

soft mewling coming from deep within her. Gently, he coaxed her lips apart until their tongues intertwined, the flames between them leaping higher.

They clung together, before he lifted her up. He clasped her to him, pressing her back against the wall as his lips seared a path down her chin to the pulse in her neck. Her hands knotted in his hair.

"I knew you'd be hot," he groaned against her.

The words seemed to spur her on, as if she had something to prove to him, to the world. To someone.

Her heat seared him, and he wanted to take her right there on the carpeted entry.

With infinite slowness, he lowered her, their bodies sliding together. But when his hand drifted higher to her breast and he cupped the fullness, for half a second she sucked in her breath and he felt sensation shudder through her before her gentle whimper cut off with a startled gasp.

As quickly as it had begun she stopped and pushed at his chest.

"No," she said, pulling away, her breath as ragged as his own. "I can't do this."

"Why not?" He kissed the line of her throat.

"No, no, no. That's not why I'm here. This isn't what I changed my mind about. I didn't come back here to kiss you." She touched her lips self-consciously, then she forced her arm to her side. "No. No kissing. Just because Grady and I have . . . broken up, doesn't mean I should throw myself into your arms on the rebound."

"Rebound?" he demanded tersely, his heart pounding hard in his chest, a warrior's heat burning through him.

"Exactly. I am not going to fall into anyone's bed, including yours. Besides, who knows what really got into

Grady? People get cold feet all the time—and say mean, hurtful things."

She cringed, and he had the distinct feeling that she might have said something she regretted.

He felt a barely contained fury. At her. At himself for his own foolish burning. "Then why are you here?" he demanded. "The penthouse? Did you decide to take the apartment after all?"

Her pert little nose wrinkled, and she bit her lip in a wry grimace. "Well, no, not that either."

She visibly gathered herself, and he could practically see her brain working. She was on the verge of something, but he couldn't imagine what. Her gray eyes darkened, color rose in her cheeks, and he would have sworn tears threatened.

"As it turns out—" Her lips started to tremble, before she raised her chin bravely. "I'm here about the job."

His brow furrowed in confusion.

"You remember. The job taking care of your sisters," she explained, her bracelets jangling, jarring in his mind.

A job? His sisters?

Hell.

He still couldn't believe he had mentioned the position in the first place, then hadn't simply told her straight out that she had gotten it wrong.

But he knew why. With her sitting there in Bobby's Place, so beautiful, so fragile, sipping her champagne cocktail with double sugar cubes in a bar that catered to a beer and margarita crowd, he had wanted to wipe away that vulnerable look in her eyes. Without warning, time had turned back, and she was the little girl in crinolines, too pretty to touch, like a doll kept behind glass, no con-

tact with the real world. A fantasy. A dre
his own world of dirt roads and an endlessly
seem manageable.

That night, like now, he had wanted to to
as he had when he was ten years old.

He cursed himself and relished the ruthlessness that he could feel just below the surface. He had survived by maintaining an ironclad control over every aspect of his life. And a slip of a woman who barely came to his chin when she wore those ridiculous high heels wasn't going to undo him.

"I find it hard to believe that you really need a job," he said.

"Need?" The single word squeaked out of her. "*Need* is such an unflattering word. Think of it as helping out."

"Helping?" he asked incredulously.

"Exactly, as in me helping you, and you helping me. What are friends for if not to help each other when they're in a jam? Think of it as a temporary arrangement while I pay off some bills and until you can find someone more qualified to take care of the girls. I'm nothing if not helpful."

"Yeah, you've got Mother Teresa written all over you."

Those gray eyes narrowed and flashed. "I wouldn't exactly describe you as a knight in shining armor," she said, then slapped her hand over her mouth. "Sorry," she mumbled. "I shouldn't have said that. I don't know what is happening to me."

He shook his head. "Tell me the real reason you need a job, Vivienne. Is your father having some kind of financial problem?"

Horror whipped across her face. "Of course not. My father is fine. He's just out of town, as I said, and un-

_chable." She shrugged daintily. "Besides, my bills are my responsibility. So I need a job."

"From my vantage point, it seems like you can hardly take care of yourself, much less my little sisters. Even temporarily."

She sucked in her breath, making him curse.

"I'm sorry, Vivienne, really," he offered gently. "But this isn't an option."

"Of course it is!"

This was crazy. Sure, he was drawn to her. Just looking at her made his blood heat. But hire her?

"It won't work," he told her with the hard-edged business voice he used to intimidate an opponent.

"Why not?"

Max was rarely questioned, and only by his teenage sister. The last thing he needed was a woman who would promote the very habit that was starting to wear on his nerves.

He focused on Vivienne. "The answer is no."

"That's the best you can do?"

He must have made a face, because she dropped her arms and her expression became determined.

"I can do this," she stated with conviction. "I really can. And I'll be good at it. Just give me a chance."

His jaw clenched as he stared at her. She wasn't afraid of him, probably had never encountered the word *intimidated*. A pit bull in ruffles.

"How about a loan?" he suggested, feeling a little desperation of his own. "I could do a loan. As big as you want. Pay me back whenever you can. No rush."

He'd insulted her—he could see it in the red that surged into her cheeks.

"I couldn't accept a loan. I have more than enough debt as it is."

"Fine, consider it a gift. How much do you need?"

"I don't want your money! I don't want anyone's money. I'm going to find work and clear up this mess. Besides, you offered me a job."

"Actually . . ."

He stared at her long and hard. Just a few simple words would clear up the misunderstanding. He had never intended to offer her employment, had only wanted to point out that there were all sorts of things people do. But he couldn't bring himself to say the words.

He cursed himself for the flicker of emotion this woman stirred inside him, hated that somehow she brought to the surface a weakness he had thought long buried. He had hammered out a life of strength and re-moteness, keeping people at a distance so he could stay focused on the task at hand—the task that had consumed him since he turned nineteen. Surviving.

He had believed that feelings had been burned out of him long ago. But just the sight of this woman, the memory of her as a child, turned his thoughts upside down.

Hell, yes, he wanted her out of his life.

But there was another reality he had to deal with be-sides what this woman made him feel, and that was the undeniable fact that Nicki and Lila had run off every maid, housekeeper, and nanny he had hired. Only he and Patricia could control the girls. The rest of the Landry clan had given up long ago.

Since then, the stream of women Max had interviewed hadn't provided him any hope that they'd be any better.

Nicki was a handful, and Lila followed her older sister like a puppy dog.

Right or wrong, he was desperate. And while Vivienne Stansfield wasn't a good answer, she was the only answer available just then.

"I really do know a lot about girls," she added hopefully, as if she could sense he was wavering.

His brain raced for an alternate plan. One that would get her out of his office and someone else into his house by Sunday night to take care of the girls when they returned from Patricia's apartment. But nothing came to mind.

His eyes narrowed against the emotion that gripped his chest—something he hadn't felt in years.

"Hell." He hesitated. "I know I'm going to regret this, but *if* I hire you, you'd have to stay at the house."

"Overnight?"

"Is that a problem?"

"Why do you need me there twenty-four hours a day if you're there after work?"

"I can't always get home, and I don't want the girls in the house alone at night."

"Then I'll stay when you travel."

His jaw muscles ticked. "I don't always know when I won't be coming home."

"You can leave town without even taking the time to get luggage?"

"It's not always about travel."

"Why else wouldn't you come home—" She cut herself off, then scoffed in disbelief. "You mean you go out with women, then . . . then . . . don't go home?"

"Not since Patricia moved out," he stated tightly, before he shook his head. "Why am I explaining? This won't work."

Vivienne put her hands up. "Fine, I'll stay nights."

His eyes narrowed as he debated. "You'll have to cook."

"Consider it done."

He hung his head. How had he gotten himself in this position?

"Just give me a chance, Max."

The conviction and enthusiasm that had tried to surface on her features dimmed. Suddenly he realized that she was still fighting hard to hold on, hold back emotion, not give in. If nothing else, he understood that.

"You won't be disappointed," she whispered. "I promise."

He groaned.

Her hands curled up in little hopeful fists, and she caught her breath. "Please, Max, tell me I have the job."

Seconds ticked by, options ran out. "Temporarily," he conceded. Though little did she know that given his sisters' ability to run people off, he doubted she'd last longer than twenty-four hours.

She all but gasped her relief, then squealed her delight as she flung her arms around him, only pulling back when the heat started to resurface.

"Ummm, well," she said, clearing her throat. "No more of that."

Suddenly she was Ms. Demure—if anyone with sexy pink lips and incredible legs underneath a scrap of material that was a sorry excuse for a skirt could be considered demure.

She clasped her hands. "When's payday?"

He growled, though he did provide a date and an amount.

"Great. When do I meet the girls?"

"They get back Sunday afternoon around five. You can meet them then."

"Perfect. Just give me your address."

Reluctantly, he did.

"Fine. I'll go home and pack a few things, then I'll be there."

She turned away, then stopped. Slowly she pivoted back and cringed. "I'm going to need a tiny bit of help."

"Already?"

"Funny."

"Believe me, I don't see anything funny about this. Tell me the problem."

"Gas. I ran out when I pulled in across the street."

My Wedding Diary

THINGS TO REMEMBER

1. Never get mad
2. Nix showing emotion of any kind
3. Don't take self too seriously
4. Stop pathetic habit of writing in wedding diary when no longer going to be a bride!!!

Though quite frankly, who else am I going to confide in? My mother? Hardly. My father? Not an option. Max? I don't think so. Which leads to the dismal reality of my life. I have no friends or available family to talk to. Not that I'm mad about that. (See #1 above.) And not that I would burden them anyway. (See #2 above.) My problems are completely and utterly minor on the scale of problems. I mean, really, there are people starving in Ethiopia. (See #3 above.) So my choices are to vent in a no-longer-valid wedding diary, or to no one. (Ignore #4 above.)

Chapter Seven

Sunday afternoon, at five exactly, Vivi arrived at Number 15 Pinehurst Drive. She sat up straighter in her car, determined not to give in to panic. Everything would work out just fine.

Over the weekend, she had held out hope that her father would call and she could straighten out this mess before Sunday afternoon even arrived. Surely he had simply moved the money or invested in stocks and bonds. Or . . .

Well, she hadn't been able to come up with any other reasonable explanation, especially when she remembered the missing jewelry.

Unfortunately, her father hadn't called, though several bill collectors had.

As a result, the thought of getting away from her father's Sutton Place condominium wasn't altogether unappealing now that she had joined the ranks of debt-ridden individuals who were hounded by an assortment of thug-like Mob types wielding baseball bats.

Max's house wasn't far from the condo, just farther up the mountain in the Coronado Country Club. At first sight, his home was gigantic—a sprawling hacienda with creamy adobe walls, terra-cotta tiles on the roof, and an abundance of beautifully trailing wisteria blooms covering an arbor that arched over the long drive to the garage out back. The house was impressive, perched on the edge of the rolling green golf course.

She had grown up in the Upper Valley, on a ten-acre estate. The property had been sold after her parents divorced, her mother downsizing again and again until she lived out of a backpack in India. Her father had downsized as well, now living in the condo where Vivi had been staying while she planned the wedding.

Vivi shuddered. Missing fathers. Canceled weddings. Puny penises. And now she had a job. She hardly recognized her life anymore.

Shaking the thought away, Vivi gathered her suitcases. She clicked up to the entrance of Max's home in a leopard-print skirt and café au lait top, then stared at the door. Then stared just a little longer.

"This is not a problem," she told herself firmly, setting down the luggage, adjusting her skirt one last time, before ringing the bell.

Seconds passed without a response. Ringing again, she stood there. Just when she would have banged the brass knocker, the door was pulled open and she peered down at a very serious-looking young girl. Despite the thick Coke-bottle glasses she wore, she looked just like Max.

Silence ticked by as each of them absorbed the other until Vivi smiled brightly and said, "Hello, I'm Vivi Stansfield."

The door was pulled open wider, revealing another girl, older, no doubt the fourteen-year-old. She also looked like Max, even if she was staring at Vivi with a scowl.

"Who are you? One of my brother's nimrod girl-friends?"

This from the sneering teen who looked like a cross between Morticia from *The Addams Family* and a bad-boy rapper from MTV. Everything she wore was black and baggy, and her hair fell into her eyes. Instantly, Vivi saw that with the right makeup and clothes, the girl would be pretty. Very pretty.

Project, she nearly enthused.

"Actually, no," Vivi said instead. "I'm not one of your brother's girlfriends."

"Then you must be the new nanny," the younger of the two surmised.

Nanny? Her?

Vivi hadn't quite thought of it in those terms. But she could do nanny.

"I'm Lila," the little one said, the seriousness on her tiny features softening with a mix of disbelief and awe.

Unlike the older sister's, Lila's clothes were a mis-matched assortment of colors. Red scarf, purple belt, pink sneakers with hand-drawn daisies on the canvas. Even her glasses were a bright shade of blue.

"And you're beautiful," Lila breathed, pushing her frames up on her nose. "You look like a doll."

The older one snorted. "Yeah, like a Barbie doll with fake plastic hair and a painted-on smile."

Vivi blinked. "Do you write for the *El Paso Tribune*?"

"Huh?"

"Nothing, nothing. Is your brother home?"

"Yes." Then silence.

"Could you tell him that I'm here?"

"Not a good idea," Lila supplied.

"Why is that?"

"He's working out in the gym upstairs. But he'll be finished any time. He's into the whole healthy heart thing. I think he's a little too into the exercising myself, but you know how old people get when they're trying to stay young."

Vivi eyed the little girl curiously, then turned to the teenager. "You must be Nicki."

She got a scoff for an answer.

"We should wait for Max inside," Lila suggested.

Leaving the suitcases on the patio, they went to the kitchen, which was a great space of high-beamed ceilings, white walls with Spanish arches, and a terra-cotta tile floor. Brushed chrome appliances accented the room, and just beyond the windows the hill-swept golf course spread out like a carpet.

Nicki sat down at the table and opened *Spin* magazine.

Lila offered Vivi a vacant chair, then sat next to her. The eleven-year-old cupped her chin in her palm. "Have you been a nanny for long?"

Without looking up from the magazine, Nicki snorted. "Does she look like she's *ever* been a nanny?"

That's when Lila smiled, a wide pull of lips that lit up her face, a laugh spilling over as she tilted in her chair like a teapot and looked under the table at Vivi's shoes. "No," she decided. "But she looks wonderful and fun."

"You're here."

All three of them whirled around at the sound of the voice. Max leaned up against a doorjamb, his arms crossed on his chest, those dark blue eyes glittering, his hair combed back and still wet from a shower. He didn't have on a sports coat, but he looked nearly as dressed up since he wore navy slacks with a white button-down shirt. His loafers sported tassels. Still formidable. Vivi wondered if he even owned a pair of jeans.

Lila sat Indian style in the chair. "If you're referring to Vivi, she is here. How'd you find her?"

Max smiled with a hint of devilish amusement. "I think it's safe to say that *she* found me."

Vivi rolled her eyes. But his gaze turned slow and heated, turning her eye roll into a blink.

"I didn't think you'd show up," he said.

She forced her mind away from how good he looked and how out of sorts she felt. "I'm nothing if not responsible."

Max chuckled, his mood appreciably better than the last time she'd seen him.

"That's right, you're Miss Never Drive over the Speed Limit," he quipped, pushing away from the wall.

"Funny."

The girls watched the exchange closely, then Nicki flipped her magazine closed. "You've outdone yourself, Maxwell. You've hired a woman who looks like a party cake, who no doubt knows more about getting into your bed than making one, and who probably can't spell the word *nanny* much less be one."

Vivi's mouth fell open. Max glowered. Lila sighed. "Nicki," she said beneath her breath, "give this one a chance. She's nice."

Nicki scowled, then stood. "I've got homework to do."

Max and Nicki stared at each other hard before the teen actually smiled with malice, then shot Vivi a hatred-filled smirk as she slouched out the door. Almost reluctantly, Lila followed. Seconds later the television flared on.

Vivi faced the empty doorway, speechless. It was one

thing to read about someone's dislike in the newspapers, but quite another to hear the words uttered to her face.

Ouch.

"They're lovely," Vivi offered.

Max didn't move for long seconds, his face a mask of stone. "I apologize for Nicki. But she's . . . a teenager."

"And that makes it okay to be ill-mannered? Not that I care for me. I'm used to it. But clearly something is wrong."

His jaw tightened. "Nothing is wrong. Nicki is just being fourteen."

"Which implies?"

She could feel the shift in him, the low simmer of frustration that started to rise.

"She's filled with hormones that make her do and say things that she doesn't really mean."

She looked at him incredulously. "Did you read that in a teenage how-to guide somewhere?"

"No, I raised five other kids."

"Score one for Max. Good answer."

He took the steps that separated them, like a predator stalking. Instantly her heart lodged in her throat and her pulse pounded like an African drum. But she stood her ground.

Stopping mere inches away, he studied her, much as the girls had earlier. Her senses leaped when his gaze drifted low. She could feel the heat of him as it swelled around them.

A sudden, undeniable surge of lust stabbed through her, making her dizzy. It amazed her how this man made her feel. Hot and aching, a little of the wildness she had tamped down for a lifetime bubbling over.

It was all she could do not to lean into the promise of

his eyes. He wanted her just as badly as she wanted him. The knowledge was heady.

But then he cursed.

"What was that for?" she demanded.

"You make me crazy. This isn't going to work. I've hired you to take care of my sisters, and the minute I see you I'm—" He cut himself off and ran a hand through his hair.

"You're what?"

His eyes narrowed. "Even crazier. Look, I think we can both see that this is a mistake. Let me give you some money and you can go get a job somewhere else."

"You can't fire me!"

"Think of it as having never being hired."

"But I was hired. And unless I don't perform my duties, you can't fire me."

"Says who?"

"Say . . . says . . . some government type who won't cotton up to an employer recanting a job offer."

"Cotton up?"

She sliced him a look. "The fact is you need a caregiver and I need a job. We've been over this. Besides," she reasoned, an unexpected sense of pleasure washing through her, "I think Lila really likes me."

Max stared at her long and hard, and she would have sworn he knew she was right.

"Fine, you can stay, at least until you cross me, and then you're out. Remember, we said this was temporary. Understand?"

"Perfectly. Now, where should I put my things?"

"I'll show you your room."

After a few less than kind comments about the sheer number of suitcases she had, they made short work of bringing her belongings inside. Or rather he made short work of it, since he hardly allowed her to do a thing. He might not want her there, but he was still the perfect gentleman. It was hard to imagine they still made men like him.

He led her through the house of tile floors and high ceilings. Everywhere she looked there were skylights and plants. It felt warm and tropical, like a world far removed from her own.

Yet one more step away from her former life. She wasn't sure if she was scared, terrified . . . or strangely elated.

They came to two sets of stairs. One led off to the left, the other to the right.

"Your house is beautiful," she offered, as they climbed the left set of stairs, which overlooked a foyer.

"Thanks."

"Did you build or buy?"

"Built."

"How long have you lived here?"

"Eight months."

But the words didn't register when he stopped in a bedroom. She realized they were in a separate wing of the house.

"Whose room is this?" she asked even though he was setting down her belongings. "Okay, it's mine. But"—she glanced at a connecting door leading to another bedroom—"who sleeps in there?" She grimaced and pointed. "Is it an overlarge guest room, perhaps? An extra master suite just in case you have some really, really important company? Or do your sisters go for hunter prints instead of rock star posters?"

"I hope you're not going to use that Valley Girl talk in

front of the girls. When I relented and hired you, I consoled myself with the idea that a woman of refinement and society would be influencing Nicki and Lila, not the trendy, Oh-my-gosh-that-is-awesome sort of sisters that I already have."

"Is that your way of saying you don't want to answer my question about the bedroom?"

"That is my bedroom, and—"

"And? We aren't finished with the 'that is my bedroom' part! Where are the girls' rooms? Why am I not by them?"

"Unless you want to sleep on the foldout couch in the den or in the maid's room near the utility area, this is the only room available. And believe me, the door will be closed and locked from now on." Then he shook his head, picked up her Louis Vuitton bags, and headed toward the door, forcing her back a few steps to get out of the way.

"You're right," he added. "What was I thinking? The maid's room will do. You *are* the help."

"Me? I mean, yes, me. I am the help, but on second thought, I see no reason why I can't be perfectly fine right here."

His smile turned wicked, teasing, which surprised Vivi as much as it worried her.

"But really, I shouldn't treat you any differently than every other nanny I hired."

That got her attention. "*Every* other nanny you hired?"

"Well . . ."

Suddenly this tall, dark, manly man looked distinctly sheepish.

"Max?"

"It's nothing, really. I hired a few, but they didn't work out. It's no big deal."

"It's sounding less like a *no big deal* than it sounds like a definite big deal. Why didn't they work out?"

"They couldn't handle the . . . responsibilities."

"How many nannies have there been?"

"One or two."

"Are you sure?"

"Or six."

"Six?" she screeched.

"In as many weeks."

"What kind of sisters do you have?"

He shot her a scowl. He wasn't teasing anymore. "The regular kind." He set down the bags. "All you have to do is feed them, clothe them, drive them to and from school, see to it that they get to all those things they do in the afternoons, and take care of the house. At night, make sure they do their homework and get them to bed on time."

Her mind raced at the thought of taking care of two girls who had run off six other women—no doubt experienced caregivers with a great deal more knowledge than she had.

"Also," he continued, looking her up and down, "I'd like you to take the girls shopping for clothes. Maybe you could steer Nicki away from all that black."

Vivi told herself to stay calm. She could do this. How hard could it be? Besides, her father never stayed away longer than a month. Maybe two. "I'd love to take Nicki shopping," she said. Though she didn't add that as much as she liked the idea of a project, she didn't think a girl who had said she looked like a party cake was going to be all that keen on taking fashion advice from her.

"Now for the rules," he said.

Rules? Her brain was already on tilt, but she didn't think asking him to slow down was a good idea.

He locked his hands behind his back and started to pace. "Nicki isn't allowed to date."

"Don't fourteen-year-old girls and boys do things like go to the mall?"

"It's not the *boys* I'm concerned with. It's the seventeen-year-old seniors, specifically the seniors with bad reputations, who interest her. So unless it's another freshman who's going to take her to the Ice Cream Shoppe on a Saturday afternoon, there's no dating."

"Fine."

"And keep her away from that place called Raiders."

"She goes there?"

"Not with permission. My sister-in-law took her shopping last week. Nicki disappeared. Randi got frantic and called the police. They found her at Raiders. From what I gather, there's one senior in particular named Brandon Bonner who she's got a huge crush on. He hangs out at the place."

"Does he like her?"

"I don't think he knows she exists."

"I'm happy to keep her out of Raiders. But why on the one hand are you really strict, then on the other, you let her dress like Morticia? I'm not clear on the psychology here. If you want her out of the black, why not just tell her to change instead of sending me out shopping with her?"

"Clothes are one thing," he said tightly. "Spending time with deadbeat seniors is another."

She held up her hands in surrender. "No problem. You're the boss. What else? What about Lila?"

"Lila is a good kid. Not nearly the trou—" He cleared his throat. "Not nearly as energetic. She won't push you at every turn." He stopped and considered. "Also, I don't want the girls watching horror movies."

"Okay."

"No junk food."

"Not a problem."

"No play dates with kids whose parents you haven't met, or with parents who aren't home."

"Check and check."

"Are you writing this down?"

"I have a mind like a steel trap."

He grumbled something. "I'll leave you a list."

"I'll look forward to it."

Max gave her a look and it was all Vivi could do not to slap her hand over her mouth. She really had to get the hang of being an employee.

"That's about it, at least for now. The girls ordered Mexican food for dinner," he added. "If you want something else, there's plenty in the refrigerator."

"What about you?"

"I'm going out."

"Already?"

"What is that supposed to mean?"

"I just got here."

There went that stern look again. "This isn't a date, Vivienne."

"Oh, darn," she said with exaggerated sweetness. "I'm crushed."

She swore he just might strangle her, but the fact was it didn't take a rocket scientist to see that these girls needed attention. Their brother's attention. She knew all about elusive parents and eating alone.

"What I meant was that, call me insane, maybe you should spend a bit of time eating dinner with your sisters, find out what they're doing in school, or at the very least stay long enough to make sure I'm not a mass murderer or debauched kidnapper with a criminal past."

"Are you?"

"Joke all you want—"

"I'm learning from you."

She shot him a scowl. "I just think it's odd that you would bring in someone new, then disappear."

Max tilted his head, his blue eyes flashing with a speculative gleam. "You really don't want me to leave."

Instantly his mood shifted and he came closer. She remembered how it had felt when he took her in his arms, the command of his lips on hers. The heat, the desire. The kiss they had shared was everything Grady had said she knew nothing about.

The thought leaped into her head that this man could teach her. He could show her the intricacies of intimacy. Lessons of a sort.

And just as soon as the idea was born, shock followed in its wake. What was she thinking? Intimacy with a man for the sole purpose of learning how?

She scoffed silently at the absurdity, the ridiculousness of her even considering such a thing. She was Vivi Stansfield, who had waited twenty-five years, not to mention until she was engaged, before having sex. And now she was wondering about lessons?

Raising her chin, her voice going stiff, she said, "Now, Mr. Landry—"

"Formal, are we? I like it. Why don't you add a few *Yes, sirs* and *No, sirs* to your repertoire?"

"Next you'll be asking me to put on an apron and sit on your lap."

"Not a bad idea." He was so close he could touch her. "What is it about you, Vivienne Stansfield, that makes me crazy one minute, then want to laugh the next?"

She wrapped prim indignation around her like a shield. "Hard to say. But with your sisters close by, this probably isn't the best time to find out."

She wheeled around, intent on fleeing, but his strong hand flattened on the doorjamb, blocking the way. He was so tall, making her feel tiny and delicate, even desirable. Not at all like an untouchable china doll.

Vivi managed a dry, croaking squeak. "What? Do you have a few more instructions for me? Or better yet, how about a few of your witty insults?"

The words stuck in her throat, making her voice crack, though that didn't stop her skin from tingling.

Ever so gently, he reached out and touched her lips, sending sensation racing through her. Despite every ounce of her that knew better, she wanted to lean into him, to feel his lips brush against hers.

But he only chuckled, then ran his fingers down her jaw to her neck. He stopped at the pulse in her throat. His blue eyes darkened with sensuality.

"I haven't insulted you once," he stated, the words a deep rumble of sound.

Inhaling slowly, she couldn't seem to move, forward or back. "Once? No. Try a half dozen times."

"Name one." His fingers moved lower.

"The 'I can't believe I hired you' comment."

"That was a statement of disbelief, not an insult."

"You say tomato, I say tomahto."

"Are you ever serious?"

"Not if I can help it."

"Did it ever occur to you that if you were serious every once in a while, you might not be in this situation?"

The words hurt, cutting deep to that place that made it harder to keep the panic at bay. But she had spent years perfecting the skill, and she wasn't going to let this man or this situation undo all her hard work.

Her eyes popped open, her mind cementing. Raising her chin, she fell back on old habits, those things that kept her safe. "I'm convinced that the whole thinking thing is overrated."

Max shook his head and smiled as he looked at her mouth. But just when she knew he would have dipped his head and kissed her, a voice rang out.

"Max! The food's here! I need some money!"

"Ah, dinner," Vivi said, relief making her knees weak. At least that's what she told herself it was. "You know, on second thought, I see no reason for you to eat in. Tacos, ugh. So not you." She gave an exaggerated shudder. "You can have dinner with the girls some other night."

Chapter Eight

Max gave Nicki some money for the delivery guy, then startled everyone a few minutes later when he entered the kitchen.

"Is there an extra burrito for me?" he asked, his blue eyes smiling.

Vivi was too surprised to respond. One, because he had changed into jeans, and two, because he looked great—better than great.

He still wore the same starched white shirt, but now it was tucked into faded button-fly denim, soft but clean, that molded to his butt and cupped his crotch like a lover. His hair had dried, winging back from his forehead, making her want to reach out and run her fingers through it.

Lila didn't appear surprised by his attire, but she was surprised by the fact that he was there. "You're eating with us?" she asked, her eyes even larger than usual behind her glasses.

"Don't look so shocked. I thought it would be a good time to catch up."

"Great." Nicki rolled her eyes.

"Nicki," Max warned, retrieving a plate, sitting down, then helping himself to dinner.

Vivi watched the Landrys, all varying images of the

other. Not only did they look alike, but they picked up their burritos the same way, then tilted their heads at the exact same angle as they took a bite. Tickled, thinking they would make a great nature vs. nurture experiment, Vivi picked up her fork and knife and cut off a small piece. Just as she was taking it toward her open mouth, she froze when she noticed all three of the Landrys staring at her in astonishment.

"What?" she demanded.

"You're eating your burrito with a fork and knife," Nicki scoffed.

Vivi hardly knew how to respond. But no one said anything when Lila quietly got up and retrieved a fork and knife for herself. When she saw that everyone was watching her, she said, "I think it's a good idea."

"Sheesh," Nicki muttered.

Vivi wanted to hug Lila tight. "As I recall, the three of you were catching up."

Lila appeared thrilled at the prospect of discussing, as she called it, the educational trials and tribulations of junior high.

"That's right," Lila said with a nod. "Let's talk about school. What do you want to know, Max?"

Her brother sat back and seemed at a loss. Clearly quality time with his sisters was at a minimum. "What did you learn this week?"

Lila snorted. "That most eleven-year-olds can't use the word *penis* without laughing."

Max choked, Nicki's mouth fell open, and Vivi cringed at the reminder of her own unfortunate penis episode. However, no one had been laughing during hers.

"I don't get why," Lila continued with the seriousness

of a Nobel Laureate, "that word causes such an uproar. Penis," she said, tilting her head one way. "Penis," she tried again, her chin jutting forward. "I just don't get it."

By now, Max's jaw had turned to stone.

"Maybe it's the fact that Ms. Pearl is teaching health this year," Lila reasoned, "in a coed class. It's no secret that every boy at Morehead Middle School has a crush on her. Though you'd understand that, Max, since you have a crush on her yourself."

Vivi cocked her head. "You're infatuated with your sister's teacher?"

"I am not," he responded, caught off guard. "I took her out. Once."

"Actually twice," Lila supplied, "if you count the way he swept her off her feet at the parent-teacher conference—"

Vivi was aghast and mouthed, *At a parent-teacher conference?*

"—and took her who knows where afterward. She was extra nice to me for an entire week." The child leaned closer to Vivi with a knowing sigh. "My brother's a real Romeo, so it shouldn't have been a surprise. But who knew he was so great that he could get my grade average up from an A to an A+? As far as I'm concerned, he can date all my teachers." She *hmm*ed. "Though I haven't had much luck getting him to ask out my PE teacher."

Max glowered. Nicki snickered.

"What's wrong with her?" Vivi asked.

"*She's* a *he*," Nicki supplied.

"One of those big burly jock guys that have gone to fat, but hey," Lila added, "I could use all the help I can get in gym. I mean really, when am I ever going to use chin-ups and rope climbing in the real world?"

"I think it's about maintaining your health," Vivi offered.

Nicki sneered. "This from a woman who probably thinks push-ups apply only to bras—"

"Stop," Max warned.

"Oh, great." Nicki rolled her eyes. "Trying to show off in front of the new nanny."

"I've had enough." His blue eyes blazed with anger. "I'm tired of your mouth, young lady. If you can't say anything nice, don't say anything at all."

An intense fury came over Nicki. The teen threw down her napkin and nearly knocked the chair over when she leaped up.

"I've had enough too. I hate this house. I hate you pretending to care," she accused Max. "And most of all I hate her," she spat, pointing at Vivi. "I'm fourteen years old, old enough to take care of myself. I don't need a nanny, especially some spoiled Barbie doll."

Then Nicki ran out of the room.

"I take it our catching-up dinner is done," Lila lamented. After a second, she got up from the table. "Thanks for trying, Max." She leaned close to Vivi and said, "I like you even if you are spoiled."

Vivi didn't know what to say as Lila disappeared. Vivi's family wasn't known for *any* kind of displays of emotion, good or bad. Part of her was embarrassed. But another part, one she hardly recognized, realized that Nicki was hurting, which made her lash out.

Max sat very still, and Vivi wondered about this family. Reaching over, she patted his hand. "Hey, you've got to start somewhere. I think it's great that you tried."

With barely held control, Max shot her a scowl, then he stood. Seconds later, he pushed out through the swinging kitchen door, leaving Vivi alone with the sudden feeling that these people might actually need her, whether they realized it or not.

Doubt tried to surface. She had spent a lifetime trying to fix things and help people, even though she had never been able to fix her own family.

Exhibit one: Her parents' divorce.

Exhibit two: Her mother preferring to plan the now nonexistent wedding from India.

Exhibit three: Vivi didn't have a clue where her father was or why he had taken her money.

Was she crazy to think she could be any more useful to Max and his sisters? Or, by being an outsider looking in, without a vested interest, could she help this man understand things he was too close to see?

Her chin rose. Maybe, maybe not. But she was there, in the house, and she had to at least try.

She was dreaming again. Of penthouses and rolling plastic cups, of a shimmering touch that sent a jolt through her body.

And peppermint.

Vivi wrinkled her nose, rolled over, and tried to burrow deeper into the mattress. But the smell of candy wouldn't go away, and slowly she woke. With a yawn and a stretch, she opened her eyes. And gasped.

"Lila?" she yelped.

The girl sat in a chair beside the bed, her chin in her palm, her elbow on her knee, staring at her.

"You must have been having some dream," the eleven-year-old announced.

Red seared Vivi's cheeks at the memory of just the kind of dream she was having. Max. Touching her.

Making her body tingle in front of a giant window, the city spilling out below. "I wasn't dreaming," she lied. "Is something wrong?"

"Nope. Not a thing."

"Then why are you here?" She glanced at the clock. It was only seven in the morning.

"Seemed like a good idea to make sure you didn't oversleep. It's your first full day and all, so you probably don't realize that we have to leave for school in thirty minutes. It takes ten minutes to get there if we hit all the lights right, but nearly sixteen if we don't. Not to mention I figured it might take you a little while to get all those party clothes on."

"Thank you," Vivi said with a big fake smile.

But the girl didn't budge, and Vivi realized she wasn't going to, just in case anyone was tempted to drift back to sleep.

"All right, all right." Vivi pushed up from the mattress. "There. I'm up. Now let me get ready." She glanced at Lila. "And don't you think you should too? Bathe, dress, brush teeth, and whatnot?"

Lila laughed out loud. "Whatnot. That's a great word." She leaped off the chair. "I've been making a list of excellent words and interesting facts."

"Great. Glad I could help."

"Did you know that it is virtually impossible to brush your teeth without your thumb?"

Vivi pulled on her wrap. "What?"

"Wow! What is that?"

Straightening in surprise, Vivi surveyed her attire. "This? It's a robe."

"Robes are made of terry cloth and make a person look like a frump."

"Is that one of your new words?"

Lila giggled. "No, but I've been adding stuff about thumbs. Did you know that the thumb is one of the things that makes us superior to other species?"

"Can't say that I did." Vivi headed for the bathroom.

Lila followed. "Most people assume it's just the brain."

"Where did you learn all this?"

"In science. It's in our book." Lila eyed her. "You have heard of books, haven't you?"

"What do I look like?"

"I don't think I should answer that."

"Good idea. Now, really, go get ready for school."

"I am ready."

Vivi raised a brow.

"No offense," the girl stated, "but I'm not sure that someone who wears feathers and high heeled slippers really gets what works in junior high. But," Lila continued, "while you might be clueless about my clothes, I was hoping you actually knew something about breakfast."

"Breakfast?"

"As in making it. It's number two on the list."

"What list?"

Lila extended two pieces of paper. "I found these on the hall table."

Vivi took the sheets, studied the bold strokes scrawled across the creamy vellum, and knew immediately it was from Max.

"It's a time schedule and a list of dos and don'ts," Lila explained. "Personally, I think the no-junk-food rule is overly optimistic. I mean, *no* junk food in a day and age when they serve it in the cafeteria at school?" Lila leaned close. "I think Max hasn't stepped into the new millennium yet."

Vivi glanced down at what was indeed a detailed timetable of what to do when and a list of everything they had gone over yesterday. Clearly the man was leaving nothing to chance.

"Speaking of your brother, where is he?"

"Gone. To work. When he's in town, he usually leaves around six. And I doubt that after last night's disaster, he'll be hanging around for another catch-up dinner anytime soon."

Vivi reached out and touched the girl's hand. Lila stared at their overlapping fingers.

"I'm sorry it didn't work out so well last night."

Lila stared a second longer. "Thanks," she said awkwardly. She started to go, then hesitated. "I'll fix cereal this morning while you get dressed. But tomorrow you might want to get up earlier. Once we finish, Nicki and I'll meet you at the car so we don't risk being late."

Indeed, Nicki and Lila were sitting in Vivi's convertible, top up, windows down, when she came out. Without a word, she got in, then headed down the hill. Quiet reigned for the first few minutes until they pulled onto Thunderbird Drive.

Vivi broke the silence. "We have a big day after school."

"Shopping," Lila acknowledged. "I had a memo from Max this morning."

"A memo?"

"He's busy," Lila explained.

"Yeah," Nicki added. "Busy sleeping with anything in a skirt."

A sizzle of something shot through her. Jealousy? Absolutely not. A hot flash? A fever? Surely she was getting sick, because she did not, in any way, care whom Max did or did not sleep with.

"Whatever the reason," she responded crisply, "that isn't my business. Shopping, however, is. I'll pick you up after school, then we'll go someplace special. Perhaps Bon Vivant."

"Yeah, right," Nicki said.

"We're kids," Lila offered with an apologetic shrug. "Not flashy rich women from across the border or old ladies trying to look like rhinestoned fluff dolls."

Vivi blinked. She loved Bon Vivant.

Vivi was thankful when they made it to the junior high school, where Lila piled out. "Pick me up right here at three-thirty," the child said. "Please don't be late."

A flash of panic darkened the girl's eyes, but then she smiled and slipped into the crush of students making their way through the blue metal doors.

"What was that about?" Vivi asked.

Another scoff. "She doesn't want you to be late."

"Of course," she said past gritted teeth. "Why didn't I get that?"

Next Vivi hurried to Coronado High. The car had barely stopped in front of the high school when Nicki opened the door.

"I'll pick you up here after I get Lila."

"Don't bother."

Swiveling in her seat to stare at the girl, Vivi asked, "What do you mean?"

"I'll take the bus."

"The bus?" Where was her list?

Nicki gave her a sarcastic, openmouthed gape. "As in public transportation," she said, dragging out the words.

"But we're going shopping."

"With you? I don't think so."

"Listen, Nicki, I'm sorry that you don't like . . . this situation."

Nicki snorted.

Vivi persevered, her voice taking on a determined edge. "But your brother said I was supposed to take you shopping, so I am taking you shopping whether you like it or not. Be here after school."

"Or what?"

Good question.

"Just be here, Nicki."

Vivi drove away nearly shaking, and praying that the teen would be there when she returned so she didn't have to figure out what the *or else* would have to be.

But she refused to let Nicki get to her. She had other things to worry about just then. Namely, a list a mile long of all she had to do before she picked up the girls after school.

My Wedding Diary

A BRIDE MUST BE FLEXIBLE

Since I'm no longer going to be a bride, does that mean I don't have to be flexible? I doubt it.

Okay, I'll work on flexible since, admittedly, I'm not off to a great start. But surely I can do nanny better than I did bride-to-be. I really do know how to cook. Though I'm a little iffier on taking care of children, not to mention cleaning and laundry. But how hard can it be?

Chapter Nine

Daytime Schedule

6:30: Wake girls.

Vivi wrinkled her nose. So Lila had woken *her*. Tomorrow she'd set the alarm.

7:00: Breakfast.

Okay, maybe an hour earlier.

7:30: Take girls to school. Nicki—Coronado. Lila—Morehead.

Done! Vivi smiled in triumph.

8:00–3:00: Straighten house—cleaning lady comes once a week.

She could do that.

Laundry. Clothes in chute.

Sorting and soap? Well, fine.

Plan menus.

She could plan with the best of them.

Grocery shop at Pricemart. Charge to my account.

Not a problem. Whether it was food, clothes, or stiletto heels, she loved any kind of shopping.

Cleaners. Find bag in front closet.

Easy.

3:30: Pick up girls.

Already planned.

The list went on regarding afternoon extracurricular activities, dinner, homework, then bed. Nine for Lila. Ten for Nicki.

All, in her opinion, very doable.

Vivi didn't waste any time and got started, walking around the house with her cup of coffee, determining what needed to be straightened. The den had a few cushions out of order. A newspaper left out. The television still on. In quick order, her charm bracelet dangling, she took care of it all.

Den. Check.

The girls' rooms were exact opposites of each other. One was neat, the other a disaster. It was Lila's room that looked as if a cyclone had hit it, with clothes and books everywhere, while Nicki had a place for everything.

Once she had Lila's things straightened, she went across the house to Max's room. Massive bed, those hunter prints. All very masculine, with a military precision, so like the man, controlled and contained, not even a pillow out of place.

She almost looked in his closet and the drawers in his bureau, just to see. She could imagine the suits, shirts, and pants lined up like soldiers, the socks and underclothes in perfect stacks. But she decided against it on the outside chance she'd get caught.

Next on the list, laundry. Heading to a utility area just off the kitchen, she found a washer, dryer, every soap known to man, but no dirty clothes—until she pulled open a small, elevated closet and out came a pile of blue jeans and underwear.

"Ah," she mused to herself, "the chute."

After that, Vivi got the laundry started, sipped her café latte, and began working on a grocery list.

Lost to the task, she couldn't have been more surprised when she glanced up at the clock and saw how
much time had passed. She still had a zillion things to
do. If she didn't hurry, she'd be late picking up the girls.
This was no way to enter the hallowed halls of sainted
nannydom.

Grabbing up her keys, then wasting another five minutes searching for the cleaner's bag, she dashed out the
door and wheeled over to Tailor and Martinizing, before
she careened up and down the aisles at Pricemart like a
contestant in an Everything You Can Grab in Twenty
Minutes melee, throwing things into the basket with
record speed.

She hurried to the cash register, cringing when she
couldn't bring herself to cut off an elderly man so she
could go first. She waited impatiently in line. Finally it
was her turn.

"Cash or credit?"

"It's a charge to Maxwell Landry's account."

That got the checker's attention. The thin, curly-haired
twenty-something looked Vivi up and down.

"You're the new nanny?" she asked, one overplucked
eyebrow raised above too-blue shadow.

"Yes," Vivi said tightly.

"What's your name?"

"Does it matter?"

"If you want to charge this stuff on Mr. Landry's account, it does. I have to make sure you're authorized."

"Oh."

"Yeah, oh," the woman sneered, much like Nicki.

"Vivi Stansfield."

The woman's eyes went wide. "As in *the* Vivi Stansfield?"

Was it possible to say no and get away with it? "None other than."

The woman whistled, then pressed one long fake nail on the inhouse phone. "Harvey, we got Mr. Landry's new nanny here." Pause. "Vivi Stansfield." Pause. Smile. A sly glance, then, "Yeah, that's the one. Standing right here."

Vivi would have melted into the floor if she could have, but she stood her ground, pulling her shoulders back. In all her twenty-six years she had never fallen apart—with the one exception of hurtling herself into Max's arms. That had been a moment of weakness. No question. She hardly understood it, especially when she had never fallen apart before. Not when her parents fought. Not when her parents divorced. Not when her mother decided she didn't want to be a mother any longer.

Vivi certainly wasn't going to fall apart now when some snide checkout girl at Pricemart was getting a laugh out of her being a nanny.

The woman hung up. "You're approved. Mr. Landry called you in this morning."

Managing a tight smile, Vivi waited while the groceries were rung, bagged, then pushed out to her car by a bag boy. She thanked him when he finished, drove back to Max's hacienda, then shuddered twice at the mess that still sprawled out over the kitchen. When Lila had said cereal, Vivi hadn't realized she meant Cream of Wheat cooked on the stovetop.

Vivi counted the minutes until she had to leave, kicked off her mules, put the groceries away, then started to clean.

She shoveled toast and thick globs of now very cold

cereal into the disposal. After she nicked the first finger-
nail, she gave up trying to be careful, then started to
scrub the pan. When she finished and the kitchen
gleamed in the streaming sunlight, for half a second she
stood back and felt a moment of strange pride, until she
remembered the wash.

With a gasp, she dashed to the laundry room,
crammed clothes into the dryer, shoved another load in
the washer, then found the clock: 3:25.

"Oh no!"

She didn't even glance in the mirror as she flew back
out the front door, leaped into her car, then streaked back
down Thunderbird. Traffic on Mesa was heavy, slowing
her down. Wheeling onto school property, she drove like
a fish swimming upstream through the kids flooding out
in a wave. She finally pulled up to the curb, fifteen minutes late, and Lila all but dove into the car. But before
Vivi could utter a word, Lila said, "We better hurry and
get Nicki."

Indeed, by the time they made it to the high school,
Nicki stood there like a knot of fury. Slamming into the
car, the girl folded her arms over her chest.

By then Lila had relaxed, and only seemed relieved
that Vivi had arrived and all had turned out well.

But before Vivi could drive off, a cocky teenage boy
leaned his head in and said, "Hey."

Nicki's eyes went wide and she sat up straight. But
when she started to say something to the guy, he looked
right past her to Vivi.

"Cool car."

Vivi looked back and forth between the two. "Thank
you. Your name is?"

"Brandon. But my friends call me Boomer."

Ah, the infamous senior that Max had warned her about. From the look of rapture on Nicki's face, Vivi knew Max hadn't exaggerated.

"Hey, Brandon," Nicki said shyly.

"Uh, hey." He looked back at Vivi, his cocky teenage smile turning sexy, and said, "Who are you?"

Vivi felt the moment Nicki deflated. Gone was the sneer. Gone was the sarcasm. Gone, even, was that moment of insecurity.

"Can we go?" Nicki asked with sharp, truncated syllables.

Vivi wanted to wring Brandon Bonner's neck. "Sure."

Vivi accelerated, practically taking Brandon "Boomer" Bonner's head off, and turned left into traffic, ignoring the honks.

"Brandon Bonner," Lila mused, leaning forward between the bucket seats, "is nothing but trouble. I mean really, how can a guy with a name like Boomer be such a girl magnet?" Lila sighed wearily. "They say all he has to do is look at a girl a certain way and off come her panties."

Vivi almost wrecked the car.

Lila didn't notice. "He has a brother who is nicer. Steve. But he's the A-plus all-American type that doesn't get the girls nearly as steamed up."

Vivi had to consciously close her mouth, then looked at Nicki, then at Lila in the rearview mirror. "Yes, well." She cleared her throat. "I'm sorry I was late. Hopefully that just gave you a few extra minutes to spend with your friends."

Lila sat back. "I don't have a lot of friends."

For half a second, Nicki's hard expression softened. "You'll find some, kid."

The moment lingered in the car, the sharp edges of the day wearing off. Vivi took it in, savored the unexpected bond between the two sisters. How bad could things be if they shared that kind of love?

They didn't say another word until they pulled up to the Sunland Park Mall.

Once inside, Vivi tried to muster some excitement for shopping, which was odd, since she loved to shop. But generally it didn't come after a day of errands and general housekeeping. Her legs actually pulsed from so much running around.

The threesome went from store to store, finding virtually nothing, agreeing on even less. Clearly they had different tastes. No surprise there.

Then, finally, Vivi found something that she and Nicki might actually agree on. She turned with a flourish, whipped out a deep blue pair of velvet bell bottoms, and said, "Voilà!"

But Nicki was gone.

Lila stood holding a multicolored sweater up in front of a mirror, but Nicki was nowhere to be seen.

"Lila, where's your sister?"

The girl's eyes went wide. "Nicki?"

Trying to remain calm, they searched the entire store with no luck. After that, they branched out into the mall. But there was no glimpse of Nicki.

They had her paged on the public address system. They asked the security guard to search as well. But not a sign.

"How can I have lost a teenager?" Vivi cried, her cool long gone, alarm in full force.

"You know," Lila began, "I bet she's at this place in the parking lot of the mall."

"Raiders? Number eleven on Max's list of don'ts?"

"That's the one."

Vivi moaned, raced out of the mall, then scrambled across the tarmac in her high heels, Lila following along in her wake.

They saw Nicki the minute they walked in the door.

"Wow," Lila said. "What a dump."

Nicki must have heard them, because she turned around, her blue eyes going wide. But then her features hardened when several of the older boys she was with whistled at the sight of Vivi.

"Who's the babe?" one asked.

"Damn, is she sweet," commented another.

Vivi muttered about insensitive men when Nicki wheeled out the door. Vivi and Lila followed, blinking into the harsh afternoon sun. When their eyes adjusted, they saw Nicki leaning back against a roughhewn column, one Dr. Martens boot crooked behind her against the wood, a cigarette in her hand.

"You can't smoke!" Vivi blurted.

The small group the girl stood with jerked around. Nicki groaned, threw down the tobacco, ground it out with a furious stamp, then started away from the building.

Clicking after her, Vivi came up beside her. Vivi grabbed her arm. "Nicki, please."

"I hate you!" she bit out.

"Okay, fine. I get that. But hating me is beside the point. I can't allow you to smoke or go to Raiders."

"My friends are there."

"I don't think those kids are your friends."

"You don't know the first thing about me or my friends."

"Maybe I don't, but I do know that your brother doesn't want you at Raiders. Of course I'm happy to bring it up with him to see if he'll reconsider."

That got Nicki's attention.

Praying the girl would follow, Vivi headed back across the parking lot. Lila caught up, and when Vivi glanced to the side, she sent up silent thanks that Nicki was there too—scowling, angry, and unhappy, but there.

Nicki muttered, "My brother doesn't care where I go or what I do."

"Clearly you haven't seen his list."

"So what. Tell him, see if I care. He'll ground me, take away my allowance, then go on his merry way."

Vivi's response cut off when she made a wrong step and broke the heel of her favorite mules. But that was the least of her problems when she saw her bright red convertible hooked to the back end of a tow truck.

"Oh, my gosh!" was all Vivi managed to say.

"Wow," Nicki breathed.

Thank goodness Lila was there. "Excuse me, sir."

A short, balding man popped out from underneath the car, brushed off his pants, and smiled.

"Howdy there, ma'am."

Snatching up her broken heel, Vivi regained her wits and marched forward, holding herself with importance despite a limp. "What are you doing with my car?"

The man grimaced. "Sorry, but it's my job to repossess this here vehicle." He flipped a lever, and the thick black straps pulled tight before the front wheels of the car lifted off the ground.

Lila looked on with wide-eyed astonishment. Even Nicki appeared surprised.

"But you can't do that," Vivi insisted. "It's my car."

"Tell that to the bank that carries the loan. You must not have made payments in a real long time if they're repossessing it."

"A loan for the car?"

Her father had told her it was hers. Bought and paid for as a graduation gift. Why would he lie?

"Sorry," the man said one last time, before he hopped into the truck and pulled her auto away.

The three females stared.

"Wow," Lila breathed.

"Man," Nicki added.

"Dear Lord," Vivi whispered. "What am I going to do now?"

Chapter Ten

"You what?"

His voice reverberated through the executive offices of MBL Holdings, and several of his vice presidents turned to stare.

"Now, Max, calm down," Vivienne said to him over the phone. "It's not as bad as it sounds."

Drawing a deep breath, Max sat back in his leather chair and stared at the mountains without seeing them. What had ever possessed him to give Vivienne Stansfield a job?

But he knew. He had fallen for the memory of a little girl. And Lila's unexpected smile.

The second he had stepped into the kitchen doorway and seen his all too serious little sister tip over and look at Vivienne's crazy shoes under the table, then announce she thought the new nanny was fun, had sealed his fate. God, how his heart had jarred to see her act like the girl she was. And Vivienne Stansfield had been the one to make it happen.

"Start from the beginning," he said with resigned patience into the phone.

"Well, you see, we were at the mall, buying winter

clothes, just as you instructed. Granted, we hadn't found anything yet, at least nothing that—"

"Forget the clothes. What happened to your car?"

"Ah, yes. That. It's gone. So we need a ride."

"Gone as in broken down?"

"Not exactly."

"Gone as in stolen?"

"Heavens, who knew there were so many options for gone?"

"Vivi," he warned.

He could all but hear her wince over the phone line and he knew he wasn't going to like her answer.

"Gone as in towed," she explained.

"Your car was towed?" His jaw ticked and he felt an unfamiliar pulse banging at his temples. The woman was going to give him a stroke. "What did you do, park in a No Parking zone? A handicap spot? In front of a fire hydrant?"

"That is completely unfair. I would never park any-where other than a clearly marked space," she stated defensively. Then she hesitated again, before she whis-pered into the receiver. "However, based on my recent, most unfortunate run of bad luck in the money depart-ment—"

He couldn't believe he actually snorted.

"—I'm guessing it's another one of those pesky little payment problems," she finished.

"Hell," he swore. "Where are you now?"

"Outside of the mall, standing at the door to Dillards. The security guard who circles the property is starting to look at us funny. We really could use a ride."

"Don't move. I'll be there in ten minutes."

He slammed down the phone, grabbed up his sports

coat, and headed for the door. "Hattie, I've got to take care of something."

"But, sir, you have a five o'clock meeting with a prospective client."

He muttered yet another oath under his breath. He had never cancelled an appointment in his life—until Vivienne Stansfield walked through his door.

"Reschedule. The girls are stranded and I have to get them."

"How did that happen?" Hattie asked.

"Don't ask."

It took him less than ten minutes to get there as he shot between the rugged desert mountains that framed Mesa Street. He saw them immediately when he pulled into the parking lot outside the department store. Nicki wore all that damned black, Lila in her ragtag assortment of rainbow colors, and Vivienne. How had Lila described her in the note he had gotten that morning?

The beautifully wonderful Barbie doll nanny.

He couldn't disagree. Long legs, short skirt, jangle of bracelets, and those damned pink lips that did crazy things to his head. He almost smiled at the thought, until he remembered that the woman had turned his well-ordered world upside down—all in less than twenty-four hours under his roof.

At the curb, his sisters and Vivienne stood frozen, staring at him. He must have looked as murderous as he felt since each one of them grimaced before Vivienne raised her hand in a quick, cartoonlike wave. He didn't wave back.

Reluctantly, they came toward the car, Lila nudging up her glasses, Nicki scowling, Vivienne smoothing her hair. She was also holding one of her shoes.

When the girls climbed into the backseat, Vivienne waited one long second, then slid reluctantly into the front.

"Hello!" she said with forced cheer.

He could see the guilt just below the surface. Then he glanced at Nicki. She looked guilty, too, though he couldn't imagine why, since despite her run-ins with principals and teachers, he doubted his sister had anything to do with a towed car.

"What's wrong with your shoe?" he asked Vivienne.

"Oh, this?" She held it up. "I broke a heel walking across the parking lot."

It wasn't until they were heading toward the exit and Nicki hurriedly glanced away from Raiders that Max knew something else had happened.

He eyed Nicki in the rearview mirror, then glanced over at Vivienne as he stopped at the light in front of the teen hangout. "What were you doing walking around the parking lot?"

Vivienne got very still.

Lila gasped.

When Nicki scrunched down in the seat even farther, he noticed that Vivienne glanced at the teen, her brow furrowing, before she returned her attention to him.

"There's a lot of parking lot between the car and the mall," she explained.

"You weren't for some reason walking back and forth between the mall and Raiders, were you?"

"Raiders? Why would I want to go to a place like that? Oh, look. The light's green."

To prove the point, someone honked.

"Saved by the horn," Lila supplied under her breath.

After one long, contemplative glower, Max drove

them home. The minute he pulled into the driveway, Lila and Nicki leaped out of the car. Vivienne did the same.

"Not you," he said to the nanny.

Nicki sneered, then leaned close to Vivienne. "Don't think that your not telling on me is going to make me like you any more."

Vivi knew Max couldn't have heard, but he knew enough to call out, "That's enough from you."

Nicki instantly got angrier.

"Go inside and stay there," he commanded. "You are in charge of Lila until I return. Vivienne and I are going to figure out her finances."

That took Vivi's mind off the teenager fast enough.

Vivi waved his comment away. "Now, really, Max, that isn't necessary."

"If your car was towed, I'm guessing it is."

It didn't take more than a minute or two to get to the Sutton Place complex. Using her keys at the front door, Vivi went straight to the kitchen and tossed her shoes in the trash. When she returned, she found Max walking around her father's living room, seeing the few things she had added to make herself feel at home.

Suddenly she felt awkward, exposed. Grady had rarely come over, and was generally in a hurry to be somewhere else when he did. With her father out of town, his condominium had become a place where she could be herself, and as Max walked around, she suddenly saw the place through someone else's eyes.

A pen with a puff of feathers on the end next to a stack of bright pink stationery with "Vivi" scrawled across the top. The cherry red pillows thrown over the surprisingly sterile furniture.

Her eyes narrowed as she remembered that the place was rented. Could the furniture be rented as well?

Where did the lies end and the truth begin?

Her father had always been the richest man in town. The king of El Paso. Why would he rent? Why would he take her money?

Her head throbbed with questions she didn't know how to answer.

Max stopped in front of a shelf of photos and noticed one with her holding a trophy.

"What is this?" he asked.

She stared at the picture until she felt an ease seep through her. Foolishly she had pulled out her favorite photos and lined them on the bookshelf. "First runner-up for the Miss Teen Homemaker of America contest."

Max looked as if he had swallowed the small gold-plated trophy of a woman in an apron.

"I know, it's hard to believe," she conceded. "My mother was in her militant feminist stage and was appalled that I had entered much less come close to winning. But I was really good at it. We had to sew a dress, plan a menu, and make a dessert." Given her new job, she was inclined to regret that Home Economics 1A hadn't taught much beyond cooking and sewing. She could have used a lesson or two in the basics of home maintenance.

She shot him a pleased smile. "I should have won first place."

"Why didn't you?"

Her smile turned wry. "The judges said I got carried away."

He raised a brow, a hint of humor surfacing. "You?"

"Funny. I prefer to think that I took artistic license."

His glance ran the length of her fluttery clothes. "With the dress you had to make?"

"No, the dessert." She cringed. "I had just seen an old *Titanic* movie, and before I knew it I had shaped my baked Alaska into an iceberg."

He laughed out loud, looking at her as if seeing her for the first time. When his laughter trailed off, he shook his head and moved on to the next framed photograph.

Her heart stilled when he picked up her very favorite. She had been eleven, horrible-looking in braces and barrettes. Smiling, arms extended as she displayed a row of Christmas gifts spilling out of boxes and wrapping paper.

Max studied the photograph, a slow, crooked smile curving his lips.

"My awkward phase," she admitted. "But it was a great Christmas." She felt the poignancy of that year return as if it had been only yesterday. Both her mother and her father had been in town, and they'd had a "family" dinner together even though they were already divorced.

Just the three of them, like a real family during the holidays, no new stepmother to take her father away.

"Is that a flowered push-up bra?" Max asked, then peered closer. "And a doll?"

"Yes." She smiled indulgently. "My father wasn't sure what an eleven-year-old was supposed to want. I was living with my mother then, and I rarely saw him."

Max turned to look at her, his brow furrowed. "Didn't you always live with your mother?"

Vivi adjusted the tangle of bracelets on her arm, making sure each of them lined up. "I did for a few years, until my mother started traveling more than usual.

It only made sense that I should live with my father after that."

He studied her much as he had studied the surroundings, and her awkwardness grew.

"What?" she demanded.

"Nothing. I didn't know that your mother left you like that."

"My mother did not leave me. She was finding herself. There's a big difference."

"Not to a kid," he offered with a wealth of kindness.

She felt something rise up in her. Confusion? Sadness? Gratitude that someone understood?

"I was fine with it. I understood what my mother needed to be happy."

His brow arched, but he didn't say anything. But when he turned away, she could tell he didn't believe her.

"Either way," he said, "while I'm certainly not one to cast stones, even I know that Lila hasn't been interested in dolls for years, and I can't imagine this bra is appropriate for any eleven-year-old girl. A thirty-year-old hooker, maybe."

Whatever she had felt before evaporated, and instinctively she defended her father. "Unfortunately for me," she said tightly, "I hadn't learned the memo system of communication that you and Lila have mastered."

Max only tilted his head and smiled. That heart-melting, knee-fusing curve of lips that made her heart beat faster.

"Touché," he offered.

The phone rang, then rang again.

"Are you going to answer that?" he asked when it rang a third time and she didn't make a move.

She stared at it in horror, then forced a smile. "Nope. If it's important, they'll leave a message."

Her voice whirled through the room, tinny and cheerful, followed by a beep.

"Vivi, this is Velda from Velda's Salon. I'm sorry to have to call, but the checks you wrote to us last week have bounced. I'm sure it's a mistake, but if you could, please give me a ring."

The answer machine beeped to an end.

"Check*s*? As in plural?" Max inquired. "To one beauty shop?"

Almost instantly, the phone started ringing again.

"I take it you aren't going to answer that one either."

"Can't see why I should."

"Miss Stansfield, this is Lionel Neesan from the El Paso Tribune. *I'm writing a piece on your father and wondered if you might know where he is."*

Dread raced down her spine, then she nearly jumped when Max came up behind her.

"You never did say where your father was."

"I told you, he's traveling."

"You didn't tell me where."

"You ask a lot of questions."

"You don't like to answer. My guess is that you don't know where he is."

His tone caught in her mind. A mix of sympathy and pity. Her thoughts hardened defensively. She didn't want anyone's pity, least of all his.

"My father is an adult," she stated. "He doesn't have to leave me an itinerary. He'll call."

Max turned her around to face him, his strong hands gentle. Her heart started that slow, steady rise to awareness. He took her in, his gaze lowering to the pulse in her neck. He didn't even have to touch her for her nipples to tighten.

She felt seared by his heat, her nerve endings raw. She felt the need to lean close and forget imperfect desserts and flowered push-up bras, fiancés who wanted other women and fathers who didn't bother to mention where they had gone. And that was ridiculous. She didn't need Max or anyone. She had always managed on her own.

And what was all this emotion that she kept feeling?

"I better check the mail," she whispered past the lump in her throat.

He didn't move out of her way, and she brushed against him when she headed for the front door, the feel of his eyes burning into her back.

Don't think about Max, she told herself, breathing deeply, counting, when she came to the row of metal mailboxes lined up along a single wall. Sliding her key into the slot, she nodded with determination as she pulled open the little door. Instantly, bright white business envelopes slipped out to land at her feet.

One by one, she picked them up, then stared at each. Wanting to run away as far as she could, she shook her head and returned inside.

"What are those?" Max asked when he saw the pile in her hands.

Instead of answering, she opened each one, her mood growing bleaker by the second. When she was done, she forced a smile. "Surprise! More bills," she said.

"Hell. Let me see."

"Max, I do not need your help. I'm a grown woman, and I'm going to make sense of the situation on my own."

She waited for him to make some damning remark, but it never came.

Crossing to her, he tugged the envelopes away, his blue eyes locking with hers. "Sometimes we all need help, Vivienne."

Her pulse slowed. Perhaps it was panic being pushed back, or perhaps it was the novel experience of suddenly not feeling alone.

"I'm still happy to lend you the money—"

"Absolutely not," she whispered.

He smiled at her, then took her hand and guided her to the tiny kitchen table. This was a different man who sat down next to her, the impatience left behind as if he had wiped it off his feet at the door. This was a man who solved problems all day long in a business world far more complicated than hers.

With a caring that surprised her, he brushed a strand of hair from her face. "If you won't take the money, then at least let me help you determine what needs to be done."

After she had spent days refusing to give in to confusion and betrayal, his simple words made her feel something she hardly recognized. Sweet and soft. And cared for. It was a sensation that drew her in and made her want to run in the opposite direction at the same time.

Over the next half hour, they went through each of her accounts, her bank and credit card statements, and a whole stack of wedding bills her father had insisted he would pay. Now creditors were sending them to her.

After that, Max and Vivi calculated just how much was owed, and determined what she could cancel and what companies would give her refunds on wedding items she hadn't yet received. All the while she prayed the end result wouldn't be so bad.

Between the information she supplied and the phone calls she made, Max tallied her debts and balances. The final result was not as bad as she feared. It was worse.

A vise clamped around her chest.

"You spent five hundred and fifty dollars at Velda's Salon?" he asked, stunned. "No wonder she called. How many times can you get your hair done in a week?"

Breathe in, breathe out.

"I do my own hair."

"Then what are you doing at Velda's Salon?"

"I pay for women with difficulties to get their hair cut and styled, to get makeovers to help them get a fresh start." She forced herself to be calm. "Sort of like projects," she tried to enthuse.

Max's blue-eyed gaze bored into her, and for half a second she was certain she saw his hard stance softening. But then he spoke. "You need to stop worrying about other people's problems and start worrying about your own. Look at this. Three hundred and ninety-five dollars charged at Nicks and Nacks. What kind of a doodad costs that kind of money?"

She wondered if she should put her head between her knees. "Doodad?"

"Don't change the subject."

Or maybe breathe into a paper bag. She'd heard that worked. "I'm not, I was just marveling that not only is there a word like doodad, but that you would use it. Have you mentioned it to Lila? She's making a list of interesting words."

"Stop marveling at Lila and the English language and do a little marveling at the sheer amount of money you spend. You could run a small country on your budget. Good God, look at this. A two-thousand-dollar country club bill—in the bar. That's an awful lot of champagne cocktails."

Insult piled onto panic.

"What do you do there every month?" he demanded.

She felt dizzy. She didn't do anything there. It was her father who spent time at the country club. Why would his bills come to her?

As much as she had not wanted to admit it, the week before her father had left town, he had been distracted. He hadn't looked good. His last wife had left him six months before, and Vivi had assumed his usual post-divorce prowl was keeping him up late.

"Last I checked," she said, searching for the calm, flip voice that had always served her well, "you weren't my keeper."

"No, but you have every creditor in town, not to mention every bill collector within a six-hundred-mile radius, breathing down your neck. And believe me, as much as I'd like to think of myself as a generous employer, you aren't making close to what it will take to pay off these debts."

She stared at bright cherry red pillows on the no doubt rented sofa, and it was all she could do not to hum. She wanted to be alone. She wanted Max to go away.

After long, silent seconds, he said, "Okay, this is the deal."

He proceeded to give it to her straight, telling her how long it would take to pay off the obligations based on minimum payments. She'd be old and haggard by the time that happened.

Pressing her eyes closed, she held back a groan. "You

mentioned that I have weekends off. Maybe I could get a second job at the Taco Bell. I saw they were hiring."

"You need more than a second job. You need a miracle."

She swallowed hard, swallowing back emotion, searching for flip. "Maybe I'll apply at the nearest street corner and see what kind of business I can drum up."

She felt the shift in Max, the censure riddling through the room.

"You know I'm joking," she said with a wan laugh.

But Max still stared at her.

Vivi rolled her eyes. "I mean really, do I look like the type who could even get business at a street corner?"

"Yes."

Straightening in surprise, she said, "It's all the pink, isn't it? Or the short skirts?"

"When are you going to start being serious, Vivienne?" he asked sternly.

But right then, serious wasn't going to help. Serious didn't change anything that mattered. Serious would come soon enough when she woke up alone at two in the morning, thinking of all that was wrong, wondering how the world as she knew it could be crumbling, her perceptions false. She had believed in her father. She had believed Grady loved her. She had never guessed he thought her a cold fish in bed. She hated to think that something so superficial bothered her the most.

That's when she got mad, breaking yet another of her rules, the sensation rocking through her, foreign and unfamiliar. She got mad at herself. At Grady. She felt like flying away from this mess and herself. She wanted to be someone different. She wanted to let loose, be wild, live like there was no tomorrow. She wanted to forget about being perfect, because look where it had gotten her. Wildness slid through her veins like champagne bubbles, pushing her on.

She smiled through lowered lashes, then moved closer to Max, walking her fingers up the buttons on his shirt. "I am serious."

Max went still. "This is not the time to play games, Vivienne."

She pressed her hand against his chest. "What kind of games did you have in mind?"

"How about the Opposite Side of the Room game."

"How do you play?"

"You stay on the opposite side of the room from me."

A sizzle of power slid through her at the thought that she was making this strong man uncomfortable. Biting her lip, she skimmed her hand lower. "I never would have taken you for a prude."

Just when her fingers got to his belt buckle, he grabbed her hand. The heat that had been on simmer flared bright and hot.

Suddenly the game turned dangerous. Respectable, impatient Max Landry disappeared and she found a man no woman should toy with.

He took her hand away from his belt and placed it back on his chest. "You want to play, sweetness?"

The "sweetness" part was a really bad sign, and she knew she was in over her head. Every ounce of her wildness disappeared like a black cat in the night. She cursed her stupidity, then cursed herself for starting something that she was a fool ever to have believed she could control.

"Now, Max," she said, her voice not so steady.

He didn't respond, only pulled her close, reeling her

in, his grip like a manacle on her wrist, until their bodies touched. The sensation was a shock, the press of his hard thighs against hers, the heat of him burning through the layers of their clothes.

She tried to tug free.

"Not quite so fun when the shoe's on the other foot," he said, his breath brushing against her ear as he nipped the delicate shell.

"Other foot?" She tried to concentrate. "Interesting choice of words, given my love of shoes. In fact"—she summoned up a look of outrage—"can you believe how irresponsible I was for buying those leopard mules at Shoe Haven?" She gave an exaggerated scoff.

"Too late for distractions," he said, his voice sending shivers along her skin, making her tremble.

Then he leaned down and captured her mouth with his own. He kissed her. Softly. Exceedingly soft. His arms came around her.

She knew it was foolish to give in, crazy to melt against his hard frame, playing a game that neither of them could win. But when his palm brushed against the tip of her breast, she managed only a feeble protest.

"Let's talk about a budget," she murmured. "Fiscal responsibility." Her fingers curled into his shirt. "Plus columns, minus columns." She inhaled, breathing him in. "Just the kind of serious, no-fun topic that I imagine you love."

The other side of his mouth crooked up, pulling his lips into a full smile. "Or not."

Then he lifted her up in his arms.

Chapter Eleven

He wanted her.

He wanted her with a driving need that pulsed through his body like a flame he couldn't douse. He wanted to bend her over the small kitchen table, gently bite her neck, and drive his hard shaft deep inside her heated center.

But that's all he wanted. The sex. Nothing more.

Vivienne Stansfield was complicated and spoiled, and he wished he knew how to purge her from his mind. But her body turned his control to putty, and he alternately wanted to damn her and fuck her at the same time.

His body reeled with the desire, every nerve ending pounding and alive. He couldn't remember the last time he had wanted a woman so badly. Perhaps never.

He was a man who had sex often, with many women, careful to protect them and himself. He had sex with a single-minded detachment. Giving pleasure, gaining release. But he never got emotionally involved.

Vivienne was different. She made his skin grow tight across his abdomen and his cock pulse with a driving ache. She made him want to consume her, peel the petals away with his tongue until she screamed out and trembled with longing.

But he had promised himself he wouldn't give in to the need to take her, to sink deep. Because need of any kind, he had learned long ago, made him weak.

But now he felt his control slipping. The vulnerability in her eyes, the way she tried not to want him but did, undercut his always ironclad ability to remain detached.

Like a dying man, he gave in and kissed her again, lowering her body as his lips grazed hers. Feeling greedy for more of her, he cupped her hips and moved her against his erection. Her soft moan sent fire rushing through him.

Gently he pressed her back against the wall and pushed one breast high, his thumb finding her nipple beneath the silk of her blouse.

Her pale gray eyes turned the color of a turbulent sky. Her hands came up, clasping his arms, undoing him even more. He could feel her uncertainty, her hesitancy, as if she hardly understood what she was experiencing. But he knew. He recognized the craving inside her. Another reminder of how she wanted him, but was afraid of that desire, sent a bolt of heat through him. It was all he could do not to push her to the floor and lick the sweet center of her until she realized what her body could feel.

But he knew that would frighten her. It was too much, too fast, and he understood that this woman needed to be taught about the power of her body.

The hot Indian summer sun of October lowered on the horizon. Vivienne felt the hard definition of Max beneath his shirt, making her feel tiny and fragile. She could lose herself in him, she realized. She could lose herself in the strength of his body. Like a drug, his touch made the world seem distant. She realized that this man didn't see her as too perfect, someone to put on a pedestal. And when his fingers began to work the buttons of her blouse, it was all she could do not to rip the material off herself.

His lips trailed back to her ear, his breath sending shivers through her body. He undid the fastenings with an ease that should have given her pause. But the sensation of air hitting skin overwhelmed her thoughts when her blouse fell open.

He coaxed her lips apart, his tongue twining with hers. When she groaned, he pulled her even closer.

"You taste as sweet as I remembered," he murmured.

"You've been thinking of this?"

A deep, guttural chuckle rumbled in his chest. "You know I have."

"What else have you been thinking?"

"Hush, Vivienne. Stop talking," he commanded, brushing a kiss across her mouth. "I want you."

The simple, straightforward statement brought an electric current of feeling curling low in her belly. Then his hand slipped under the fluttering edges of her blouse and he found bare skin. She could feel the change in him. She could feel his desire, and she didn't want to say no.

In all the time she had dated Grady, he had never made her feel desired. Important? Yes.

But this was different. This was a wild yearning that burned in Max's eyes, a heat that said louder than words what he wanted from her. Sex. Hard, demanding sex. It didn't matter that she was Vivienne Stansfield. In fact, if anything held him back, it was that.

She focused on Max, saw his dark gaze glittering as it raked over her, nothing polite—only an animal desire. But when he glanced up and their eyes met, she saw something else. Something deeper that made her think that this heat would burn him up.

The thought surprised her, and her mind narrowed against the idea. She was the one in danger of being hurt by giving in to a man who clearly didn't like her.

Her instinct was to race back to the world she was used to, the one that despite its flaws she knew how to manage and survive in. She didn't need this complication in her life added to her laundry list of complications. But somehow she couldn't make reason penetrate the hunger that filled her, pushing her farther away from who she was. She no longer cared why he was there. She wanted to feel his touch.

When he swept her up in his arms, she didn't protest, and when he laid her down on the sofa, she went willingly. His gaze bored into her as if he couldn't get enough.

With infinite slowness, he leaned over her and kissed the pulse in her neck. Then lower, making her body quiver and want. The intensity was nearly overwhelming and she felt herself stiffen.

"Relax, sweetheart," he crooned. "Just lie back. Close your eyes."

"But—"

"No buts."

Kneeling, he pushed her blouse to the side, unfastened the front clasp of her bra. Then he brushed his palm over her nipple, just barely, before he cupped her breast, his thumb circling, working its magic.

"Do you understand the power of your body?" he asked, the words a low rumble of sound along her senses.

She opened her eyes. She must have looked as confused by the question as she felt, because the glimmer in his gaze flashed with what she could only call anticipation of what he was going to show her. A passion, something special, something sacred. *He* would show her. Her skin burned just from the look, and when he bent his head and pressed his lips just above her breast and nipped at the skin, her body leaped with fire.

He dipped his head and took one nipple deep in his mouth. She sighed, instinctively arching her back. His tongue laved the tender bud. Her body burned for this, burned to be touched. She had been waiting for this since she walked into his office and saw the chiseled strength of him through the glass.

He touched and caressed, licked and sucked. Her mind spun as her body arched to him. She began to understand that he was opening a secret place inside her, as if he had known something was there that she had sensed but had been afraid to give in to.

He did things to her body that she had always been afraid to admit she wanted. And this man would accept nothing less than her full submission.

A tight knot formed in her mind and she tried to push up from cushions. Max pulled back and looked at her.

"I can't do this," she whispered.

"You can, Vivienne."

She stared at him. "It's too much. I feel like I'm burning up."

His brow furrowed as if he didn't understand. Or maybe it was that he understood too well.

"You have an incredible passion inside you. Don't be afraid of it."

"I'm not. I mean I don't—have passion inside me.

Really." She tried to laugh. "Remember me? The ice queen. No passion here."

The glimmer in his eyes returned. "But there is" was all he said, as he came over her.

He bore his weight on his elbows, one hand framing her face. She savored the solidness of him as he bent to taste her, their tongues intertwining. And she was lost.

She sought the feel of him, wanting to touch his heat, his skin. His shirt fell away, then hers, their clothes tangling together.

Somewhere in the distant recesses of her mind, she heard the phone ring. Once, twice. But she didn't care. All she wanted was more of what Max was giving her.

His lips trailed up her skin to her ear, as his hand went lower.

Her voice on the answering machine filled the room.

"Hi, I'm not here. But please leave a message."

His hand slipped between her thighs. Pure heat rushed through her as the beeping sound echoed.

"You want this," Max murmured against her. "You're wet and hot."

Then another voice. Male, but not as deep. Older.

"Vivi . . ."

Her name entwined with heat and the kind of sensation she had never felt in her life. But her body yearned, overriding all else.

"It's your father."

The words jarred, and her mind froze.

"Sorry I haven't called before now, but I've been extremely busy here."

"Oh my gosh!"

Vivienne pushed at Max's chest so hard that they both tumbled to the floor between the coffee table and sofa.

"Hurry! I have to answer the phone!"

The more she scrambled, the more they twisted together, until finally Max got control of her and set them both upright.

"Daddy! Don't hang up!"

But he couldn't hear her, only kept talking.

Vivienne launched herself across the room, tripping over a pillow that had fallen to the floor. When she finally jerked up the handpiece, the line went dead.

She stared at the phone in disbelief. "Daddy," she whispered, as a stunned shock settled through her.

Frantically she pressed Play to listen to the message again. "Maybe he left a phone number."

"I didn't hear one," Max said.

"Don't say that!"

Her father's voice flared a second time. Sorry she wasn't home. He'd call back when he could. Then he hesitated, before adding for her not to worry. Things were going to be all right. Just give him a bit longer. Followed by the click, then her own voice.

"Daddy!"

A desperate echoing word left to shimmer as the last of the Indian sun burned itself out completely.

She stood there for what seemed like ages. Not moving.

Her hair trailed down her back, so dark it seemed like a spill of midnight. She was beyond beautiful, Max thought. The curves, the flawless skin. And his body screamed to finish what they had started.

But he could see something more, deeper than desire, deeper than beauty. The same thing he had seen in her before, as if she were something precious kept under glass. Easily broken. And he felt the need to protect her, keep her safe.

The thought filtered through his mind, and for half a second, another memory hit him. Of Vivienne at eighteen, dressed in a beautiful gown, surrounded by other girls in white who stood next to their fathers.

The Symphony Association Debutante Ball.

A series of rich girls, but Vivienne was the one who stood out. Because of her beauty, and because she was alone.

But the memory shattered in the nearly dark apartment when Vivienne turned around to Max.

"I missed him."

"He'll call back."

"Will he?" The words clearly surprised her as much as they surprised him. He saw her tense.

"For your sake, I hope so."

She pulled her blouse on. He watched as she took a deep breath, her perfect chin rising, and he knew she was fighting for the calm that continually amazed him. Her life was in shreds and she had an amazing ability to rise above worry. He'd never seen anything like it. But why was that? Because she refused to believe that bad things could really happen? Or was it that she thought that through sheer determination she could keep her world from turning upside down?

Something inside him shifted. Yes, she was all about facades and extravagant exteriors. But he realized, standing there, that while she might be spoiled, and while she might hold the real world at bay, it came at a price.

My Wedding Diary

THE WEDDING BED
Multiple Choice

Question: In the last four, long, nerve-racking days I have ...

A. mortified Lila when I showed up at Morehead Middle School thinking it'd be "fun" to have lunch together.

B. "ruined" Nicki's life by pulling up to Coronado High with the top down, Barry Manilow's "Copacabana" playing on the radio.

C. nearly had sex with Max—without the benefit of a "wedding" or a "bed."

Answer: An abysmal and utterly depressing All of the Above!

What was I thinking?!!

Chapter Twelve

Vivi closed the diary when she heard Nicki roll out of bed at six on Friday morning. Walking over to the closet, Vivi put the slim volume toward the back, behind the box that held the tiara her father had given her a lifetime ago. For half a second she thought about throwing the book and the tiara away. Then she muttered to herself when she knew she couldn't do it.

She headed downstairs to make breakfast for the girls. Thankfully she'd hardly seen Max in the last four days, other than to argue about her towed car. She hoped the trend continued—hardly seeing him, that is, not the arguing part—since she had no idea what she would say to him if he brought up the whole nearly-having-had-sex thing.

She concentrated on blueberry pancakes instead.

Upstairs, Nicki stretched. She always woke early because getting all that black eye makeup just right wasn't easy. And the fingernails. Who knew that black polish chipped so easily and looked totally gross if it wasn't redone practically every day?

So she woke at the crack of dawn. If she could help it, she wasn't going to be fourteen and never been French kissed for long.

Today they had a pep rally during last period, which meant she'd get to see Steve Bonner. Steve was just a year older than her, but was so good at football that he was on the varsity team. He was pretty popular, even if he was just a sophomore.

For reasons she didn't get, he was nice to her. Probably because they had gone to school together since grade school. But it was his older brother who she had a total crush on.

Brandon Bonner.

Nicki exhaled a melting sigh at the thought of Brandon. Where Steve was the all-American type, Brandon was a bad boy. Brandon always had some cute girl hanging on his arm. What Nicki would do to hang on his arm herself.

Knowing Brandon would definitely go to the pep rally because of his brother, Nicki couldn't wait to get there in hopes of getting Brandon to notice her. They'd be perfect together. She knew it.

Finishing her makeup, she went to her dresser. Last night she had decided she had to go for it today at the pep rally. She'd wear her favorite black low-cut jeans with an awesome T-shirt she had found in Max's castoffs. Black with the group Guns N' Roses on the front. She had cut the bottom half off, so it hit just above where her jeans started.

It was hard to imagine that Max had ever done anything remotely wild in his life. She hated that he was always gone, and when he showed up it was with some dictatorial command, as if he thought that was the best way to parent.

She knew he was busy, but it really ticked her off that he didn't spend more time with her—no, with Lila, she told herself firmly. Nicki reasoned that she didn't need the attention so much, but Lila was just a kid.

Nicki knew there was the whole Max-shouldering-the-responsibility-of-the-world thing, and sometimes she did feel guilty—or even kind of bad for him. But if he'd just spend some time at home, maybe tell her something about her mother or father every once in a while, things wouldn't be so hard.

She was always having to snoop around to find out anything. She wouldn't even remember what her mom looked like if it weren't for pictures she'd found, and she had no clue about her dad because he took off and Max didn't have a single photo of him.

Not that she blamed Max for burning or ripping the photos up, which is what she suspected he'd done. What kind of a dad bolted on his family?

To make matters worse, the guy had never even come back after their mom died, leaving eight kids, including a baby who was barely one year old.

Nicki found the shirt, pulled it over her head, then went to her closet for her jeans. Practically humming, she got them out, then tried to put them on. At first she was so caught up in the anticipation of Brandon noticing her that she didn't think too much about having a hard time getting the jeans on. Then it hit her. They weren't going to go on. They were too small. They had shrunk. They were ruined and there was no way she could wear them to school.

Furious, she screamed.

Within seconds, pounding came from every direction. Standing there with the pants clutched in her hands, she watched her door burst open. First Max flew in, then Lila.

"What's wrong?" her brother demanded.

He had a demented with worry look about him, and Nicki had a moment of regret for having made such a scene. But then Miss Priss came in, and all feelings of regret vanished.

Vivi held a spatula in her hands and wore a stupid frilly apron around her waist and, unlike Max and Lila, her hair wasn't sticking up in every single direction. She looked beautiful. Like a fairy princess. With these really great shoe things with tons of feathers flying all over the toes.

Nicki hated her even more.

"My jeans," Nicki bleated.

Max's expression went from warrior mode to disbelief. "You screamed because of a pair of pants?"

"Not just a pair of pants. My favorite jeans that I have to wear today! And they're ruined. Look at these!" Nicki turned and glared at Vivi. "What did you do to them?"

Vivi stared at the pants like she couldn't figure out what they were. "I washed and dried them."

"You put them in the dryer?" Nicki whirled on Max. "See? She's horrible. She doesn't have a clue how to do anything. Including dress. What are you wearing?"

Vivi's weird gray eyes went wide, then she stared down at her foofy clothes. But before she could say anything, Max stepped farther into the room with that look about him that could only mean trouble.

Uh-oh.

"I've had enough of your attitude. You will apologize to Vivienne."

"I will not! And who are you anyway? You aren't my dad. You don't have any say about what I do 'cause you're never here."

She turned away and threw the jeans in a heap. She could feel her brother behind her, could feel the anger in him and the frustration, and she hated what she had said. She wanted him to walk up behind her, wrap her in his arms, and tell her that everything was going to be all right.

But he didn't. "You will apologize," he commanded.

Hating Max and Vivi in that moment with every fiber of her being, she bit out the words. "I'm sorry."

She heard the minute Max turned and left.

It was Lila who walked over and wrapped her tiny arms around Nicki. It felt good, and she wanted to give a hug back. But somehow she couldn't.

"Go get dressed, kid, and hope like hell you have something to wear that isn't ruined."

Sniffing through her tears, Lila ran to her own room, slamming herself inside.

Vivi still stood there.

"Just leave," Nicki hissed.

The woman must be a moron, because instead of leaving, Vivi walked over and picked up the jeans.

"What are you doing?"

"They didn't shrink that much."

Nicki gave her a drop-dead look. "Like it matters. Ruined is ruined. Now just get out."

Clearly deaf or maybe just as stupid as she looked, Vivi took the pants, then headed for the door. But when Nicki finally thought she would be left alone, Vivi stopped.

"I know what it's like when you feel as if you're all alone in the world."

Nicki felt her heart pound and a prick of sappiness

trying to burst out. She couldn't move, couldn't get the words out to tell Vivi to shut up.

"But that's no reason to work so hard to reject everyone before they have the chance to reject you."

Tears suddenly burned in Nicki's throat. But she didn't give in. Instead, she got a hold of herself, turned to the woman, and gave her the evilest eye she could manage. "You don't know what you're talking about. You don't know the first thing about anything. And I wish you'd get the hell out of my life."

They stared at each other for long seconds like the worst of enemies. Nicki expected Vivi to crumple like a wilted flower and start to cry. Good. She wanted her to hurt as badly as she did.

But of course stupid Vivi had to go and surprise her and ruin everything.

"I can fix your jeans before I take you to school." Then she turned and finally disappeared.

Sure enough, by the time breakfast was on the table— a major gross meal of weird eggs, sausages, and pancakes that were ruined by blueberries—the jeans were folded over the back of her chair.

For reasons Nicki couldn't imagine, her eyes burned and her throat got tight yet again. She hated it when that happened.

Lila sniffled at her place, and Nicki felt even worse. She wanted to say she was sorry, but couldn't seem to get the words out.

"Do the jeans look okay?" Lila asked feebly. "I helped Vivi fix them."

The tear thing got worse.

"Maybe you should try them on and see if they fit."

Not knowing what else to do, feeling Vivi watching her from over by the stove, Nicki took the pants and changed into them in the laundry room. They were kind of damp, but not bad. But most amazing was that they fit, actually better than before, since they had been kind of big to start with.

Not sure if she were relieved or mad, she came out.

"Are they okay?" Lila asked hesitantly.

With her heart still lodged in her throat, Nicki sat down in her chair. "Yeah," she managed to say, "they're okay."

Lila looked relieved. "We sprayed them with water, then we tugged on either end, then Vivi put them on! Well, she kind of put them on, then did squats and all sorts of things before she ironed them. I'm glad they're okay now."

Vivi didn't say a word, she just brought over two slices of cinnamon toast and set the plate down. Nicki's favorite from when she was a little kid. But when Lila reached under the table and linked her finger with hers, Nicki took her slice and gave it to her little sister.

"But you love cinnamon toast," Lila breathed.

"It's okay. You can have mine."

Then suddenly everything was back to normal between them, and she felt the tears start to recede.

Vivi still didn't say a word, not anything, and finally Nicki rolled her eyes and mumbled, "Thanks."

Just that, and stupid Vivi got this really big smile and said, "I'm sorry I shrunk them."

And then, thank God, it was time to go to school, which was a total good news/bad news scenario.

Vivi had to use Max's car since hers had gotten towed away. Last night, Nicki had heard the two of them arguing about cars. Max had said he'd lend her one, but he said it in that voice of his, all superior and impatient, that really made a person want to shove the offer in his face.

Even though Nicki hated Vivi, she could hardly blame her when she got all huffy. Vivi had ended the conversation by saying she'd deal with the car situation on her own. She'd even added a snippy "Just you wait and see" that almost made Nicki smile.

Until then, Vivi was using Max's Mercedes, driving them to school in the gigantic car, nearly getting them killed when she seemed to forget they weren't zipping around in her little red convertible.

Amazingly not dead, Nicki got to school and walked into C Building in hopes of catching a glimpse of Brandon Bonner.

She saw him the minute she walked in and realized that it was crazy to wait until the pep rally. This was it. This was her chance. Bucking up her nerve, she puffed out her flat chest to make it look bigger, then walked toward him.

Not two feet from him, she stopped in her tracks. "Please, please, please see me," she whispered.

Then it happened. He turned around, just enough so that they came face-to-face. She opened her mouth to say hey, but she froze when some girl called out to him.

It was all Nicki could do not to grab his arm. Her fingers tingled from holding her books so tight to keep from making a fool of herself. And that's just what would have happened if she had said hi. Because when she looked closer, saw the light that sparked in his eyes, she could see that he was looking at Mindy Wasserstein, dressed all in pink lace and rhinestones.

Brandon walked over to Mindy and slung his strong

arm around her shoulders just like Nicki had dreamed he'd do to her. And that was when she started rethinking all the black.

Early the next morning, Nicki took action. It was Saturday, and Vivi was gone for the weekend. Quiet as a mouse, Nicki walked to the stairs and peeked over the banister. Once she was sure that Max had left for the day, she flew down her set of stairs, then back up the other side to the opposite wing of the house.

Patricia, the sister who took her and Lila on Saturdays and Sundays, had said she'd be there at ten. So Nicki had time.

She raced to Vivi's bedroom. With her heart pounding in her ears, Nicki hurried to the closet, yanked open the accordion doors, and found a rainbow of color leaping out at her. Yellows and pinks, blues and greens. Not to mention shoes. Nicki had never seen so many, every one of them with very high heels.

She remembered Mindy, remembered the way Brandon had looked at her wearing clothes that looked like they came out of this closet.

Flopping down on the floor, Nicki started with shoes. Leaning in, she saw some of the storage stuff Max kept in the closet. For half a second Nicki thought about pulling out and digging through the old photos she had found once that he kept of all the kids, even some of their mom. But there was no time for pictures.

Hurrying, she found a blouse and skirt that weren't half bad if she imagined it as something Mindy would wear. That's when she noticed the small satin box she had never seen before at the very back of the closet.

Biting her lip, then glancing back toward the door,

Nicki decided it wouldn't hurt to look. Inside she found the most beautiful tiara.

Feeling something close to awe, she put it on her head, then pushed up from the floor very carefully to see her reflection. The sight surprised her. She looked like a princess. Her. Despite the black, despite the anger even she could see on her face, the simple crown made her feel freer, lighter. Special.

"What are you doing?"

Nicki about had a heart attack until she wheeled around and saw that it was Lila. Her little sister stood in the doorway in her usual confusion of mismatched colors, staring at her like she had gone mad.

"Go away!" Nicki hissed.

"You can't be in here! You're going to get in trouble."

"If you don't tell, no one will ever know."

"But what if Max finds out? He'll be so mad."

Lila got all teary-eyed again, making Nicki feel guilty.

"Don't cry, Lila," she cajoled. "I'm just trying stuff on. Besides, Max isn't here, and neither is Vivi."

But thoughts of tiaras and Vivi evaporated when something like a gunshot exploded outside.

Chapter Thirteen

Vivi sat in the car, her fingers gripping the thin, old-fashioned steering wheel, her body still vibrating from the chugging backfire that had echoed along Pinehurst Drive when she turned off the car. Her mother's faded, dark green Oldsmobile 88 had seen better days. About three decades ago. But when her mother was in town, she insisted on driving it.

Her father called it her mother's rebellion. A nuisance to society. A decrepit bucket of bolts. The more her father lamented about the vehicle, the more Isabelle took pride in driving it, tooling around town with the windows open, her hair covered with a gossamer scarf, the ends trailing out the window.

It didn't take a brain surgeon to figure out that her mother did it to get under her ex-husband's hide, cruising past the El Paso Country Club golf course while Jennings played, making a point to honk whenever she saw him standing with his friends.

Jennings Stansfield was all about the appearance of the women in his life. A beat-up old car driven by his first wife, and the mother of his only child, infuriated him. Which, of course, was the point.

Vivi had never understood her father's need to show

off, as she thought of it, or her mother's need to throw tasteless sorts of things in his face. But Vivi had never questioned. Though the minute she had pulled the vehicle out from behind the downtown service station where it was kept during Isabelle LeBuc Stansfield's many travels, Vivi felt a prick of her mother's rebellious blood flowing through her veins.

Not that she would stoop as low as her mother to get back at her father. The fact was she needed a car. And this hardworking, if unfashionable car perfectly suited her new life.

With the door squealing in protest, Vivi pushed it open, waved at the neighbor who peered suspiciously out a multipaned window, then went to the trunk. She had to work the key a few times, then actually gave the metal a good hard thump with her fist, before it popped open.

Her charm bracelet jangled against the rim when she reached in to pull out one of the many suitcases and bags she had loaded into the car.

"What happened?" a voice said.

Vivi jerked up to find Nicki and Lila standing in the drive, their eyes wide, their mouths open, looking at her with the same accusing suspicion as the lady next door. But it wasn't their faces that made her suck in a slow, painful breath.

"Where did you get that?" she asked quietly.

Instantly, Nicki's hand flew to her head and to the tiara Vivi's father had given her years before.

"Close your eyes. I have a birthday surprise for you."

Her father's voice, surprising her. She was six and feeling grown up. And very, very special beneath her father's attention.

"For me," she breathed.

Then he held out the crown. "For my princess."

Foolishly she had cherished those simple words, hadn't even minded that he made her wear it when he took her out on the makeshift stage the following day when he had opened the plant in South El Paso. The crowd had been huge, overwhelming. It was the first time she had felt like a china doll.

"This cheap thing?" Nicki demanded, pointing to the crown with a belligerent scowl.

But the teenager's cheeks were red with guilt and little Lila looked as if the world would fall apart.

"What kind of a grownup has a stupid tiara hanging around? Do you wear it to bed?" Nicki sneered.

"Nicki, stop," Lila pleaded.

The fourteen-year-old's face hardened as she ripped the thing off her head, then walked over and shoved it into Vivi's hands.

"Take it. I sure don't want it."

For long irrational seconds, Vivi stared at the gift, alternately wishing her father were there, and damning him.

"What is all this?" Nicki demanded. "More suitcases? Can't you live with the ten thousand of them you already have here? You need another fifty million to make it through the next week or two? And why the hell are you here? Are you so much of an airhead that you don't get the words *weekends off*?"

Vivi wrinkled her nose. She was more than ready for the weekend off. But after she had retrieved her mother's car from the service station downtown and made her way to her father's condo, she'd had an unfortunate visit from the landlord.

Though if she were honest about it, by the time Mr. Sandoval knocked on her door, she wasn't even surprised when he told her she had to move out. Three months' worth of her father's rent checks had bounced, and now the man had a tenant ready to move in. One who could pay.

In a daze, Vivi had packed up the rest of her belongings, then headed for greener pastures—or rather the only pasture available to her just then. Max's house.

But she wasn't about to share all of that with a fourteen-year-old handful or an eleven-year-old who had too many problems to deal with as it was.

"What were you doing in my room?" Vivi asked sternly.

"Nothing."

"You obviously were going through my things if you found the tiara. I hardly call that nothing."

Nicki shrugged. "So we were looking at your lame clothes."

Lila gasped. "*You* were looking. Not me, Vivi. Really. Nicki thinks that if she wears clothes like you, she'll get that awful Boomer Bonner to like her."

This time Nicki gasped. "That is not true. I would never wear your bimbo stuff," she declared, her cheeks bright red, "and I sure don't want some guy to notice me looking like some dumb slut."

"Watch your mouth," Vivi snapped.

For a second, all three of them were surprised. It was the first time Vivi had reprimanded the girl.

Nicki recovered first. "*You* watch it. You are not my boss."

"I beg to differ." Just like that, the words popped out of Vivi's mouth.

Not that Nicki was particularly impressed. "Beg all you like," she scoffed, preening at her wit. "It's the weekend, and weekends I'm free of you."

To prove her point, a car pulled up into the driveway.

"Patricia!" Lila yelped, relief welling up in her blue eyes.

A woman who couldn't be more than a few years older than Vivi, and who had Landry stamped all over her, got out of the car. She was beautiful, the promise that Nicki showed beneath all the black and scowls having been realized in this woman. Her hair was dark, her eyes were a bright blue, and her lips pulled into a genuine smile.

"Hello," she said, extending her hand. "You must be Vivi. I'm Pat Landry."

Vivi saw a true warmth in her expression, and instantly she liked her. "I'm glad to meet you."

"Great tiara. I always wanted one." Pat laughed, the sound sweet and nice, without an ounce of coyness. "And sorry I'm late. I had to get some tickets out before I left this morning. Clients always seem to wait until the last minute to let me know they are taking a trip. The next day."

"Clients?"

"I work at Landry Travel—"

"She's the president," Lila explained proudly.

Pat smiled and ruffled Lila's hair. "Easy to be president when your brother buys the business for you."

"Really?" Vivi asked. "He bought it?"

"Yep. He's helped all of us after we graduated from college. And graduating is a must."

"Wow," she said without thinking.

Pat looked at her with amusement. "Wow?" Then she

smiled, her blue eyes softening with a deep love that somehow hit Vivi right between the shoulder blades.

"He's the nicest man I know," Pat said. "I wish I could find someone like him to marry."

Vivi must have made a face, because Pat chuckled. "I take it you don't agree."

"No. I'm mean, it's not that. . . . It's just . . . well . . ." She shrugged. "Wow," she repeated, "I'm just surprised. Though of course I shouldn't be," she rushed on.

"Girls, go get your stuff."

Nicki and Lila raced inside. Once they were gone, Pat looked at her. "Why did you take this job if you don't like Maxwell?" she asked boldly.

Vivi's thoughts jarred, and she felt the automatic need to whitewash everything. But something about this woman made her believe that the question wasn't a way to find some weakness, something to exploit.

"I'm broke."

This time it was Pat who was surprised. "You?"

"That seems to be a recurring theme."

"Oh, well, I just didn't realize. I thought maybe you were here because you wanted access to Max."

"Believe me, access is not what I'm here for. Especially to a man who'd just as soon fire me as say hello."

Pat suddenly laughed, then leaned forward like a girlfriend telling secrets. "He can be intimidating, can't he?"

It was an amazing feeling, this unexpected closeness that she had missed by attending schools all over the world, never in any one place for long. A shiver of giddiness raced through her.

"I'll say," Vivi said. "Just one look and it's all I can do to stand my ground."

The woman studied her. "But I bet you do stand your ground with him." She nodded. "Good. He needs someone like you in his life."

"To drive him crazy?"

"To turn his perfectly ordered world upside down a little. Don't get me wrong, I love Max. And he truly is sweeter than he seems."

Vivi wondered.

A smile pulled at Pat's lips and she glanced off into the distance. "I swear it's true. Deep down he cares a great deal. He's always looked after us. He wasn't the type of big brother to pretend he didn't know his younger brothers and sisters, ever. He was mature for his age even when we were growing up. I thought he could do no wrong." Pat hesitated, her brow furrowing with both poignancy and memory. "When I was in sixth grade, Max was a really popular eighth grader. Everyone loved him. The teachers, the other kids. He was an amazing athlete, smart, funny. I was a nerd, as shy as they come." She shook her head as she remembered.

Vivi could barely make out the picture Pat painted. A funny Max.

"I was fat and dumpy and wore thick glasses just like Lila's. But he was never too busy or too cool to pay attention to me. That year I was eleven, soon to be twelve, and with so many kids in the house, my mom didn't have time for much besides keeping the place together. I remember waking up one night with the worst pain in my stomach that I had ever felt. Next thing I knew, I was bleeding."

"Bleeding?"

"I'd started my period, but I didn't know that at the time. I was convinced I was dying."

"But then your mother explained everything?"

"I didn't tell her. I hated to add a dying kid to all of her problems. So I stuffed my underwear full of tissues and went to school."

"Ugh."

"Ugh is right. The next thing I knew I felt blood everywhere. I was on the verge of death, I was sure, but too damn mortified to let anyone know. When I wouldn't get up to do a math problem on the chalkboard, Mr. Henderson asked what was wrong."

"Did you tell him?"

"I couldn't. And suddenly the entire class had turned around to stare at me. Bleeding to death seemed the best option." Pat shook her head and smiled. "I asked him to get Max for me. I told him it was an emergency. A few minutes later my brother came in, so tall and wonderful. Every sixth grader in the class sat back in awe. Mr. Henderson hovered, trying to overhear. But the minute Max saw my face, he knew something was really wrong. He kneeled down in front of my little desk and leaned close and said, 'What is it, Patti?' I could feel my lip tremble, I was so afraid to say a word. Then it burst out in a horrified whisper. *I'm dying!*"

Pat leaned back and laughed, though Vivi could see the shine of tears in her eyes.

Vivi felt her own tears, felt a strange tightness in her chest.

"Thank God, Max didn't panic or even act like I was crazy. He just asked me what was wrong. I told him I was bleeding, *there*, and when he glanced down, he didn't hesitate more than a second before he smiled at me and said I wasn't dying at all. Before I knew it, he had me out of the chair, his favorite sweatshirt tied around my waist before I got up, and he took me to the nurse's office."

"What did your mother say?"

"I don't think she ever knew. The next morning there was a library book on my desk with a note from Max telling me that it would explain everything." Pat straightened and gathered herself. "Max really has spent his whole life taking care of us." She looked at Vivi. "It's been a huge responsibility, but he did it. And it hasn't given him a lot of time to be that boy who cared so easily."

Vivi felt the twist in her heart for the obvious love and respect Pat had for her brother. As an only child, Vivi found the protectiveness she sensed in Pat was as foreign as it was intriguing. Vivi had always wanted brothers and sisters. And when she had said yes to Grady's proposal, she had believed that at last she'd be able to have a family of her own.

The girls returned, backpacks in hand. "Come on, Pat," Lila said. "We've got to go or we'll be even later than we already are."

"Sorry," Pat said to Vivi. "On Saturdays we usually go to the movies. You want to go?"

Nicki went stiff with fury.

Vivi quickly declined, though she would have loved it. "That is so nice, but I can't. Thanks anyway."

The three sisters who looked so much alike started getting in the car, the love and the caring among them only heightening Vivi's awareness that their older brother no longer seemed to know how to make the connection to them.

Before she could think she blurted out, "Pat!" The idea was pulling together at the same time the woman turned back. "What do you think about having a picnic on Monday since it's a holiday?"

"A picnic?"

"For all your brothers and sisters and their families. I know the girls are off. It'll be fun. And if you could call everyone, I'll make the food."

"Pat," Lila almost whined from inside the car. "Hurry."

"We're going." Pat looked at Vivi for a second more, then smiled and nodded. "Okay, that sounds great. How about Cloudview Park at noon? I'll make sure everyone is there."

"Great!"

It took Vivi only a matter of minutes to put the tiara away and cart the rest of her belongings upstairs. Max was nowhere to be found, which was best, she told herself, because she wanted all the picnic planning done before she surprised him with the good news. Wouldn't he be amazed that she had remembered his mention of picnics and softball? Obviously he loved both, and what better way to get him to spend time with the girls and the rest of his family?

Vivi's heart just about burst with enthusiasm and purpose.

Sitting down with a cup of tea, she started making her plans. The food they would eat, the games they would play, and the songs they'd sing. Okay, maybe no songs.

Instantly she was back in her days of Miss Teen Homemaker of America, planning the event, coordinating the schedule. When she had a glimmer of memory about being the runner-up, iceberg and all, instead of the winner, she disregarded it. A picnic was a picnic.

Once the menu was planned, she glanced at the clock. It was nearly noon and Max hadn't returned. She really wasn't disappointed. She wasn't.

She went to Pricemart and shopped, buying everything she needed for Max and his family. Over the next hour, she readied hamburgers and hotdogs for the grill, whipped up gigantic batches of potato salad and coleslaw, then started on dessert. By the time she had everything ready, the brownies in the oven baking, it was five o'clock and she had the biggest mess she had ever seen. And still no Max.

With no help for it, she rolled up her sleeves, turned on the radio, then started to clean. After a minute, she started to tap her foot. After five, she started to hum. And when Aretha Franklin came over the wires, Vivi bit her lip, glanced around the empty kitchen, then couldn't help herself from belting out "R-e-s-p-e-c-t" in time with the music.

Perfect veneers dropped away. She swished her hips and sang along as she rinsed bowls, stacked dishes, and did Aretha proud. But her eyes went wide when she did one hugely impressive jumping jack turn . . . and came face-to-face with Max.

Vivi screamed. Massively manly Max jumped back. Then, after one sharp glare, he started talking to her—or more specifically, it looked like he was lecturing her.

Mortified that she'd been caught, she didn't turn down the volume. She wasn't too keen on knowing what he had to say. At least that was the decision until a woman walked up beside him.

She was beautiful. That is, if you liked perfectly elegant mixed with scads of perfectly proper shoulder-length blond hair, a hint of foundation, a dash of blush, and the requisite low-heeled pumps of the Symphony Society crowd.

Max turned off the stereo with a click.

After a second, the woman raised an expensively plucked brow. "Who's this?" she asked, looking Vivi up and down.

Vivi took off the brownie-stained apron and set it aside. If she hadn't prided herself on liking everyone she met and finding something to appreciate in all people, she would have hated the woman on sight. Or maybe it was the strange way the woman made her feel by standing so close to Max.

But she didn't care, Vivi told herself firmly. She didn't dislike this obnoxiously elegant woman.

Vivi peeled back a wide smile. "Hello, I'm Vivi. And you are?"

"Max's date."

Bitch. Oops, sorry.

Max got that look about him, stern and commanding, as he glanced at the woman. "Nell," he said in a really unfriendly way.

Nell smiled shyly, abashed, though Vivi could tell it was only for show.

Hmmm, something not so perfect about their date.

"Nell, this is Vivi Stansfield. She's helping me out with the girls."

"Ah, the new nanny." Nell regained her superior footing as if she had never lost it and gave Vivi another once-over. "Surely you're not *the* Vivi Stansfield that we read so much about."

Vivi had to fight really hard to keep the smile in place. "Afraid so."

Nell looked pleased. She glanced back and forth between Vivi and Max, then said, "I'll just go make a call, then freshen up."

With little more than a superior smirk, she turned and left the room.

Gone, just like that. As if she had nothing to worry about by leaving the two of them alone.

"Excuse me," Vivi started to call after her.

But Max caught her arm and held her there as the kitchen door swung closed.

"Whatever you were going to say," he stated, "don't."

Vivi gave him an indignant glare. "She wasn't even threatened by me."

He raised a brow.

"Not even the least little bit," she complained.

"Have you looked in the mirror lately?"

With a scowl, she glanced in the chrome bread box, yelped, and leaped back. "I look terrible!"

Max chuckled. "Now you know why I jumped."

"Very funny." She tugged her arm away.

"Why are you here?"

Her mind scanned for an answer, since she wasn't in the mood to admit to being evicted, especially with Miss Perfect out there getting more perfect. "Time off is overrated. As a dedicated employee, I thought I should be here."

Max leaned back against the counter and crossed his arms over his chest. She could tell he didn't believe her, and just when she thought she'd truly have to confess, he spoke. "Are you staying here over the weekend because you're trying to avoid Grady?" he asked sternly.

Avoid Grady?

At first she was confused, then she was elated. Saved. "Yes! That's it. I'm still trying to get over my ex-fiancé."

That wasn't a lie. Whenever she allowed herself to think about it, it seemed impossible that they weren't getting married anymore—that *she* wasn't getting married anymore. She had the dress, the wedding cake top, even her wedding diary filled with notes.

Who wouldn't want to avoid facing the reality of that, if not the reality of Grady? And just because she'd had the sudden insight that they weren't right for each other, that didn't mean she didn't feel badly about everything. But no reason to explain all of that.

"It only makes sense that I wouldn't want to be home alone in my apartment, moping around, stuffing my face with chocolate. And what else would a reasonable person do when this city is filled with potential land mines that remind me of Grady?"

Max scowled, but Vivi was on a roll and couldn't seem to stop herself. "That field where we played in the snow. The busy streets filled with yellow taxicabs, where we walked hand and hand—" She cut herself off.

"Why doesn't this sound like El Paso?"

Vivi grimaced. "Okay, so maybe that was Jenny and Oliver in *Love Story*, but still, I have memories and I deserve to drown in them for a few days, and why not drown here rather than . . . somewhere else?"

The change in his mood happened swiftly. Max pushed away from the counter and he didn't stop until he was directly in front of her.

"Are you going to tell me why you're here or not?"

Just standing close to this man did strange things to her nerves. Awareness and heat made her skin tingle with the memory of his hands touching her, his lips coming down on her—

"Am I a horrible kisser?"

Immediately his body tensed. "What?"

She couldn't believe she had asked. "Sorry, it's just that, well, I wondered."

"Too late, I'm already wise to your circuitous method of conversation meant to evade and distract. Why are you here?"

"I was serious. But forget it," she managed to say, staring at the broad expanse of his chest. "I have a tiny problem."

That warrior's tension of his sizzled through him, and she knew if she looked up, his dark brow would be furrowed. So she didn't look, just sighed and realized she couldn't hide from this problem any more than she could hide from the rest.

He touched her then, gently, just one strong finger to her chin as he forced her to meet his eyes.

"What is it, Vivienne?"

She hated the way he refused to call her Vivi. Somehow the use of her given name felt intimate and knowing, catching her off guard, making her say and do things that normally she wouldn't do.

"I was evicted."

That certainly doused the flames.

He stood there a second longer, his finger frozen at her chin, then, "Have you always been this much of a disaster?"

"You flatterer, you."

Max dropped his hand away. "First the credit cards, then the car, now the apartment." He hesitated, and she could feel the intensity of his gaze burning into her. "Are you sure you're telling me everything?"

"Of course I am. What else could there be?"

"God only knows." He looked at her long and hard,

then finally said, "I don't think you're simply overdrawn. I think your father's the one in financial trouble and in the process is pulling you down."

Vivi reeled, a wealth of emotion careening through her. Hot and cold. She turned away and looked out the window. "My father would never hurt me. My father loves me. He wouldn't do that." She started to pace. "It's all a misunderstanding, and just as soon as I find him—" She froze. "I mean, as soon as I get him on the phone, he'll explain how all of this is a horrible mistake. You heard that message. He sounded fine. He told me not to worry."

Max watched her, could all but feel the stress as she tried to keep that crystalline facade around her. Since the night he had seen her in Bobby's Place, she continued to hold on to her faith in Jennings Stansfield. Admirably. She had not given in, as he could tell she wanted to. But now he saw the cracks were deepening.

"Daddy, where are you?" he could barely hear her whisper.

Max was certain she had forgotten he was there, and he felt the hard knot inside him try to slip.

With this woman it was always the same. Her laughter and strength would give way to reveal vulnerability. In those moments she seemed frail, and his frustration would give way to need. Need to slip deep inside her thoughts—and her body. Take her completely. And in doing so, once and for all, extricate her from his mind.

But could he get her out of his mind?

Then, as had happened again and again since she walked into his office, he remembered, the memories swirling back. Back to that night of the debutante ball. The girls dressed in shimmering white satin. He in a tux.

But unlike the dates and fathers, Max had been a waiter moonlighting to make ends meet. All that juggling to keep his brothers and sisters afloat. The exhaustion.

The minute he saw Vivienne, everything had evaporated but her.

She had been sleek, wearing the same glittering tiara she had worn as a child. And like that day when he was young and saw her on the stage, he had felt the need to reach out and touch her.

Her father was nowhere to be seen, no doubt downstairs in the bar or running late.

Forgetting himself as he always did when he saw her, Max didn't think about who he was and walked toward her. But just before he would have said her name, the look in her eyes stopped him.

She stood alone, her porcelain features held in a perfect smile that didn't match the darkness in her pewter eyes. Then a woman who had to have been her mother walked up in attire that he could only describe as earth mother chic, saying, "I'm sorry, sweetheart. But you know Jennings. Can't be counted on for anything."

"Don't say that," Vivi had stated with the staunch belief of a young girl who adored her father.

Max saw the look of bitterness that almost swallowed Isabelle Stansfield. She saw her daughter's unwavering belief. And constant disappointment.

Now, standing in his kitchen with her, Max felt the same weakness inside him as he had felt that night. The need to take her in his arms and solve her problems.

As he had done so many times before, he reached out to her. But this time he touched her.

As if he had no will of his own, Max ran his thumb

along her jaw. Barely a touch, but her breath caught, her pale gray eyes darkening.

He thought of the afternoon in her apartment, touching her, watching her passion.

Unable to help himself now, he traced her mouth with the tips of his fingers. Like the ten-year-old boy, he felt himself shake. She was beautiful, as beautiful as she was to him when he had first seen her.

Her breath went ragged the second his fingers grazed against her skin, her brow furrowing in panic and concern. But just when he thought she would pull away, she sighed and stepped into his arms, clinging to him. And he was lost—lost as he had been growing up, lost as he had been for so many years when he had nearly drowned after his father had left, then his mother died. Suddenly he clung to Vivienne, their mouths slanting together.

"Max," she breathed, her fingers curling into the back of his shirt.

Running his hands down her spine, molding her to him, he could feel her curves. His erection was swift and intense. He felt feral and reckless and he wanted her closer. He wanted to be inside her, just like that. From a simple kiss to need in a heartbeat.

He sensed her own desire, but sensed as well a certain franticness, as if she didn't understand how quickly things had flared between them.

Then suddenly she pushed at him, her tiny hand flattening on his chest. "Why do you want me?"

The question jarred in his mind. "What?"

Her lips were slightly swollen from his kiss, her eyes glazed with sexual awareness. "What is it about me that makes you want me?" she asked, confusion mixing with desire. "Over and over again we're drawn together. But I don't know why."

He saw in her expression that she truly wanted to know, wanted to understand. But how could he explain when he didn't understand it any more than she did, and liked it even less.

Suddenly he was back in that hotel, back on that debutante night, reaching out. Like a young, innocent fool, he had wanted to step in when her father had deserted her. The knight in shining armor coming to her rescue.

But just as he was about to, just as Vivienne's eyes settled on him, her name was bellowed through the great hall.

"Vivi!"

Vivienne had grown still in her white debutante gown, then turned, worry replaced by a joy that kicked Max in the midsection. Everyone there turned as well, ensnared by Jennings Stansfield as he strode into the gold, gilt, and crystal chandelier opulence of the hotel ballroom, larger than life.

While Max had served plates of food and poured water and wine, Jennings had presented his daughter, the most beautiful girl there. Max had been forgotten— that is, if she had ever noticed him at all.

Now, all these years later, he didn't understand what he felt. Part of him wanted her, but part of him couldn't look at her without thinking about the years of struggling to keep his head above water.

"Hey," she said, with a laugh that didn't show in her eyes, "don't worry about it. It was a silly question."

Red crept into her cheeks and she started to turn away. Unable to help himself, he caught her arm.

"I think a better question is why do you keep ending

up in my arms. Why do *you* want me? It's time you faced up to who you are."

Whatever embarrassment she had felt before melted away, and her eyes flashed. "Who is that, Max? The pampered princess that everyone accuses me of being?"

"You tell me. Are you really a woman whom everyone has misjudged? Or do you even know?"

She sucked in her breath. "Why are you doing this?"

He looked at her hard, then said, "Maybe because we all have to realize who we have been before we can truly understand who we have the potential to become. I'm willing to help you, Vivienne. Your father isn't here, and my guess is that he either can't or won't bail you out of this mess. And short of taking my offer of money, or being a nanny for the rest of your life, you'd better find something you can do."

They stared at each other, and just when he would have damned all else and pulled her back, Nell called out.

"Max! I'm ready."

My Wedding Diary

THINGS TO DO

8. Ignore Max. He doesn't know the first thing about me. I'm strong. I care about people, and I've survived a lot worse than he can dole out.

9. Do not feel embarrassed about lifetime dream of wanting to be a bride—hasn't most every girl wanted the same thing??

10. Organize laundry room

11. Come up with a way to make more money

12. Under no circumstances ask Max why he didn't come home last night!!

Chapter Fourteen

Early the next morning, the house was quiet. It was Sunday, the day before the picnic, and Vivi stood in the kitchen, thinking—not obsessing, she promised herself—about Max.

As if the thought made him appear, he pushed through the swinging door. He wore workout clothes and a towel slung around his neck. And before she could stop herself, she sniffed indignantly and said, "Had a little sleepover, did we?"

So much for #12 on her list.

Max raised an incredulous brow. But it seemed to her she had a little leeway in the snippy department since he was the one who had kissed her, then waltzed out the door with another woman. Who could blame her for being a tad on the testy side?

But rather than giving her the opportunity to indulge in some really good verbal venting, allowing her to find out if indeed he had slept with the woman, Max only smiled, grabbed an apple, tapped her on the nose, went to his room without a word, showered, changed into golf clothes, then disappeared.

An hour later, she was so frustrated and antsy that she even started missing the girls. For half a second, she felt the whole life-falling-apart panic start to rise like a tide. But in the next, she knew the only solution was to do something productive.

She had already determined that the laundry room needed to be organized. But how?

A dry board with colored markers hung on the wall in the laundry room and there were several colored baskets stacked in a closet. In a matter of minutes, she came up with a color-coordinated plan for doing whites on Mondays and Thursdays, darks on Tuesdays, bright colors on Wednesday, and bedding on Friday. She designated a whole separate basket for clothes that couldn't be put in the dryer. There would be no more laundry calamities in the Landry household if she could help it.

After that, she moved on to her closet and drawers. Not to organize, this time, but to find a way to start dealing with her debt.

It's time you faced up to who you are.

Vivi scoffed. She would show Max Landry who she was. She was someone who could manage on her own and manage well, thank you very much.

By noon, Vivi had made three stacks. One of clothes that still had price tags on them and could be returned, another of items that she felt certain she could sell on consignment, and a third for every piece of Louis Vuitton luggage she owned.

By five, Vivi had finished the returns, dropped off the clothing at Cathy's Consignment Corner, and made a deal with the largest luggage dealer in town to sell her perfectly good, nearly new luggage. The feeling was exhilarating. When she counted the money at the end, she didn't have near enough to pay off all the bills, but it was a start. And most important, she could pay Velda from the salon for the styles and makeovers she had done for the women Vivi had sent in.

To celebrate, Vivi rummaged up enough change to take herself to the Charcoaler for a burger. She fired up the Olds, bringing the neighbor back to the window like a lightning bolt, then sailed off, barely managing the thin drive-thru at the burger joint in the lumbering car.

With burger in hand, not even splurging on cheese, she docked under an awning, scaring everyone within a half mile when the car kaboomed to a stop.

But Vivi was fast becoming immune to this different kind of stare from strangers. Not the "Is that the Vivi Stansfield who everyone talks about?" stare. Rather the new "What in the world has happened to Vivi Stansfield?" gawk.

Oddly, it was freeing. No more concern about giving the wrong impression. She had already given it, and it was hard to go from bad to worse when she had already hit *worse* six days ago.

The first thing the next morning, Vivi leaped out of bed.

"Picnic day!"

Realizing that she had yet to tell Max about the plan, she dashed to his bedroom, only to find it empty.

She wasn't going to think about the fact that she had become obsessed with a man who didn't even like her. She pulled on her brand-new flannel robe and terry cloth slippers she had bought at Wal-Mart to replace her favorite marabou and satin wrap that now hung at Cathy's Corner.

Heading downstairs to the kitchen, trying not to be disappointed that Max had yet again not come home, she stopped dead in her tracks when she found him standing bare-chested in front of the refrigerator, drinking orange juice straight out of the carton.

Awareness whispered through her at the sight of muscles rippling in his arms, his abdomen washboard hard, dark hair wisping away beneath the waistband of his button-fly jeans, then disappearing to places Vivi knew she'd better not think about.

"Would you like me to get you a glass?" she asked, after having to clear her throat.

Max lowered the juice, his lips tipping guiltily. But the guilt gave way to something sensual when he took her in, one dark brow rising. "Look at you all in flannel. What happened to the feathers?"

Foolishly pleased at the look on his face, not to mention that he was there and not at Nell's, she waved her hand shyly. "I thought I'd take a break from the feathers. Wal-Mart flannel is a definite must-have this season."

Max chuckled as he returned the juice to the refrigerator, then leaned back against the closed door. "Flannel, feathers . . . you'd probably look sexy as hell in a burlap bag."

She pulled the robe tightly around her. "I bet you say that to all the girls . . . late at night . . ." She eyed him. "When you don't come home."

"Keeping tabs on me?"

"I am not."

"Then how do you know if I came in last night or not?"

"Did you?"

"As a matter of fact, I did."

"How about the night before last?"

"Slept right here."

"What about Little Miss . . . I mean, Nell?"

"She works for me."

"But you went out with her."

"To see a commercial listing. The owner flew into town and was leaving early the next morning."

"Nell said it was a date."

"Nell likes to cause trouble."

Vivi was unaccountably pleased, and she started to smile before she realized what she was doing. "Not that it mattered," she said with great seriousness.

He came closer, his smile widening. "Did you wait up?"

"Me? Never."

"Sure you didn't." Then he stopped, and sniffed the air. "What is that?"

"What is what?" Panicked, Vivi cupped her hand over her mouth and breathed.

Max smiled. "Are you wearing perfume?" His smile turned wicked. "Vivi, you didn't have to spiff up just for me."

"Spiff up?" she asked, her arms extended.

"I'm partial to flannel, and you smell awfully sweet. I think you waited up for me last night."

She thought of her long bath in scented silky oil and how she had indeed listened for him to come in until she finally couldn't keep her eyes open. "Absolutely not."

"Liar."

"Go stuff yourself."

"Mmmm, I like it when you talk dirty."

He took a step closer. She took a step back.

"Now, Max, this really isn't a good idea. We already got carried away once. No sense in pressing our luck again."

"Or what will happen?" he asked in that deep, rumbling voice that turned her insides to jelly.

"You know what will happen," she snipped, backing around the center island.

"We'll end up on the sofa and you'll be grabbing me by the hair and saying, 'More, Max, more, more, more!' "

Vivi's eyes went wide and she gasped, planting her hands on the granite top. "I never said any such thing!"

"Think back. In your father's apartment. You and me. Remember now?"

Actually, she hardly remembered anything except that her body had turned traitorous, and she very easily could have said that and more—more, more. Ugh.

"I really don't like you," she stated crisply.

"I don't believe you," he teased with a molasses-slow grin. "If I were a gambling man, I'd say what you'd really like is to leap into my arms."

A noise worked its way free from her chest as that recently all-too-available emotion surged up and she launched herself across the slab of granite. She probably would have gotten her nails into his skin, but he had the agility of a panther and sidestepped out of the way.

"Whoa," he said, surprised and amused, grabbing her wrists to keep her from actually doing some damage. "If you're not careful, you're going to hurt someone."

"I'm trying to hurt *you*."

"Tsk, tsk," he admonished with a devilish smile. "Who knew you were the violent type?"

He pushed away and headed for the door. At the last minute he turned around, pulled a set of keys from his pocket, and tossed them to her.

Too startled to do anything but catch them, Vivi stared at the ring. "What are you doing with my keys?"

Max shrugged. "I fixed your car."

Vivi's mouth fell open.

"Don't look so shocked. There isn't a guy born and raised on the south side of town who can't tune an eight cylinder in his sleep."

But it wasn't the car that held her attention. "You're from the south side?"

"Born and raised. This is America," he quipped. "There are plenty of poor kids who make good."

"No doubt. But I'm not as sure that there are so many who did it while raising seven brothers and sisters. That really is incredible."

Her compliment made this controlled man shift his weight awkwardly. "Anyone in my position would have done the same thing."

"I wouldn't be too sure about that." She considered him for a moment. "Do you miss it?"

"Miss what?"

"The south side?"

The question surprised him, and she realized that he was on the verge of saying absolutely not. But then he seemed to drift back, seeing the shadow of memories, she was sure.

"Sometimes I do."

"What do you miss the most?"

"The smell of chili and tamales when you walk down the street. And the music, guitars and mariachis, coming from the shops."

"You must have been happy growing up."

Every trace of softness evaporated. "Mainly I wanted out. But all of a sudden I feel like everywhere I turn, I find something from my past that makes me remember."

"Is that so bad?"

He drew a deep breath, then he focused on her in a

way that made her skin tingle. "It depends on the memory."

She braced her hands on her hips and smiled at him.

"What?" he asked.

"Nothing."

"That smile is not nothing."

"I'm thinking that deep down beneath your gruff exterior is a very nice man."

He snorted.

"A nice man who might like me just a little more than he's willing to admit."

He scowled, but when his hand shot out to grab her wrist, she danced away.

"Face it, Landry. You're a regular sweetheart. A real gem of a guy."

One dark brow rose and he took a step toward her. But they were saved from another verbal clash or falling into a wild embrace on the kitchen table when the phone rang.

Muttering something about impossible women, he grabbed up the receiver. "Hello?" Then, "Good morning to you too, Pat." He leaned back against the counter, his bare feet crossed at the ankles. "Yep, she's still here." He looked Vivi up and down before he seemed to freeze and his expression went hard. "What are you talking about? I haven't heard a word about a picnic."

"Oops, I forgot to mention that," Vivi interjected.

Max listened for a few more minutes before grunting into the phone and then hanging up.

"What is this about a picnic?" he demanded.

"It's going to be great."

"What are you trying to do?"

"I'm not sure what you mean."

His eyes narrowed in accusation. "Why would you plan a picnic for my family?"

Vivi made an indignant noise. "I was just trying to find a way for you to spend time with your brothers and sisters. I don't mind telling you that I've noticed a distinct division between you and them. And what better way to bridge the gap than a day of great food and games?"

"What is it with you and fixing things? There is nothing wrong with my relationship with my family," he stated.

"Really? So when was the last time you did something with them?"

"I'm busy."

"Ah, yes, which explains your system of memos with your eleven-year-old sister."

"There is no system. She memos me."

"And that sounds normal in what country?"

His jaw cemented. "My family is my business," he stated coldly, then headed for the door.

"But you'll go to the picnic, right?" she called after him.

He pushed out of the room with a curse. "Yeah, I'll be there."

"Great! And thanks for taking care of my car!"

He only grumbled, and as soon as the door swung closed, she did a little victory dance. "You're bad, you're bad." Then she raced upstairs to get ready.

Two hours later, rain threatened the picnic, but that didn't dampen Vivi's excitement. She hadn't accepted Max's grumbled invitation to ride with him to Cloudview Park. She drove herself, pulling into the single available spot in the crowded lot.

She saw Max the second she arrived. He was taller than most, but it was his cool command that separated him from the crowd. He stood with an easy smile on his full, sensual lips.

That was what most people noticed. But Vivi saw the always tightly held control just below—and she saw as well that Max gave a proud nod when she turned off the car. No chugging, no explosion, just the smooth purr of an engine disengaging.

Max watched, and he even shot her an "are you impressed?" raising of an eyebrow. But his pride turned to amazement when he got a look at her clothes.

"What?" she demanded when he came up to the car.

"We're here for barbeque and baseball, not a fashion show."

"Oooh, do I look that good?"

There went that murderous scowl again. Though why he was bothered, she couldn't say. She had on a Girl Scout's Honor T-shirt, tennis shoes, and pants. Of course, Girl Scout's Honor was spelled out in sequins, but what was she supposed to wear? After her trip to the consignment shop, she didn't have a lot left and she couldn't afford to turn around and buy a whole new less-sequiny wardrobe.

Max didn't have time to comment or murder her when she leaned into the car for a container of potato salad. Seconds later, the rest of his family joined them.

There was Raymond Landry and his wife of five years, Randi, and their three kids, Roger, Regina, and Rebecca.

"Oh, wow, all Rs," Vivi said.

Next came brother Gabriel, his wife, Fatima, who took the potato salad from Max, and the cutest little daughter named Missy. They were a well-dressed family, all spitshined clean with mother and daughter in matching picnic clothes.

"Great outfits," Vivi offered, hardly able to fathom so much family.

Next came younger brother Jim, wife Petra, and little Jimmy, followed by Pat's on-again, off-again boyfriend, Joel. Seeing this group of people, Vivi felt a pierce of poignancy that made her throat tighten. Clearly there were tensions and back stories to all these relationships, but there was an unmistakable bond as well.

Vivi had the distinct feeling that they could get on each other's nerves, say whatever they wanted within the family, but no way would they let someone from the outside try to mess with any one of them. As revealed in Pat's story about Max protecting her when she was young, this family clearly cared about each other.

The group cheered when another Landry showed up. It was as if a lightness blew in with the dark clouds that were gathering. He was Christopher Landry. He wore a military haircut and some kind of a military uniform, and the minute the brothers and sisters saw him, they circled around.

"Chris!"

The soldier hugged and shook hands, swept up the kids, and even pulled Nicki into a brotherly embrace when she hung back.

"Hey, punk," he said.

Nicki smiled reluctantly, almost shyly, her tense little body easing. Max looked on, a mix of fierce love and pride etched in his bold features. It wasn't until the rest of the family was done with Chris that he found his oldest brother. A devilish smile cracked his young face, then he strode over and the two men gave each other bone-crushing hugs.

The strength of their love was palpable, and more unwanted emotion swelled in Vivi's throat.

"Hey, Max," Chris said.

Max held him at arm's length. "You look good, kid. Pilot training is treating you well."

Chris chuckled. "I wouldn't go that far."

Despite the impending bad weather, the picnic was off to a great start, and Vivi felt her own sense of pride. She might not have brothers and sisters, but she loved bringing this family together.

The park was crowded with kids and adults. An official softball game was going on with real referees, while the other fields were taken up with informal games.

Chris turned and saw Vivi for the first time. Clearly not shy, he whistled appreciatively. "Who are you?"

Max stepped forward, but before he could say a word, Lila perked up. "She's our new nanny."

Chris took a step closer to Vivi in a way that reminded her of his older brother.

Nicki snorted. "Yeah, like the really *old* new nanny. Way older than you," she clarified.

"Old?" Chris looked Vivi up and down. "I doubt it, but I'm happy to do the older woman–younger man thing."

The siblings hooted, except for Nicki—and Max.

"Chris," he said, his voice a command. "Keep your thoughts and hands to yourself."

Everyone there but Chris quieted instantly. The youngest brother only glanced back, lifted a brow, and smiled, his hands raised in surrender. "So, big brother, that's the way the wind blows."

Max glowered, Vivi's mouth rounded in an O, and Nicki scowled. "As if," the teen muttered.

"Come on, everyone, I'm starving," Chris announced, taking the potato salad. "Then can I assume we're up for some serious softball?"

Vivi rummaged around in her Naughty & Nice tote bag until she produced two softballs she had found in the garage. Next she produced bats and mitts from the trunk.

Max shot her a teasing grin. "You really do know what a picnic is."

Vivi rolled her eyes and shoved the equipment into his arms, then retrieved the rest of the food.

Chris winked. "I feel a winning streak coming on, big brother. When was the last time you played?" He laughed. "Do you even remember how?"

Max's features took on a competitive gleam. "I'll show you how to play the game, little boy. Come on, let's eat."

And eat they did, everyone devouring the *regular* food Vivi had made. Or at least most of it was regular.

"Wow," Chris chirped, kind of choking. "What's this?"

Everyone looked.

"A hot dog," Vivi supplied.

Chris didn't look convinced.

"It is. It's just stuffed with caviar and wrapped in Gruyère cheese."

"Oh," he managed to say, swallowing hard.

Max leaned close, smiling against her ear. "I see your regular food has gone the way of your baked Alaska."

Vivi sniffed. "No sense in being completely boring."

Patricia sat down beside her. "I love your hot dogs," she said with a fond smile as Max headed off with the other men to congregate around the very regular hamburgers.

Vivi laughed. "Thank you."

"I'm glad you thought to do this," Pat said.

"Your brother wasn't as enthusiastic about the idea."

"Like I said before, Max needs his world shaken up."

"Why is everyone so afraid of him?"

"Not afraid. It's respect and gratitude. If he hadn't taken over the responsibility for all of us, who knows where we'd be? Certainly not together. He gave up college to take care of us. We owe him a lot."

"Dropping out doesn't seem to have held him back."

"No," Pat said thoughtfully. "For as long as I can remember there's always been something in him that kept him going—something that drove him to succeed no matter what. I've always wondered what it was. Even before our father left, Dad wasn't much help. Perhaps Max wanted to show him."

"Did you ever hear anything from your father?"

"Nope. It's like he vanished. I guess deep down we've all held on to the selfish hope that he wanted to return, but couldn't."

Chris came up behind them, then Max.

"Time to pick teams," Chris announced. "I get Vivi on my side."

Max blinked. "Her?" he said, the very same time Vivi said, "Me?"

Chris only smiled. "Yep."

"Oh, well, I couldn't, really."

"Why?"

"For starters, I've never played. I saw myself more as a

cheerleader or spectator." Vivi shrugged apologetically. "You know, 'Go team.' "

"Not on your life," Chris said. "Anyone who stuffs hot dogs with caviar is bound to be full of surprises."

Sure enough, when places were taken, Vivi found herself chosen for the first time in her life. No more playground games where kids lined up and she was the little girl in the too perfect dress that no one wanted on their team. This group actually gave her a starting position.

Max watched with a mixture of bemusement and chagrin when Vivienne turned out to be such a good sport and actually looked as if she was enjoying herself. She also looked hot as hell and was definitely a distraction— for just about every male within a half-mile radius.

But when Chris came up behind her, practically swallowing her with his arms as he showed her how to hold the bat, and Vivi blushed the deepest shade of red he had ever seen, Max had had it.

"That's enough!"

"But, Max," Chris said with unabated good humor. "I'm just showing little Vivi here a thing or two about the game."

Whatever he was doing, it worked. For all her sequins and perfect hair, Vivi got out there and hit the ball so hard that Max nearly missed catching it because of sheer surprise.

"You nearly killed me with that ball," he bellowed from the pitcher's mound after it had come straight for his head.

"And that's a bad thing?" she asked with an innocent smile after she had run to second base.

But for every bit of frustration that mounted in Max, his family liked her more and more. Everyone, that is, except Nicki, whose animosity grew and festered. The more the family liked Vivi, the more Nicki's already simmering hatred began to bubble over, until at the very end when Vivi managed to catch a pop fly and win the game for her team, Nicki stormed off toward the concession stand.

Vivi came up next to Max. "I can't do anything right with her," she said, staring at Nicki's back.

"This has been going on too long," he stated. "It's time I had a talk with her."

Vivi hesitated, grimacing at the thought that she'd probably only make things worse, but wanting to find some way to turn things around herself. "Please wait until you get home. For now, let me talk to her."

Max looked doubtful, but Vivi didn't wait for permission.

She followed Nicki, ignoring the rumbles of thunder that drew closer. She watched as the girl stopped in front of the guy Vivi recognized as Brandon Bonner.

In the dim confines of Raiders, or even poking his head into her car, he had looked like trouble. But out in the open he looked like bad news in the worst sort of way. Sinfully good looks combined with an insouciant stance that spoke volumes about belligerence. Vivi had the fleeting thought that Max Landry might have looked much the same at his age. Then she dismissed the idea as ludicrous given Max's controlled reputation.

Nicki stood there in a kind of strange slouch and batting black eyelashes, clearly trying to get the boy's attention with little success. It was painful to watch.

The longer Brandon ignored her, the more desperate Nicki became. Forgetting that Nicki hated her guts, wanting to mitigate the awkward situation, Vivi walked up and interrupted.

"Hey, Nicki!"

But if she thought to help, she was mistaken. The boy turned and ran his gaze over her, then said, "Hey, yourself. You're the girl with the awesome car."

Great.

Nicki's face went bright red with fury. "Yeah, the awesome, *repossessed* car."

"Wow," Brandon said. "Cool."

Cool?

But before Vivi could respond, Mr. Cool glanced up at the sky, mumbled something about not wanting to get wet, then made a dash for the parking lot.

"Do you have to take over everything?" Nicki demanded.

"I was just trying to help."

Thunder rumbled, lightning cracked the sky.

"Help?" Nicki demanded, her voice rising. "Like you know anything. Haven't you figured out that no one likes you—at least no one that matters. Not Max, not even your own father."

Vivi's head came back.

"You think because you're pretty and rich you can get away with being stupid and incompetent," Nicki spat. "But you're not that pretty and you sure can't be all that rich if you're working for us."

Vivi couldn't speak.

"I read the newspaper this morning," Nicki sneered. "Your dad bolted. And even some lame fiancé of yours dumped you."

Confused, Vivi stood very still, unable to think much

less move, as the skies finally let go of a light rain that dusted her hair. "What are you talking about?"

Nicki rolled her eyes. "Did you really call yourself the Christmas Bride?"

Vivi tried to make sense of the words. "How do you know about that?"

"Don't you read the paper? They said that even if you had managed to keep your fiancé, your father doesn't have the money to pay for a wedding." But Nicki cut herself off, her eyes going wide at something.

Slowly Vivi turned and found Max standing there. While looking at Vivi, he told Nicki that it was time to leave and Pat was waiting for her in the car. Nicki dashed away just as the sky opened up completely and it began to pour. But neither Max nor Vivi moved.

"Where is this article?" Vivi asked numbly.

Max tried to take her arm. "We'll talk about it at home."

With a calm she didn't feel, Vivi pulled away. "Tell me. What article?"

His expression grew even more grim. "In the morning newspaper. Your father defaulted on several of his loans."

"Defaulted?" She wanted to be incensed at an outrageous lie. She wanted to believe it was impossible. But she realized it all too easily could be true.

Vivi blinked as the concession shop behind them banged closed. She stared at the pouring rain that soaked through her clothes. Within minutes the park was deserted, dirt turning to soupy puddles, her Oldsmobile waiting in the lot like a lonely holdover from days long past.

She counted to ten, then twenty. She felt weak, her

knees starting to shake, though she wasn't cold. Pressure built at the back of her eyes, her throat tightening. She told herself it was the rain and mud, not Nicki or her father or even the strange unsettling sexual dance she kept playing with this man who stood so close, his hard, penetrating gaze unnerving.

Rain surrounded them, but Max didn't leave her, drops clinging to his dark lashes, spiking them together, making his blue eyes glitter.

"As soon as I heard," he began to explain, "I put in a few calls. Your father has defaulted on three outstanding loans. He has thirty days to make good or he'll be forced into bankruptcy." He hesitated. "My guess is that he's not on vacation, but out of town trying to find financing. Also, I learned that this isn't the first time it has happened. He has been struggling off and on for years, Vivienne. And he's left a lot of people in the lurch."

Her mind reeled.

"Are you all right?" he asked, his voice a gruff whisper of sound nearly drowned out by a clap of thunder in the distance.

She stared at this man, seeing a disquieting mix of emotions on his normally implacable features. The usual censure was there, but now something else mixed in. Not disgust, but pity. And that made her sick. "No wonder everyone hates me."

His gaze never broke from hers, and he looked at her hard. "Not everyone," he whispered.

His words made her heart go still, filling her with the same empty, hungry feeling he always stirred in her, a need that sank as deeply as the pain sinking into her soul. It was difficult to breathe as she looked at him, then impossible when he took the steps that separated them.

Then she was in his arms, holding on, their mouths coming together in a hungry demand, as if they could somehow move beyond the barriers of clothes and even of life.

Desperate and intense, Max pressed her up against the baseball diamond backstop, her fingers sliding back into the chain link as he touched her, leaning down to taste her skin like a starving man giving in.

Mindless of the empty world around them, Vivi gave in and Max trailed his lips along her jaw, then lower. She realized that she wanted this, wanted more of his obliterating touch—had wanted it every day and every night since she met him. This man, for reasons she didn't understand, had the ability to wipe her mind clean, erase all else but the desire to touch him.

Pressing her breasts high through the clinging wet T-shirt, he lowered his head, kissing the fullness of each. Letting go of the fence, she wrapped her arms around his head, savoring, thinking of nothing else, tilting her face up to the wet skies. But she moved too fast, and slipped in the slick mud.

For one startled moment her eyes went wide as she lost her balance, pulling Max with her despite his straining muscles that tried to keep them upright. They fell to the ground with Max landing on top of her, his weight supported on his elbows. Mud splattered them, their gazes locking in surprise.

But then the elements were forgotten. Their mouths crashed together as he rolled her on top of him, his hands finding her hips, cupping, lifting, pressing her against the very real hardness of him. If their clothes hadn't been plastered to their bodies, she was sure that he would have damned all else and slid inside her.

Rain fell relentlessly, mud surrounded them, but they hardly noticed. He rolled them again so that he came over her.

He looked at her then, a reluctant smile pulling at his sinful lips. "I guess I was wrong that you'd never like picnics."

"Or getting dirty." She gave him a cheeky grin, feeling a relief wash through her that the despair had been pushed back, held at bay—at least for now. She would deal with the mess her father had made, but tomorrow. Later.

"No one can call me a priss ever again."

He touched her cheek. "Thank you for today."

She could see the sincerity in his sharp features. "You're welcome. You have a great family."

His lips crooked at one corner. "I do."

"I even fit in, sort of. I wasn't half bad at softball."

Max tugged a strand of hair from her mouth. "Not bad for a girl," he teased.

"Hey! Chris thought I was great."

Max's smile disappeared and his brow furrowed. "My brother is a young pup who better watch himself."

"Or what?" she whispered.

"Or I'll have to convince him that he'd better keep his hands off you. And he might not like my methods of persuasion."

"You don't want him messing with your nanny?"

"I don't want him messing with you," he stated, his voice lowering to a possessive rumble.

Sensation rushed through her, sensation that she didn't have words for, only made her think of sex and desire, yearning and heat, and the mindless pleasure she wanted to feel.

"Why?" she whispered. "Why does it matter what Chris does?"

He framed her face, pushing her wet hair back, his eyes darkened with intensity. "Because I want you." He took her hand and pressed it to him in proof.

His body was hard against her, aching and yearning. She relished the taste of him when he coaxed her lips open with his tongue.

Their need became frantic, desperate. She wanted to give in completely, and she almost did, wanting suddenly to feel the wet and wind against bare skin.

As if understanding, but knowing a public park was not the place for this, he pushed up from the ground. He pulled her up and took her hand as they ran to the empty lot.

"Where's your car?" she yelled through the wind and rain.

"Chris took it."

The rest of the family had gathered all the gear and leftovers and had departed. Max and Vivi found some old towels in her trunk, then wiped themselves clean with the help of the rain. Then Max asked for the keys.

"Keys?"

His expression was heated and sensual. "I'm not going to make love to you in a parking lot."

Her heart fluttered, and nervously she fell into the driver's seat of the Oldsmobile. But Max followed instead of going around, forcing her to move over.

When she looked at him, her mouth falling open, he said, "Women don't drive me around."

Chapter Fifteen

"Women don't drive you around?" she demanded, sanity returning like a cold splash of water.

"Vivienne, just give me the keys."

"Fine. Drive. Make Cro-Magnon Men of America proud."

He had the audacity to laugh, then, without an ounce of shame, start the car.

Vivi plastered herself to the door, all but choking on disbelief. At him. At her.

What in the world had she been doing rolling around in the mud with this man?

Yes, she was attracted to him, even if his knuckles did scrape the ground on occasion, but that was as far as it went. He was big and broad and domineering. Demanding. There was too much of him—he was too overpowering. The kind of man who took without asking.

A man like her father who'd leave her.

The thought shot through her like a punch to the chest, and just as quickly she discounted it. She would never give Max Landry the chance to leave her. She would not allow herself to feel anything for this man other than concern that he reconnect with his family. *That* she could do. *That* she wanted to do. But nothing more—especially rolling around in any fashion.

Max put the car in reverse and pulled out of the parking lot with ease. Vivi hated how he drove, the way his hand worked the wheel with a casual competence. He commanded the difficult Olds, steering it along like a fine-tuned sports car. Which only added to her frustration because it made him all the harder to ignore.

Over and over again she had found herself in his arms. But that was very different from actually having sex, plunging into the rawness of totally giving herself to a man. She might be some throwback, but to her, making love meant commitment. Or so she had told herself for years.

She knew she was old-fashioned, though she figured that it wasn't so odd given her father's constant stream of relationships and her mother's decision to be free to love where and when she chose. Growing up with a relic hippy for a mom, Vivi had been the one to wait up and make sure she got home safely. That didn't make a sexually free life seem all that appealing. And when she went to live with her father, things hadn't gotten much better. Only he didn't go out. He had the women in. No daughter should have to deal with her father's assorted wives and paramours.

As far as Vivi was concerned, sex should have meaning, a deep, committed bond. Though every time she was around Max Landry, all her beliefs flew right out the window. Suddenly a little uncommitted sex didn't sound so bad.

But she would not let this man alter her convictions.

By the time Max slid into the drive of Number 15

Pinehurst, Vivi really wasn't happy. When Max reached across the seat to take her hand, she leaped out of the car.

"Got to go! Thanks for coming to the picnic," she blurted out, then dashed into the house.

Inside her bedroom, Vivi froze when she heard Max come up the stairs and hesitate outside her door. Her blood began to pound, her skin tingling. But after one long second, he continued on to his own room.

Clearly both of them had regained their wits.

Telling herself this was how it had to be, each of them keeping their distance, neither of them giving in to this crazy attraction, Vivi went to the bath and scrubbed every remaining inch of dirt from her body. She washed her hair, dried it, and dressed in pink, low-rise terry-cloth warm-up pants and a white cropped T-shirt. She could hear Max in his room, both of them moving around like they were two magnets dancing in tandem on either side of the wall. Vivi wanted to damn all else and open the door.

But she wouldn't give in. She gathered her dirty clothes and put them in a pile. She flipped through magazines, straightened her closet, organized her lipsticks by shade. But still she felt the presence of Max as if he were standing next to her.

The phone rang, and she heard him pick up. His deep voice hummed through the wall, skipping down her spine. Suddenly she was pacing, itching to go through that door like a woman craving chocolate.

She shuddered that she had resorted to comparing any man to food. So she slammed out through her door and flew to the stairs, intent on the kitchen and the promise of some very real and very uncomplicated cake. But she hadn't gone more than a few steps down when she stopped, cursed, and hung her head. "This is ridiculous," she muttered. "You kissed him, then ran away like an immature child."

They needed to talk. She would tell him what she was feeling, have an open and honest discussion about the precarious situation they found themselves in. Nothing more.

Proudly, she raised her chin and marched to Max's bedroom. Determined, she knocked.

But when he opened the door, her breath caught. He stood shirtless, his hair still damp from his shower, all traces of mud gone. He stared at her. Feral, primal, his blue eyes burning.

She gathered herself, her mind putting in order the very real things she needed to discuss. But when she spoke, all she managed to say was "I'm not sure why I'm here."

"I didn't ask."

Then, like a current pulling her under, she was in his arms, their bodies crashing together in a tangle as he pulled her into his room and kicked the door shut.

It was crazy, insane. Two people drawn together despite the fact that they had nothing in common. His lips seared her like a brand. Her body melted against his as she tried to get closer, as if she could lose herself to sensation.

She kissed him, savoring the feel, relishing the power she sensed she had over him. She felt as much as heard the groan that rumbled when she ran her palms down his back. For a few incredible moments, he let her maintain control. She touched and kissed, took what she wanted.

Then suddenly this strong man had had enough. "Careful, princess. If your hands get any lower, you're going to find yourself in my bed, on your back, with me sliding inside you."

And this was a bad thing?

Yes!

She was the nanny.

She was here to prove that she could be independent and responsible and take care of herself.

He turned her in his arms, her back to his chest, then ran his palms up her abdomen, beneath the T-shirt. With his hands against her ribs he pulled her to him, the small of her back cradling his hardness as he cupped her breasts.

Her breath slid out in a moan when he wouldn't let her turn around, only gently squeezed her nipples between his thumbs and forefingers. She felt on fire, burning for something she could hardly name. But deep inside she knew this was what had been missing from her life. Need and yearning. Passion. The flame that made people willing to throw themselves into the fire.

His arm came across her collarbone, holding her secure, one hand still cupping her breast, pressing her high, before trailing away. Her skin felt sensitive and burning, and when his fingers slipped beneath the elastic band of her terry-cloth pants, her body shuddered.

When he nudged her feet apart, widening her stance, she obeyed willingly, only to gasp when his fingers found the curls between her legs. With one slightly callused tip, he parted her.

Her mouth fell open in a silent *ah* of sensation.

"You're wet," he whispered against her ear.

His finger traced the sensitive edges, reminding her of that day in her apartment. She made an incoherent sound.

"You're hot," he added. "Your passion is amazing."

He circled and teased, but his finger didn't slip inside her. She moved against him, wanting more. But then he pulled away.

When he turned her to face him, her expression must have shown the disappointment she felt, because his blue eyes darkened with satisfaction.

"Take off your clothes," he ordered.

Heat rushed through her, though she couldn't seem to move. After a moment, he reached out and gently pulled her T-shirt over her head, leaving her arms bound for one long second as he dipped low and ran his tongue over each nipple.

Her breath grew raspy with wanting when he tossed the shirt aside. Then he lowered his body, kneeling before her as he pulled the pink material down her thighs. He smiled when he came face-to-face with her hot pink bikini briefs, running his fingers along the elastic, sensation scorching through her. Then he tugged them free, too.

She stood naked, and before she had the chance to feel self-conscious, she saw the awe in his eyes.

"You're beautiful," he breathed.

With that the world shifted. She wanted this, had wanted it for so long. It was time she stopped being afraid of that desire. And when he worked the buttons of his jeans, then stepped free, it was Vivi who stood in awe.

He stood before her, finely made, like the warrior from earlier without the mud paint. There was no embarrassment in his expression, only some innate understanding that she knew very little about men.

He let her drink in her fill, then he swept her up and carried her to his bed, following when he laid her down.

In all her life, she had never been completely naked with a man. When she had made love with Grady, it had been an awkward grappling beneath clothes. When she had touched him, he had tensed and pulled her hand away, embarrassing her to the core.

But there was no embarrassment with Max. She understood that she could touch, feel, revel, and he wouldn't think less of her. And suddenly she understood that this man would allow her to let go of inhibition and not punish her afterward.

She wanted to kiss him, she wanted to feel his chiseled strength, but he only brushed his lips over hers before he rolled onto his side. He propped his head on his elbow, then made a sensual perusal of her body. She felt as if she had never been looked at before, not really, not seen. He saw into her, she understood.

When she grew impatient, he chuckled, then captured her hands above her head. He nipped and kissed and laved her with his tongue. Her body yearned for release. But in truth she wanted something more than that. Simply touching and seeing wasn't enough.

"Teach me," she pleaded. "Teach me about sex."

His body visibly tensed.

"I'm serious," she added, when he let go of her hands. "I want to learn about you."

Muttering an oath, Max rolled away from her, his chest and back muscles rippling as he sat on the edge of the bed. "This is about your pleasure, Vivienne, not mine."

"But I want to understand what a man wants. *I* want that."

When he didn't give in, she grabbed his arm, leaping off the bed to kneel in front of him.

"I want to know, Max. That gives me power." She smiled barely, shyly. Then boldly. "Show me what you want."

He looked at her long and hard, his pulse visible in his neck. His breath grew ragged, but he didn't move.

"Don't make me beg," she whispered.

After long ticking seconds, like a drowning man giving in, he placed his hands on her head, then gently lowered her mouth to the aching hardness between his thighs.

Chapter Sixteen

The minute he felt her lips touch him, heat was instantaneous.

It burst through him and he had to fight for control. His body strained, the tendons in his neck feeling like they would pop. Her inexpert attempts to please were nearly his undoing.

She wanted this. She wanted him.

That moved him in a way he didn't want to consider.

His body's response grew, every muscle taut when he finally began moving her on his hard shaft, her mouth tight and hot and sweet like silk, his head falling back, his fingers tangling in her hair, his muscles straining against the desperate need for release.

With an eager innocence, she moved on him, her very clear inexperience making the sensation even more intense. He was a big man in every way, and hard with desire. He wanted to thrust, but knew he couldn't. He couldn't lose the little control he managed to maintain. He barely moved, willing himself to be gentle, to teach her, not to give in to what his body craved.

He closed his eyes and tried to think of anything but the feel of her wet, slick lips gliding on him. His hands fisted in her hair, guiding her.

Arching over her, he leaned down, running his large palms along her slender back to her hips. His body felt on fire, a moan escaping from deep inside his chest.

The fire leaped higher, stronger, consuming him in a way that felt like leaping into madness. Unable to take anymore, he let out his strangled breath in a choking rush as he moved her away from him, then pulled her up and kissed her.

"You make me burn," he whispered.

He held her close as he rolled back. She was awkward in his arms, uncomfortable and fumbling, trying too hard. He alternately wanted to laugh and curse—laugh because she really was a cute piece of work, and curse because her innocence was never more evident than right now as they lay together in a way that was primal and sweaty.

"Shhh," he murmured. "Let me show you."

"Show me?"

"Like this." He spread his thighs, cradling her between them, his hands cupping her round bottom.

She pressed close to his chest and *ahh*ed, the sound a soft vibration of pleasure. Her body was made for sin, just like her mouth, with nothing prim or icy about it.

He rolled them over until he was on top of her, his weight supported on his forearms. Their eyes locked as he nudged her knees apart and settled between them. The heat of her was incredible as he buried his lips against the skin of her neck. Reaching down, he pulled one of her knees up, bringing him closer, his hard shaft sliding against her soft, slick folds, his breath ragged. He kissed her, and her arms wrapped around his neck. With his body pulsing against her, he nipped her full, bottom lip, then gently sucked. He could tell she wanted to learn, wanted to match his rhythm. It would be easy to let go, like giving in to a drug.

God, how he wanted her. He wanted to possess her completely. Sink into her, take her, fill her, ease the ache that pounded through him.

Looking into her eyes, seeing the innocent desire mixing with vulnerability, he realized he couldn't. As much as he didn't want to admit it, Vivienne Stansfield wasn't a woman he could have sex with, then walk away from. She was the kind of woman a man married. Which made it impossible to give in to her at all. She and the likes of her father were everything he had fought against since he was ten years old.

A voice in his head whispered that they were everything he had fought to become. Rich and powerful. But he disregarded the thought. He had gained both wealth and power by working hard and never giving up. He was firmly rooted in reality. Vivienne Stansfield lived in a world of fantasy—a world he would never belong to.

With a groan, his body burning for completion, he pulled away as he tried to master the need to take her.

"Max?"

Panting, every muscle taut and wired, he could see the confusion in her eyes mixing with the pale, phosphorescent gray that had darkened with power and her own desire only seconds before.

"This is a mistake," he managed to say.

Slowly she pulled away, looking betrayed and lost, touching her lips with the very tips of her fingers.

His chest heaved as he tried to breathe, tried to regain reason.

"Don't you see, Vivienne? You work for me. I can't take advantage of that."

The betrayal he witnessed turned into something else—something even more vulnerable. The glint in her eyes made it clear that she didn't believe him. And why should she? He didn't believe it either. This had nothing to do with employee or employer, had had nothing to do with that since the day he hired her.

But he refused to admit that he couldn't afford to lose control—not to anyone, and especially not to this woman who had plagued his thoughts for the last two decades.

"You're just using that as an excuse," she stated, rolling off the bed.

When she stood in front of him it was all he could do not to pull her underneath him and sink into her again and again until he was lost. Her body was elegantly curved, alabaster white with a mother of pearl sheen, her breasts heavy and full. He wanted to taste her, lick her until she cried out. Instead, he stood up and stepped into his jeans, using his mind to regain control of his arousal.

When he turned back, she still stood there, her chin raised defiantly.

"Vivienne, I'm sorry this happened. I never should have allowed it."

"Allowed it?" she demanded, huffing with every piece of her scattered clothing she retrieved. "You are the most arrogant"—she jerked up her panties—"egotistical"—next came the warm-up bottoms—"moronic man"—she had particular trouble fighting her way into the T-shirt—"I have ever had the misfortune to meet."

When finally she was finished, she looked at him. "You didn't *allow* anything. I'm a grown woman, wild and modern and I *wanted* it."

Max had to clear his throat, fighting to feel any emotion besides need and wanting. He forced himself to smile.

"What?" she barked.

"Well, if you really want to know, all that frilly pink doesn't go so well with the image of a . . . wild woman."

"Joke all you want, Max. But this isn't about me and you know it. You want me."

Whatever smile he mustered evaporated when she looked him dead in the eye.

"But you hate that," she added relentlessly. "Don't you?"

His jaw muscles began to work.

"Tell me the truth, Max. You want me, but you hate that you want me. You think I was handed everything on a silver platter, and you're a kid who had to pull himself up by the bootstraps, which makes you feel like you're better than me."

Long seconds ticked by, the rain still pouring down outside, relentless against the windows.

"I want you," he finally stated, unable to lie. "And yes, I hate wanting you. Hate burning up every time you walk into a room. But we have nothing in common—no future together when we look at the world so differently. But still you set me on fire until I think I'll burn up if I don't find a way to slide inside you, fill you until you scream your release—and mine."

She didn't move, the sound of thunder rolling in the distance, her white teeth sinking into her full lower lip.

"I'm not trying to hurt you, Vivienne."

"And comments like 'We have nothing in common' and 'There's no future for us' are supposed to make me feel good?"

"You disagree?"

"No," she whispered sharply. "We *don't* have anything in common. And there *is* no future for us."

"Then what's the problem?"

Vivi turned to look at him. "You didn't have to say it so bluntly."

"A lie's better?"

Vivi wrinkled her nose, making her look innocent and sweet despite the frustration that stained her cheeks. Then she sighed.

"*Lie* is such an ugly word," she explained. "Equivocate. Fudge. Bend the truth. All could have worked here. Any of those would have helped me avoid the awful truth that men don't want me."

She started for the door.

"Vivienne?" He caught her hand. "You are desirable."

He felt the urge again to pull her close, to prove just how desirable she truly was, but that couldn't happen.

"You are, really." But even he knew how inadequate that was, though saying more than that, allowing more than that, didn't do either of them any good. "I'm sorry." He hesitated, loosening his grip. "Are you going to be okay?"

She blinked, then focused and surprised him with a tense smile that didn't reach her eyes. "I'm fine. Better than fine."

Then she slipped out the door.

My Wedding Diary

EMOTIONAL HIGHLIGHTS

Does a pesky little urge to throw myself over the balcony like some demented drama queen count as a highlight?

Just joking. Like I said to Max, I'm fine. I swear. What do I care that men don't want to have sex with me? That certainly is no reason to get all emotional. Besides, since Max's house is on a slope, and the yard is practically right outside my second-story window, I doubt I could do much more than ruin what is left of my clothes.

Okay, so _fine_ is an overstatement.

But I am strong. And I am _not_ just throwing myself into other people's problems to avoid dealing with my own. Really. REALLY!!!!

Chapter Seventeen

Vivi stood in her bedroom, staring out the window without seeing, and thought of the issues she faced.

One, she had thrown herself at Max. And just like Grady, he had rejected her.

Clearly she was doing things wrong in the sex department.

Two, her father had defaulted on his loans. A man who supposedly had more money than God.

Three, he had cleaned out her bank account without a word.

Vivi didn't know how to take it all in. But more than anything, one thought wouldn't leave her alone.

Her life had been a lie.

Since the moment her credit cards had been rejected, she had held on, refusing to give in to the current that kept trying to wash away the sand beneath her feet. She had told herself that she was being strong.

But now disbelief and despair rushed in on her. Every emotion that she had fought off overtook her. She couldn't run any more. And as much as she didn't want to admit it, that was exactly what she had been doing. Running, hiding, putting on blinders to the truth. She had thrown herself into Max's family problems and tried not to think of her own.

But she couldn't avoid it any longer.

"My life is a lie!"

There, she said it, not that anyone heard.

Falling back on the bed, Vivi stared at the ceiling. If money had been an issue, why had her father insisted that she plan a big wedding? And why had he encouraged her to spend so much over the years?

She shuddered at her extravagance, and shuddered again at all the wasted money in nonrefundable wedding deposits.

And still her father hadn't called back, and she knew he had her cell phone number.

She glanced over at the tiara sitting in its satin box on the dresser. A stupid crown, as Nicki had said, as if she really was her father's princess.

Vivi scoffed into the air because she understood then that she *was* everything people thought she was. Not her *father's* princess, but the spoiled, pampered princess, who had spent a lifetime living in a fantasy world made of little more than smoke and mirrors.

Foolishly, in the week and a half since her credit cards had been rejected, she had held out hope that she could go back to her old life. However imperfect, it was what she knew.

She understood now that once and for all, she needed a long-term solution. She had to determine what needed to be done, then she'd do what she always did when she tackled a problem. She would come up with a plan to fix it.

At the thought, a pure, unadulterated shiver of fear raced down her spine. She had spent a lifetime trying to fix things—not always having success. But combined with that fear was a sense of determination and an amazing sense of freedom.

With no money and no desire to please her father any longer, she had the freedom to start a new life. She could let down the facade that had slipped all too often anyway. She could laugh out loud without cringing, or jump out of her seat to do the Wave and not care who saw.

Her heart started to pound and her palms got clammy. She remembered Max saying that she had to understand who she was before she could realize who she had the potential to be.

She knew he was right. And the first step was reading the whole truth of what they were saying about her and her father.

Leaping off the bed, she hurried downstairs to find the newspaper article. With ideas filling her mind, purpose pushing her on, she entered Max's office, where he always read the paper. She stopped cold when she found him at the desk which faced the door, looking at his computer screen, Chris sitting in the chair in front of him. As soon as she arrived Chris turned.

"Vivi!" the younger brother said.

She had a hard time focusing on Chris when Max glanced away from the computer and saw her. Slowly he stood. After a second, as if understanding a lady had entered, Chris followed his brother's lead and popped up out of his seat.

Max didn't notice or comment. His gaze ran over Vivi as he took her in. He studied her intently, possessively, as if trying to get some clue if she was okay or not.

He planted his hands on the desk, and instantly she

thought of how he had touched her, his palm skimming over her skin, and she felt heat rush through her.

"I hear you got caught in the rain," Chris said.

Max and Vivi stared at each other.

"Just got a little wet," she managed.

Chris glanced back and forth between the two, then cleared his throat. "I dropped Max's car off, and now I'm waiting for Pat and the girls to pick me up."

"Great," she said, barely hearing as she walked to Max's desk, the entire time his gaze never leaving her.

"Are you okay?" he asked quietly, a wealth of genuine concern in his voice.

"Great," she repeated, her heart pounding as it always did when he was near. A lock of dark hair had fallen forward on his forehead, and her fingers itched to push it back. An excuse to touch him. She clasped her hands behind her back. "In fact, I'm better than great. I wondered if you had the newspaper. I figured I better read the bad news for myself."

But before Max could respond, a picture of a house on his computer screen caught her eye. It was small, and clearly needed work.

"What's that?" She focused on the screen that displayed exactly the kind of house she had wanted. Not an impressive stone weather tower or a penthouse with stunning views. Rather a home that needed attention and love.

Chris chuckled. "It's a listing on University Avenue that a banker friend of ours wants Max to take over. It's a true dog and no one wants it."

"Including me," Max stated. He glanced back at his brother. "I don't appreciate Andy sending you over here trying to change my mind. I already told him no."

Chris shrugged just as a horn sounded in the drive. He pushed up from his chair. "I know, but he said it was important. I thought I'd give it a try. Listen, that'll be Pat. After the movie we'll drop off the girls."

The brothers shook hands, before Chris hugged Vivi in a way that made Max grumble. But Vivi hardly noticed. Her mind raced as she stared over his shoulder at the computer screen—at the old, decrepit house that no one wanted.

Once Chris had left, Vivi started to pace.

"Vivienne, what's wrong?" Max asked.

She whirled to a stop in front of him, taking in his large form, the dark hair, and his contrasting blue eyes. The nose that would have been too perfect if at some time it hadn't been broken. And today she could see the deep worry that lined his forehead.

"Nothing's wrong," she practically sang. "In fact, everything's wonderful! I've come up with a plan to fix my problems."

His expression turned leery. "Oh, no. Not more of your fixing."

Vivi didn't respond. Her mind churned with that heady sense of purpose. Pieces fell together like dominoes tipping over—as if the answer had been there all along. "I have a plan for the new, improved Vivi Stansfield. No more fantasy. No more pampered princess pretending that everything will be okay." She stopped abruptly, her eyes going wide as something else occurred to her. "It's a three-part plan!"

"Vivienne, what are you talking about?"

"First, I need a raise."

His dark brows slammed together. "I already pay you more than the average nanny."

"I'm hardly your average nanny. I want double." She hesitated, summoned up her most serious expression, then added, "Or I walk."

When his face grew murderous, she knew she had pushed her luck. "Fine. I'm willing to negotiate. Get back to me with a counteroffer."

"Counteroffer?" He looked at her as if she had lost her mind, but she forged ahead undaunted.

"Second, let me sell that house."

"You don't have a real estate license," he stated, his voice rising. Not a great sign, but Vivi had come too far to retreat now.

"But *you* have one," she clarified. "Let me do the work, then you can officially close the deal. We'll split the commission."

"That's against the law."

She waved the words away. "You can't tell me there aren't hundreds of real estate agents who have assistants who do most of the work. Let me show the property, hold the open houses, write the classified ads."

"The answer is no."

Frustration shot through her, but she held it back. "I bet you're worried about my ability to keep your house in order and get the girls to all the places they need to be while I'm doing it. Believe me, I'm a master of multitasking. Remember?"

She could tell he didn't and with good reason, since it hadn't proved to be her strong suit. But she'd never really tried. "Don't you see, this is a win-win situation, Max. You have a banker friend who wants a favor. I'm willing to facilitate the process. That's it! I'll be the facilitator. I'll do the footwork—nothing illegal in that. You'll close the deal."

He eyed her with menace.

"Please, Max." She tried to swallow the panic that tried to bubble up through her determination. "I need this," she whispered.

Drawing a deep breath, he sighed, then stood and came around the desk. "I'll think about it."

They stared at each other, their bodies suddenly so close that she had to tilt her head to look him in the eye. She felt the heat of him instantly, could smell the scent of him. "Good enough," she offered, having to clear her throat. "You can get back to me on that, too."

She remembered the third and final point to her impromptu plan and suddenly thought better of it. She had already pushed her luck, so she started to leave. But he took her hand, stopping her.

Leaning back against the hard edge of the desk, he tugged her close until she ended up very nearly between his knees.

"You said there were three parts."

Vivi grimaced. "Did I?"

She felt vulnerable in a way that only this man had the ability to make her feel. When she had launched into her spiel, she had felt modern and empowered. She had also felt the foolish need to fix more than her financial situation. She wanted to fix herself. Now, in hindsight, the third part seemed like a really bad idea.

Then she chastised herself for being weak-willed. She was twenty-six years old and every man—okay, all two of them—who she'd been intimate with had turned her away. Grady told her she didn't know how to tangle with him in life or in bed. Then she had been naked and willing with Max, and something had caused him to set

her aside. She wanted to be real. She wanted to understand what made men turn to putty in a woman's hands.

She wanted the men in her life to stop leaving her.

And before she could think better of it, she blurted, "I
want you to teach me about real life—about sex."

Confusion drew his face into hard lines, then understanding surfaced. Instantly heat mixed with desire. His
gaze dropped to her mouth. But just as suddenly he
stood and stepped away from her.

Vivi plunged ahead, her heart pounding so hard that
she felt light-headed. "No obligations, no strings attached. I want to learn. You have the ability to teach."

"What the hell?" he burst out. A vein popped out on
his forehead, and that jaw of his really started to work. "I
am not some . . . some . . . sex tutor."

"You make it sound so clinical. I was thinking more of
a friend helping out a friend. Just like the nanny thing. I
needed a job, you needed someone to take care of the
girls. We all win. But I'm still strapped with all this
Grady baggage of bad sex that makes me wonder . . .
well, I wonder what I'm doing wrong."

His eyes went glacial. "You've had sex with Grady?"

"And you're from what planet? Of course I've had sex
with Grady. I'm twenty-six years old. What did you expect? Besides, who are you to talk when it's a well-
known fact that you sleep with most anything in a skirt?"

"I do not."

"Oh, right. You're discriminating." She rolled her
eyes. "Whatever. I'm discriminating, too. I've chosen
you."

His mouth fell open.

Vivi had never thought of Max Landry as a man at a

loss for words, but just then she could see that she had left him speechless.

"I've had enough," he said finally. "I think you should go to your room and tomorrow we'll pretend this conversation never happened."

Based on his expression of sheer murderous incredulity, she could tell that he wasn't going to give in on this one.

"Fine." She shrugged, refusing to be embarrassed. "But, one, I will not forget the raise; two, I still want to sell that house; and three, just remember that you were the one who told me to go out and find myself."

Max didn't have a lot of regrets in his life. But in the long two weeks since Vivienne Stansfield presented her three-part plan, his list of regrets had grown by the hour.

Sitting back in the plush leather of his home office chair, Max took a slow sip of an eighteen-year-old single-malt scotch as the sun faded in the distance. Not a man to drink early, often, or by himself, the crystal glass filled with amber liquid was proof enough of just how far Vivienne Stansfield had pushed him toward the edge.

He had envisioned this house he had completed eight months ago as a place that would provide a true home and foundation for his family. But for the most part, his brothers and sisters were scattered all over town with families of their own.

Max felt proud of their achievements, wanted only what was best for each of them—was proud of the independent individuals they had become. But he didn't like how Vivienne forced him to see that he hardly knew his brothers and sisters anymore.

Vivi, as everyone called her, with her rosebud lips. As

long as he lived he was certain he'd never forget her going down on him. Neither would he forget rolling around in the mud as if they were no better than sex-crazed teenagers. Wouldn't the press have liked to get ahold of that one?

Yes, damn it, he wanted her. He wanted her with an intensity that made him feel as if he were burning up from the inside out. Now Vivienne Stansfield promised to change her life. And she seemed determined that he change his, too.

Vivienne had drummed up respectable clothes and had started keeping a schedule with the precision of a military drill sergeant. She had always been caring—even he couldn't deny that. But now she had added an upright exterior and irreproachable behavior. She was fast becoming everything a man could want in a woman.

Perfect, proper. And boring as hell. Damn, he missed those sequins.

Every time Max saw her now he expected her to have replaced the feathers with a whistle around her neck. But there was no whistle, just a clipboard on the utility room wall where she kept an assortment of lists and schedules, menus and helpful articles she had run across during the day. If there was a self-help book out there that dealt with becoming a responsible, contributing individual, Vivienne found it.

Which reminded him of her three-part plan.

Max grimaced over the fact that he knew it was only a matter of time before he gave in and increased her salary. Every ounce of hard-as-nails businessman softened the minute he took in the little slip of a woman with lively gray eyes.

He started to smile over the fact that Vivienne really

did want to sell the old house on University. But any hint of a smile flattened into a hard, jaw-ticking glower at the thought of the third part of her plan. What had he been thinking when he told her he wouldn't teach her about sex? Not that it should have been a regret. Was it so wrong to have done the gentlemanly thing and said no?

Hell, he should be getting some kind of award for turning her down, especially when all he could think about was spreading her sweet thighs and licking her until she came.

Unfortunately, he was wrong on all counts.

The telephone rang, but before he could answer one of the girls got it. Seconds later, footsteps raced down the upstairs hallway. "Is Vivi back from the grocery store?" Lila called out. "Some guy is on the phone for her."

Max pressed his fingers to his temples. Ever since the article had run in the newspaper, Vivienne had been swamped with attention—mainly from men who had learned that she was no longer engaged. To think she thought she was undesirable. With or without money, there was something about Vivienne that made her a prize to men.

"Tell him she's not here."

"Who's not here?" Vivienne chimed as she sailed into his office from the kitchen.

As always when he saw her, his body reacted with a primal urge to bend her over his hard mahogany desk and take her—then wrap her in his arms and never let her go. Which in turn made him curse and take another sip of his scotch. He did not want a wife. Not now. Hell, he hadn't finished raising his first family yet.

"Groceries done," she announced, clipboard in hand, long dark hair pulled back in a ponytail, her new uniform of white polo shirt with a white sweater tied around her shoulders and crisply pressed khaki pants clinging to her curves.

"Glad to hear it," he muttered over a very distinct sexual frustration.

Vivienne smiled like a nursery school teacher. "Now, now, Mr. Landry. No reason to be grumpy when it's Friday and a surprisingly warm November day."

He easily could have strangled her for being so cheerful while he couldn't seem to get part three of her three-part plan out of his head. Nights, days. He had become obsessed. And another woman wouldn't do. He'd tried.

For half a second, he nearly damned every ounce of good sense he possessed and stripped the damned khakis and ponytail holder free. Thankfully Lila came in behind her.

"Where's Nicki?" he asked.

"She's around."

Probably hiding, he mused to himself.

Nicki still didn't like Vivienne, but something had softened her hard stance toward the nanny. No one would call them friends by a long shot, but now Nicki spent more time avoiding Vivienne than coming up with bitingly mean things to say to her.

Vivienne, on the other hand, had become more determined than ever to win over the teen. Like a car wreck in slow motion, it was painful to watch. Vivienne trying so hard, Nicki avoiding her like the plague. But Max could see Vivienne's confident smile, as if deep down she knew she would win what had become a battle of wills.

"Lila," Vivienne said, "I got your favorite Fruit Roll-Ups."

"Oh, thanks!"

The minute the eleven-year-old dashed out, Vivienne said, "We need to talk."

Here it came. More of the ultimatums. More of the sex talk. He'd had enough. He decided then and there to give in. He was tired of doing the right thing. Let her twist his arm. Let her do what she wanted with him. His body responded with anticipation.

Vivienne cleared her throat and clutched her clipboard to her chest. "Since Pat isn't picking up the girls until tomorrow morning, maybe you could spend some time with them."

Max could only stare. "You want to talk about the girls?"

"What did you think?"

He stood and walked toward her. Vivi didn't seem to notice that he wasn't interested in talking about his sisters.

"They need your attention, Max. Nicki especially."

Since his father disappeared and his mother died, his life had been consumed by making a living, supporting the family, and providing guidance. He'd always been the one to make the hard decisions—and to keep them together. That was his job. And he had done it.

"Things are just fine around here," he said, stopping in front of her. It wasn't until he pulled the clipboard away that her eyes went wide.

"Max?" Her voice wobbled. "What are you doing?"

"I'm tired of talking."

"Oh." Her pulse fluttered in her neck and her lips parted, before suddenly she shook herself. "I mean, too bad." She pulled propriety and professionalism up around her like a wet suit on a diver. "I'm here to discuss

Nicki. She loves you, but she's scared to death of you and covers it up with belligerence."

He curled a single loose tendril around his finger. He could make out the faint outline of her breasts beneath her cotton shirt, and when she noticed him looking, her nipples pulled into buds. His mouth went dry and his cock tightened. There was so much he could teach her, that he wanted to teach her.

"Max, really."

His hand trailed back, tracing the delicate shell of her ear. "Really, what?"

"She *really* needs you."

Something in her voice snagged in his mind, and he studied her. For a second she looked incredibly sad, even hurt. But just as quickly, he watched as she pushed it away.

"Everyone needs to know they're loved," she said. "Like it or not, a young girl learns how she can expect to be treated by a man from how her father—or her father figure—treats her." She willed him with her eyes to do the right thing. "Let Nicki know that you think she's special, Max. Every girl deserves that."

My Wedding Diary

PRE-WEDDING PAMPER

No question that the **pamper** is the perfect **pre** to any situation.

Pre-wedding? Sure, fine, but how about pre-ventative, for those days when a woman feels really horrible. Can you beat a good, long soak in a bath filled with bubbles? Then there's a pre-carpool pamper, pre-going to the store pamper, pre-just about anything pamper, as far as I'm concerned.

Or how about a pre-date pamper...that is, if I'm lucky enough to get someone to ask me out.

Chapter Eighteen

It was six-thirty in the evening, the sun already down, when Vivi raced out of Max's office, her heart hammering as she hurried upstairs to her bedroom. She knew she was the one who had started them on this crazy sexual path with her infamous plan. But the way he had looked at her, the passion, the desire, had made her feel tiny and vulnerable.

The intensity had been there from the beginning. But this was different, as if she had unleashed something more powerful than either of them. She would have cursed her stupidity if she hadn't been running so late.

Even though Pat wasn't picking up the girls until morning, Vivi still had Friday nights off. Not that she ever really had anything to do on nights off, but this was the beginning of the new, improved Vivi and things were going to change.

Vivi took a long bath, then put on a short robe over her bra and panties as she dipped her fingers into the face mask of strawberry yogurt mixed with sugar granules that she had made from instructions in *Empowered Woman* magazine. No more expensive cosmetics for her.

After smearing a generous portion over her cheeks, chin, and forehead, she started to rub. The yogurt was supposed to smooth, the sugar granules exfoliate the skin, leaving with her with a rosy glow.

"Knock, knock?"

Vivi turned to find Lila in the bathroom doorway.

"Eck," the girl said, her lip curled back.

"Don't underestimate the ability of a good mask to clean away impurities."

"I think you look really good even with impurities," Lila said shyly.

"Ah, that is so sweet. Come in and join me."

Lila did, sitting beside her on the long cushioned bench in front of the vanity mirror.

"Sorry about how bad things are for you," Lila said without preamble.

Vivi smiled. "Thank you, but I don't want you worrying about me. I'm used to sticks and stones tossed my way."

Lila sat there for a second, then asked, "Do you think I could try your mask?"

Vivi felt a stab of pleasure. "Sure."

Clipping up Lila's hair, Vivi wrapped a towel around her tiny neck, then spread a thick portion on the eleven-year-old's face.

It was just when Vivi was showing her how to rub in an upward circular motion that they noticed Nicki standing reluctantly in the doorway.

"Hey," the teen said.

Vivi and Lila exchanged round mask-eyed glances, before saying, "Hey."

It took Vivi a second to get over the shock, then she did her best not to jump up and down with success. As casually as she could, she asked, "Do you want a facial?"

Lila nodded. "It might look weird but it feels neat in a gooey strange way."

Nicki shrugged. "Why not?"

Within minutes, all three of them sat in a row on the cushioned bench, their faces painted with yogurt and sugar, before they started in on the circular motions.

"How long do we have to do this?" Lila wanted to know.

"Long enough to make our pores throw up their arms in surrender."

Lila giggled, seeming more like an eleven-year-old than she had since Vivi first met her.

"What are some of your other beauty secrets?" Nicki asked, surprising her yet again.

"Ah, well . . ." Vivi stammered. "Let's see. There are face tips and body tips—"

"Tell me the body tips."

"That depends on the woman. Some believe that they have to be skinny at all costs. But I think curves are a better option. Personally, I like to eat."

"So do I, but I still don't have any curves," Nicki lamented.

"I'm sure you will soon. No reason for you to run out and buy fake breasts yet."

Lila squeaked. "Fake ones?"

"Of course. They sell them at most lingerie stores. Victoria's Secret sells a set that look so real they even have nipples on them."

Nicki and Lila gaped.

"I'm not kidding," Vivi added. "You put them in your bra, and voilà, instant figure."

"Do you wear them?" Lila asked.

"Never."

"Boys are totally into boobs," Lila added with a world-weary wisdom that was far beyond her years. Her fingers stilled in midcircle as she glanced down at her chest. "I don't get it."

"It's a guy thing," Vivi explained. "But I absolutely, unequivocally do not recommend stuffing your bra. It can only lead to trouble."

"What's going on in here?"

At the sound of Max's voice, the three whipped around to find him standing in the doorway, his eyes going wide at the sight.

"Eck," he managed.

Lila laughed and leaped up. "That's what I said. But it's fun. We're pampering." She raced over and took his hand and pulled him into the bathroom.

As always, the minute he was close, Vivi felt her skin shimmer with awareness, followed by a hard, jarring stab of embarrassment. Had she really asked him to teach her about sex?

But when he stopped just in front of her, seeming amused by the smell of her face mask and actually running his finger along her cheek, her knees felt weak, and the heat in her cheeks settled low between her thighs.

Then he surprised them all when he licked his finger. "Mmmm, strawberry."

Tingles ran along her spine as she exhaled sharply, and she barely noticed the questioning gaze that Nicki gave them.

"I have it on, too," Lila announced, extending her own finger for Max to taste.

He cleared his throat, then smiled. "I bet it's great."

"Vivi made it herself in the kitchen. Oh, I have an idea!" Lila blurted out. "Let us pamper you!"

Even Nicki lit up at the prospect. The teenager looked at her older brother with a yearning that she rarely showed. But Max didn't notice, and Vivi could tell he wasn't interested in a mask.

"Thanks, but no."

She thought about this man who had spent a lifetime trying to keep his family afloat. And now that they were secure, he didn't know the first thing about having fun. Or about how to show his little sisters that he cared. But Vivi knew he did.

As quickly as the light came into Nicki's face, it was gone. Even Lila's mood dimmed. Vivi could have smacked him for failing to see how important this was, especially since she had just given him the every-girl-deserves-to-feel-special speech.

"Max," she said with a hard-edged cajolement. "You really could use a little pampering."

He looked at her as if she had gone soft in the head.

"Forget it," Nicki stated.

Vivi waved the words away. "No, let's not forget it. We're talking guy pampering, no sissy stuff for your brother. Besides, look at that face. Have you ever seen skin that could use a good vigorous, manly mask?"

His hand whipped up to his jaw. "I don't need a mask."

"I get it. You're more a Lava soap sort of guy. If I had a bar, I'd use it in a jiff. You probably didn't realize that all that grit makes a great exfoliative. See, you've been fa-cialing all these years and didn't even know it." She gave him a wicked smile. "Girls, let your brother have a seat."

Looking on in horror, Lila and Nicki leaped up from the bench, tripping over each other to get out of the way.

Max didn't look happy.

Vivi didn't care.

After that one fleeting expression on Nicki's face—the hope that had blossomed over the possibility of her brother spending time with her—Vivi couldn't do anything but make it happen, even if it was with a facial instead of ice skating or bowling.

She pushed him down onto the bench with his back to the mirror and made quick work of wiping her own face clean before she retrieved the bowl of yogurt.

"Vivienne," he warned.

The girls were behind her, peering around her shoulder, and for the first time in her life, Vivi narrowed her eyes and looked at another human being with a wealth of intimidation.

Their eyes locked, doing battle. Then she said tightly, "Your sisters would love to *spend some time with you.* Remember?"

Max glanced between Vivi and the girls, seeming to understand. With a mutter and a curse, he scowled and braced his strong hands on his knees. The bench wasn't a small piece of furniture, but Max's massive form made it look as if it belonged in a dollhouse.

A startled second passed before the girls came forward. Lila adjusted easily and immediately got to work smoothing the facial mask over his chiseled features.

Nicki held back, not entirely comfortable with this new situation she found herself in—with Vivi or Max.

"Nicki, why don't you give Max a manicure?"

"A what?"

He nearly came off the cushion, but Vivi was ready for him, planting her palm on his chest.

"Really, Maxwell," she said. "Men get manicures all the time."

Max grumbled, but finally he gave in, relaxing just a

little more with each ministration to his face and hands. And when Max relaxed, Nicki relaxed as well. The second she did, Vivi leaped at the opportunity.

"Nicki, let me wipe off your mask," she said. "Lila, you keep after that callus on Max's palm."

With a few expert wipes, Vivi removed every bit of black eye makeup and orange lipstick from the teen, revealing a fresh innocence that was very unlike the Goth girl she tried so hard to be.

"Hold on a sec, Nicki. Let me do a couple more things," Vivi added, then quickly got to work. A few more seconds passed, then she stood back.

Lila gasped. "Nicki, you're so pretty!"

Max opened one eyelid, then both. "You do look pretty, Nick," he said with a wealth of emotion.

Nicki looked in the mirror, took in her face that was free of everything but a light coating of mascara and a hint of blush on her cheeks.

"I don't look like me," she whispered.

"Sure you do," Vivi said. "You look just like you."

The simple words made Nicki smile shyly. Suddenly the girls were laughing, Max reluctantly putting up with their fun, sending silent promises to Vivi with his eyes that she would pay for this.

But Vivi only laughed, painting and polishing each of his sisters, who in turned buffed and shined and manicured Max until he had the best-looking hands this side of the Mississippi River.

It wasn't until they started to paint his nails that he balked. "You are not painting my nails pink."

"Power pink," Vivi clarified. "A girl can never have too much pink or too many tiaras."

"Is that why you have the tiara?" Lila asked.

Vivi hesitated. "No, mine was a gift. From my father."
She could feel Max's scrutiny.

"He must think you're a princess," Lila decided.

Had he ever? Or was that a lie, too? She shrugged with a nonchalance she didn't feel. "Every girl deserves to believe she's special to someone. So I keep it."

"I think you're special," Lila said.

Completely unused to outward displays of affection, Vivi felt uncomfortable and awkward. But good, too. "Thank you, sweetie. I think you're pretty special yourself."

She had the fleeting thought that in some small way she had become a part of this family. But was she really? Was she kidding herself about that, too?

She turned and found Max watching her, a speculative gleam in his eyes.

"What?" she demanded.

He smiled in a way that made Vivi want to touch him and ask him if he liked her at all. Despite her bold teasing that he did, she was never sure. Which was ridiculous.

"Time for a wax," she blurted out.

"Wax?" the girls asked in unison.

"Yep. Who wants to go first?"

The girls looked ambivalent. "Maybe try it out on Max," Lila suggested.

"No way," Max said, sitting up, his predator's scowl completely overridden by the clips the girls had put in his hair. Thank God he hadn't seen himself in the mirror.

Vivi decided not to push the wax when she caught sight of the clock. "Oh, my gosh!" she squeaked. "Look what time it is."

"What does it matter? You never go anywhere on Fridays."

But Vivi wasn't listening. "I haven't done my makeup or my hair. And forget doing my nails!"

She would have dashed out of the bathroom altogether, but his bellow stopped her.

"You put butterflies in my hair!" he barked, staring at his reflection in the mirror.

"Oh, ah, yeah. But it's very Mel Gibson."

Vivi decided that wasn't the best answer when Max pivoted with military precision and gave her a burningly sensual look that had nothing to do with anger and everything to do with turning the tables. The last thing she wanted was for Max to have the upper hand.

"Now, Max, think of your sisters."

"Girls, go downstairs," he instructed, his exacting gaze never wavering from hers as he took a step toward her. "I want a word with Vivienne. Alone."

Vivi took a step back, her hip bumping into the wall. "I think they should stay."

"I don't."

Nicki and Lila stood in the doorway with eyes wide.

"Girls," he stated with a teasing menace, "I said go downstairs."

It didn't take more than that before they wheeled around and fled. Vivi tried to follow, but Max blocked her path with his arm. The minute they were alone, her heart lurched.

Max didn't move away as he pulled first one clip, then another from his hair, tossing them aside, all the while his gaze boring into her.

"All right," she managed, her voice shaky, "you want to talk, we'll talk."

He raised a brow, then took her arms with a deliberate gentleness. "Too late for talk." He backed her against the wall.

The breadth of his shoulders was a shock, though it shouldn't have been. He was so big, but frequently she forgot that because he moved with such athletic grace.

She felt light-headed at the presence of him, his strength, the scent of him—ruggedly male, intensely sensual. He bent down and nipped at her ear.

"You said you wanted to learn about sex," he whispered, his warm breath making her shiver.

"Oh, that." She choked on a forced laugh. "Silly me. My mouth runs amok before my brain can catch up."

"We'll start tonight."

"Tonight!" She could barely get the word out of her mouth. She pushed at his chest, then quickly ducked under his arm. "I can't, at least not now. But you are so sweet to offer."

Those dark brows of his slammed together. "Sweet?"

"Exactly. Totally. But really, Max, I have to get ready."

He glowered. "For what?"

Vivi's heart leaped as she hurried out of the bathroom. "I'm going on a date!"

Chapter Nineteen

Max stood in the foyer like a furnace ready to explode. He would have been pacing if he hadn't been there with Lila, Nicki . . . and Vivienne's date.

Max knew Don Galway from business dealings and as members of some of the same clubs. Max had never trusted the man. He played fast and loose with ethics and morals—and women.

Max refused to think about what he felt. Hot, angry. Jealous. Hell, no. Not jealous. But he'd be damned if he was going to stand by and let Vivienne traipse out the door with some loser who'd no doubt be happy to teach her about sex.

Max's skin stung from the creams, the masks, and the soap that had removed it all. He wondered if anyone would blame him if he strangled her.

Don glanced at his watch, then shifted his weight under Max's brutal glare.

"Vivi'll be down in a second," Lila reassured the date.

"Actually," Max stated coldly, "Vivienne won't be going out tonight."

Don's mouth fell open in surprise, then he started to protest but was interrupted by the sound of Vivi's heels daintily clicking down the stairs.

"Don!" she enthused.

"Vivi!" Lila squeaked. "You look beautiful!"

Max about choked and he slapped his hands over Lila's eyes. "Good God, Vivienne, what are you wearing?"

Lila peeled his fingers away. "It's your Girl Scout's Honor T-shirt!"

Vivi smiled the kind of smile that could bring a grown man to his knees. She extended her arms. "Do you like? My color coordinated wash system isn't quite perfected yet, and the dryer and I still aren't getting along. I tried the whole stretching thing on my top, but this time it didn't work so well."

"A top? Is that what that scrap of material is supposed to be?" Max bit out.

Don made an appreciative sound and offered her a single red rose. "Vivi, you look incredible."

She took the stem. "Thank you, Don. Are you ready to go?"

"Vivienne."

The single word echoed in the high-ceilinged foyer. Vivi turned back and looked Max in the eye. "Yes? Is there a problem with my going out on my night off?"

Max stared at her, the muscles in his jaw working. But what could he say? It was her night off. She didn't belong to him. He had no say regarding what she did on the weekends.

Vivi tossed her hair and smiled. "Didn't think so. Don't wait up," she called out, then they were gone.

Max, Nicki, and Lila stared at the closed door, none of them saying a word in the silence.

Then Lila drew a deep breath and grimaced. "I don't

mean to criticize, Max," she said, "but I'm not sure it was such a good idea to let her walk out the door."

Max's thoughts hardened. "Thank you, Lila. I appreciate your insight."

"No problem."

Then the girls disappeared, leaving Max alone with the sound of Don Galway's car racing down the road.

As dates went, she'd had better. Not that that was saying a lot, since truth be told she hadn't had that many. She wondered if there was a book she could read. *Dating for Dummies*? A place that gave lessons to women who still held out hopes of becoming a bride?

Vivi groaned and let herself in the house just past ten that night, holding her high heels in her hand, hoping she could make it upstairs without being seen.

Who knew that Don Galway could be such a creep?

The whole night, all he had wanted to talk about was her father and sex. Practically the first question out of his mouth had been. *"What's the real scoop on your dad?"* followed quickly by a decidedly lurid smile and *"How long is it going to take you to get naked?"*

Did lines like that really work in this day and age?

The foyer was quiet, and Vivi even tiptoed up the stairs in the dark to avoid Max and the girls. When she made it into her bedroom without a sound, she breathed a sigh of relief.

She even managed to remove her makeup and take a quiet bath without too much noise. But when she returned to her bedroom, her luck ran dry.

"Did you have a nice time?"

Vivi nearly jumped out of her skin and she wheeled

around to find Max sitting in the chair next to her window.

"Good God, you scared me to death."

"That wasn't my intent. I simply wanted to make sure you enjoyed yourself."

"Why don't I believe you?"

He chuckled, a devilishly sexy sound that slid along her senses. He wore those soft, button-fly jeans, one button left undone at the top, and no shirt. "Really," he persisted, "how was it?"

Wary, she said, "It was all right."

"That's it? Just all right?"

With forced cheerfulness, she answered, "It was great. There, are you satisfied? Can I go to bed now?"

"Did you have sex?"

She gasped. "Absolutely not."

In the dim light spilling through the window, she could see his slow satisfied smile. "See," he said, "you aren't nearly as forward as you keep trying to convince yourself you are."

Now she was insulted.

"I am completely forward. A tramp really." She sniffed. "I just wasn't in the mood."

Though who'd ever be in the mood for some guy who stared at her breasts all through dinner, at one point even leaning close and telling her he'd "like to meet those babies"?

Excuse me?

She had hardly known how to respond. Slap him? Belt him? Throw her water in his face?

She had asked him to take her home.

Now here she was, wanting nothing more than to

climb into bed, pull the sheets over her head, and lose herself to dreams. She'd had enough *reality* for one day.

"If you don't mind," she said, "I'm exhausted."

"Let me help with your robe."

Help and *Max*, late at night in her bedroom, could only mean trouble. Especially since every ounce of her boldly professed new stance as a Modern Woman had evaporated under Don Galway's leering gaze.

"Thanks, but I can manage on my own."

Max stood up from the chair and her heart about leaped out of her chest. He looked at her with a predatory gleam in his eye that made her feel the need to flee—though where she'd go she had no idea, since they were in her bedroom.

"Max," she warned, eyeing the comforting confines of her thick comforter and soft flannel sheets. "I think I'll just get into bed and call it a night."

But before she could make it past him, he caught her hand.

"What are you doing?" she stammered.

"I'm picking up where we left off earlier."

She felt a shiver of concern . . . and anticipation.

He leaned close. "Don't be afraid, Vivienne." He murmured the words against her neck, nipping at the skin. "We'll go slowly."

Her breath shuddered through her. She remembered that very first thought she had had of him when she saw him at MBL Holdings. Of his naked body barely covered by a sheet, of him moving slowly, deeply, watching a woman's passion. She felt panicked and totally in over her head.

"I'm really tired." She faked an exaggerated yawn, too

unsettled to know what to think. "I've got lots to do tomorrow. A full day of multitasking."

"On Saturday?"

"Never too soon to get next week's work out of the way. See, I'm going to show you I deserve that raise."

Max chuckled, a deep rumble of sound that tingled down her spine. "Tonight I thought we'd start with Lesson One."

Oh, my gosh!

"Now, Max, really."

"You said you were modern and deserved to find out about life . . . and passion. If you are hell bent on learning"—he ran his finger along her shoulder to her chin, tilting her face to his—"who am I not to help?"

There was that *help* word again.

"What was it you called me?" he asked. "A knight in shining armor?"

"I said you *weren't* a knight in shining armor."

His gaze turned steamy. "Were, weren't? Why let a mere *n*, *t*, and apostrophe stand in the way?"

She wasn't sure if he was joking or not. But decided on not when he guided her back into the bathroom.

"Call me a tad out of the loop, but what are we doing in here? Doesn't sex belong in a bed? Not that I intend on having any. At least tonight, that is. Tomorrow or the next day, and I'm in, modern woman that I am."

He only smiled, capturing her against the doorjamb, his thumb running over the fullness of her lips. "I'm going to kiss you."

Despite everything, anticipation fizzed through her like pink champagne, and a deep sighing moan followed when he gently pressed his mouth to hers. The touch was warm and tender, teaching, shaping her kiss to his. Her heart fluttered, and her eyelids closed when she felt the heat of his tongue slide ever so softly across her lips.

"Open for me," he whispered.

She did, relishing the jolt of sensation when he tasted her. He showed her what he wanted. Sucking and nipping, his arms coming around her to pull her close.

When her fingers curled into his arms, she felt his simmering desire.

"That's it, Vivienne. Touch me."

Their kiss deepened, his hands lowering to cup her hips. For one intense, heated moment, he pressed his erection against her. She could feel the hardness, could feel his deep, shuddering breath.

But just as suddenly, he pulled away. He looked down at her with a mix of heated sensuality and kindness. "You turn me into a schoolboy. You make me want to damn everything and slip inside you until I come." He lined her jaw with one hand. "But not now. This is about you."

"But I thought—"

He pressed his finger to her lips, pulled her to the chaise longue that stood against the bathroom wall, then gently forced her to sit down—just as she had forced him to do early that evening. She had a shiver of understanding that this *lesson* would be about making her feel . . . and turning the tables.

Slowly guiding her back into the soft cushions, he took each of her feet and raised them, planting the arches on the edge of the chaise, her robe fluttering down her thighs. Thank goodness she had a camisole and panties on underneath.

"Max, what are you doing?"

Her voice shook, though with a traitorous anticipation instead of indignity.

"Close your eyes," he commanded softly.

"I don't think this is wise." But she closed her eyes anyway.

When she did, she felt the whisper of his palm brush up her calf, then along the inside of her thigh. Her breath caught when his finger ran along the edge of her panties.

She barely heard the gruff sound of rumbling laughter. "Amazing. Do you even own any plain white underwear?"

"Do you have to be amazed at everything I do?" She tried to push up, but he wouldn't let her.

"Sorry," he stated—but not all that apologetically, she thought. "Just lie still and close your eyes."

"Max, really."

But he was persistent, and finally, trembling, she settled back, his strong hands spreading her feet a bit more as he kissed the inside of each knee. "Your skin is so soft," he breathed against her.

He picked up one foot and kissed the arched instep. Unable to help herself, her body tingled, yearned for whatever it was he would do to her as he lowered her foot back to the velvet cushion.

She felt exposed and vulnerable and very much alive beneath his touch.

"Keep your eyes closed," he commanded quietly.

She could tell that he moved away, and her body shivered with anticipation. But her mind careened with surprise when the next thing she felt was a feather-touch on her toes.

Her eyes popped open, and she found Max sitting Indian-style on the floor, his large hands holding a tiny brush as he began to paint her toenails with her favorite hot pink polish.

"What? Why?"

"Hush, I'm pampering."

"But what does this have to do with sex?" Then she cringed.

"This has everything to do with sex," he stated arrogantly. "Sex is about passion and pleasure. About which you have a great deal to learn."

Then suddenly she was laughing, a full, deep burst of complete joy.

"Hold still," he admonished.

Remarkably she did. She leaned back, much as he had earlier, while he painted her toenails, his head bent in concentration, a lock of dark hair falling forward on his brow.

"If I didn't know better, I'd swear you'd done this before."

His eyes glinted. "Years ago. When Pat was nine. She had a dance recital, and all the other little ballerinas had pink toenails. But she'd hurt her hand. Pat begged our mom to paint them for her."

He concentrated on finishing Vivi's small toe, then nodded proudly. She watched, felt her heart squeeze in her chest for this complicated man. "I take it your mother said no."

"She had more on her plate than she could handle." He shrugged, his broad shoulders rippling, and started on her other foot. "So I painted Pat's toenails."

"You've been parenting for a long time."

He didn't say anything, only stroked on the color with the same concentration that she suspected he applied to everything he did.

"I'd think spending time with Lila and Nicki would be just as easy," she said.

His hand stilled and he glanced up, seeming to debate his answer.

"I was eleven when I painted her toes. A lifetime ago. At nineteen I became the one person in my brothers' and sisters' lives who had the responsibility of providing a good example."

"And that ruled out painting toenails?"

"It ruled out a lot of things."

"Then why are you painting mine?"

He twisted the bottle closed and set it aside. "Because this time it's about showing a grown woman about passion. And because you turn my world upside down"—one corner of his mouth crooked—"making me crazy."

"Good crazy?"

Max shook his head and laughed. "I never thought of crazy as being anything but bad."

She tried again to get up, but his smile turned heated and he captured her wrists. "I'm not finished."

He kissed her palm, making her shiver with yearning. She couldn't move until the polish dried anyway, making her captive to whatever else he wanted to do to her. And really, who was she to deny this man a bit of retribution for all her pampering of him earlier? Crazy or not.

But when she expected his kisses to continue, he surprised her again by pulling out a bottle of lotion and pumping a dab into his callused palm.

The attention was heavenly. He massaged her hand with a competence that made her body melt, and when he finished the first, she sighed her pleasure as he took the other.

"Who knew sex could be so good?" she murmured.

With a deep chuckle and an ease that spoke of his incredible strength, he pulled her up, then slid in behind her. His hands were warm when he touched her neck, the edges of her robe falling away, catching on the rise of her breasts. He massaged and kneaded her shoulders until she couldn't hold back the moans that bubbled up. When his strong fingers sank into her hair, kneading her scalp, her whole body turned to putty in his hands.

"How does that feel?" he asked.

"Incredible."

Better than incredible, she thought as ease turned to awareness of his hands on her body, as his strong palms worked their way down her spine. His touch was intimate, making her senses come alive with a bone-deep desire. Every inch of her skin sizzled with sensation, and she began to anticipate what came next.

Would his fingers slip beneath her panties as they had before and brush against her tender skin? She knew she was wet, could feel her own heat.

Would he finally spread her legs and slide deep inside?

Just when she reached out to him, wanting to feel the hard contours of his body, he stepped away.

When seconds passed and he didn't return, her eyes opened. It took a second for her to understand, then she squeaked her protest. "Where are you going?"

He stood at the doorway, tall, handsome, looking utterly satisfied with himself. "To bed."

"That's it?" She struggled to make her muscles work so she could leap up. "You paint my nails and give me a massage and call that Lesson One?"

"Exactly."

Disappointment made her give an unladylike snort.

Max grinned. "Tsk, tsk."

"Don't *tsk* me."

"You've had enough for one night."

Then he winked at her, clicking the door shut behind him, leaving her to wonder how long she'd have to wait for Lesson Two.

My Wedding Diary

TROUBLESOME ~~BRIDESMAIDS~~ *Teenagers*

Nicki seems to live by an unspoken motto of: "I'll reject you before you can reject me."

Not that I would know anything about that. Nope, not me. Never.

I've tried to break through Nicki's shell, but regardless of my desire to help, she continues to see me as someone set down on this earth to make her life miserable—and I haven't even played Barry Manilow a single other time.

But worse than that, I can tell something's brewing in that head of hers. If only I could figure out what.

Chapter Twenty

The next morning, when Patricia arrived, Nicki convinced her that she *had* to go to the mall.

"You?" Pat questioned, glancing at her little sister as they drove down Mesa. "You hate to shop."

"I don't haaaate it," Nicki replied. "In fact, I'm into clothes and stuff now."

Pat reached across the console and pressed her hand to Nicki's forehead. "Are you feeling all right?"

Nicki shot her a scowl. "I'm fine."

"This is Vivi's doing, isn't it?"

"It is not. I just want to go to the mall, not rob a bank."

"Don't get smart with me, Nick."

Nicki gave a long-suffering sigh. "Sorry. Can we just please go? I promise it won't take long. You and Lila can even wait in the car." Nicki hesitated, debating. "I have to get a present for someone."

"All right. But hurry."

During the next ten minutes, Nicki dashed into the mall, found the store, explained her needs to the salesperson, made her purchase, brought it out to the car wrapped in pretty paper, then wouldn't breathe a word as to who it was for.

"It's a surprise," she explained.

A surprise for herself. Fake boobs with nipples, just like Vivi had said. They were really weird in an awesome sort of way, soon to be the crowning glory to the newly pink and powerful Nicki Landry. As much as she still wasn't crazy about Vivi, Nicki had to admit she was the only person she knew who dressed like Mindy Wasserstein—and Mindy seemed to know something about getting guys.

So if she had to be nicer to Vivi to learn a thing or two, fine. She'd stomach the nanny's smiles and cheerfulness. She'd put up with the way Vivi let insults roll off her back like water off a duck. She wouldn't even make any more snide remarks about Vivi wanting to be a Christmas bride. Not that the wedding was going to happen now. Nicki started to smile, then shook it away. She would do what it took to learn the ropes.

Part of Nicki actually had begun to think that Vivi wasn't *that* bad. In fact, there were times when it was kind of nice to have her around. She was smarter than she looked, amazingly, and she didn't put up with crap like all the other nannies had. Not that they had wanted to. They just had had no idea how to deal with her or Lila.

Heck, Lila's weirdness and all hadn't even fazed Vivi—as if Lila wasn't weird at all. Which was totally true, but no one had ever seemed to get that.

First thing Monday morning, Nicki announced she had to be at school early to do an extra-credit project. Hence the need for the big bag she brought with her.

Max, of course, had already gone to work, so she didn't have to do any convincing there, and Vivi fell for it hook, line, and sinker. Lila wasn't so easy, primarily because the littlest Landry had found the *surprise* the night before. Now Lila sat in the back seat of the big, lumbering Oldsmobile, her arms crossed sullenly over her chest. But Nicki knew the secret was safe. As much as Lila didn't like what Nicki was doing, her little sister would never tell.

Before a single soul arrived at school, Nicki ducked into the girls' bathroom. It was really weird putting the jelly-filled plastic things in her bra, and even weirder trying to move them around so that she didn't look like she had two small melons strapped to her chest. But by the time the other kids started showing up at Coronado High, Nicki had walked out of the bathroom dressed in one of the few short shirts Vivi had left, a skintight T-shirt with a wild-haired princess painted on the front.

Nicki tried to act like she wasn't nervous. She walked across the tile floor in the heels she had been practicing in, like a runway model walking down a stage.

"Who's the new girl?" she heard someone ask.

"Wow" came next.

"She's outstanding."

Outstanding. The highest compliment, out of an assortment of completely and utterly satisfying statements—that is, until someone else added, "Take a look at those knockers."

She wasn't so crazy about the knockers comment, but she *was* crazy about the way every guy there stopped dead in their tracks at the sight of her.

"Nicki?"

Pivoting around, she saw Steve Bonner, younger brother to Brandon.

She waved, her heart pounding, her knees feeling all

weak and bendy like licorice sticks because if Steve was around, Brandon couldn't be far away.

"Hey, Steve," she said, as cool as possible in a way she'd practiced in the mirror.

Steve looked her up and down. "What happened to you?"

He didn't say it in a "Wow, you look awesome" sort of way. It was more like "What planet are you from?" But then his brother, her wonderful Brandon, appeared like a vision on the horizon.

This was it.

This was her moment.

She tried to act cool as she smiled, even though she could feel her lips starting to quiver and she was almost certain her eyelid started to twitch. "Nothing happened to me."

Steve's scowl deepened and she was having a real hard time denying that he didn't appear happy or impressed by her new look. As Brandon came closer, still not seeing her, she had a moment of sheer stomach-churning doubt.

Maybe this was a mistake.

Maybe frilly pink power clothes were a crock and she was making a total fool of herself.

But then her mind went still, and her heart about burst out of her chest, when Brandon finally saw her. He froze, his head coming back as his gaze narrowed in focus. His dark eyes traveled over her real slow, and she had the distinct feeling that he was imagining her without clothes.

Never, ever had she experienced such a feeling. Hot and powerful, as if she could take a single finger and tip him over like a wooden soldier. And never, ever had something lived up to her expectations so completely.

"Hey, sweet thang," Brandon said, half joking for his friends to hear, half hot as hell. "What's your name?"

Like she hadn't told him a hundred times before. But that was the old Nicki. This was the new Nicki, and this Nicki was just about to say something equally hot and provocative when Steve interjected.

"It's Nicki Landry, you ass," the younger brother said.

A startled moment passed.

"Hey, Boomer, it's Goth girl!" One of the guys laughed, the others following suit.

Goth girl? They called her Goth girl?

The old Nicki tried to resurface, making her feel sick and horrible and totally embarrassed.

Brandon's hot gaze turned disgusted. Or so she thought until he told his friends to shut up. "I never knew you looked like that underneath all that black and baggy shit," he said to her. "You are totally hot."

He said she was hot!

A slow drip of confidence started to return. "Thanks," she said.

"Come on, this is crazy," Steve said. "The bell's gonna ring and you'll be late, Nicki."

Like she cared.

It was the first time in her life she'd been noticed by Brandon "Boomer" Bonner, and she was not going to ruin it.

"Hey, bro. Go to class," Brandon interjected with a really great smile. "I'll walk Nicki."

And he did.

Brandon Bonner, reigning bad boy at Coronado High, walked—or rather strutted—her to Algebra II. He lingered in the doorway, completely infatuated.

At least that was how she explained his lock-eyed stare at her chest.

She hardly heard a word Mr. Robbins said throughout math, and she didn't take a single note in English or even first-year Spanish. By the time the lunch bell rang, she had done little more than scribble in her spiral-bound notebook.

Brandon Bonner.

Nicki Bonner.

Mrs. Brandon Bonner.

Mrs. Nicki Landry Bonner. With a hyphen. Without a hyphen.

"What's that?" Missy Ramos asked.

Nicki slapped the flap shut. "Science homework that I forgot to do last night." Then she dashed out of biology and ran straight into the focus of her scribbling.

"Brandon!"

"Hey." He looked at her breasts, then met her gaze. "Are you free for lunch?"

Say you have plans.

Play hard to get.

Leave him off balance.

"Sure!"

With her heart in her throat, Nicki slid into Brandon's Ford Mustang. Then she had to hold on for her life when they drove about a hundred miles an hour to the Charcoaler. As they squealed into the narrow drive, she managed a bared-teeth smile. She ordered a cheeseburger and a Coke, and pretended not to be surprised when he asked her to pay for both of their meals.

Not that she thought this was an official date. Not really, she told herself, refusing to be disappointed.

She spent the next ten minutes trying to eat and talk

and not spill Charcoaler sauce all over Vivi's princess T-shirt. Which pretty much set the pattern for how she spent lunch during the next week.

Nicki all but exhausted herself sneaking Vivi's clothes in and out of the house, getting to school early, changing in the girls' room, and surviving the death-defying rides here and there for lunch with Brandon.

But it was worth every minute when the following Wednesday he asked her to an end of the semester party. She'd heard about it, knew it was between Thanksgiving and Christmas. And she'd heard only cool people went. That could only mean that he really, really liked her.

The plan was working, and that was confirmed the minute Brandon leaned across the console of his Mustang and gave her a quick kiss before walking her back into school.

Take that, Fourteen and Never Been Frenched. The streak was about to be broken.

My Wedding Diary

THE WEDDING GOWN
a.k.a. All Dressed Up with Nowhere to Go

Once and for all I have to put my dream of becoming a bride out of my head. It's gone. Finished. But the idea of renovating this old house makes the vanished dream a little more bearable.

Now I just need to convince Max that dreams are worth having.

Chapter Twenty-one

"I'm impressed with the change you've brought out in Nicki."

Vivi looked up from where she was digging around in her closet for a pair of platform tennis shoes, one of the few fun things she had left, and found Max standing in the door that connected their rooms. She was in a hurry, having just gotten off the phone.

She sat back on her heels, forgetting the search, forgetting the phone call. She focused on the strength of him, his glittering blue eyes and those sensuously full lips that made her think of little else besides the things he had the ability to do with her body.

"She's becoming everything I believed she could be," he added.

Ah, yes. Nicki.

Vivi was impressed, too, but she didn't dare say that because next he might ask something like "How'd you do it?" And unfortunately she had no idea.

For the first time since Vivi had met her, the teen seemed happy. Giddy almost, which made Vivi suspect there was a boy involved—Please, God, don't let it be Brandon—and maybe, just maybe, her missing shoes.

"As much as I hate to admit it," he continued with a

teasing smile, "I think you've been a good influence on her. This morning she asked me for money to buy some new things. Apparently she's tired of all that black."

Ding, ding, ding. Suspicion confirmed. No wonder Vivi was missing so many clothes recently.

"I'd appreciate it if you took her shopping again. I think this time it will go better."

"I'm happy to, Max."

"Thank you."

He started to leave through her door. Vivi leaped up and followed. Max stopped and glanced at her. "Did you want something?" he asked.

"Nope." She walked past him, then glanced back and glared at him. "Hattie from your office called. She said that your banker friend needs to move your appointment back thirty minutes. He'll meet you at the University house at nine."

Max got really still.

"Yep, she spilled the beans. I can't believe you were going to see that house without telling me."

"Vivienne—"

"Girls," she hollered out. "Quick, I've got to get you to school."

Vivi wheeled the Olds up to the small house on University Avenue. Max stood at the curb, staring at the tiny structure. When Vivi came up beside him, she swallowed back shock at the sight. She had expected a fixer-upper—but this unwanted house needed more than a little attention and love.

She never would have guessed that something this awful could exist only a few blocks over from the prestigious Rim Road. Weeds choked the lawn, grime coated the windows, and two old rockers sat out on the front porch, giving the place a very definite Beverly Hillbillies chic.

"Here it is," Max said grimly. "What do you think now?"

Words eluded her.

Max surprised her when he hooked his arm over her shoulders. "Listen, Vivienne." He pulled her around until she leaned into him. "You don't have anything to prove."

She wanted to give in, let him kiss her. But before she could, it hit her. She did have something to prove. To the world and to herself.

She smiled with exaggerated enthusiasm and pushed away from him. "This is so great, and I can't wait to get started! We're going to make the perfect team."

Max shook his head. "Do you ever take no for an answer?"

"Not if I can help it."

Another car pulled up, and a man in a three-piece suit got out. "Maxwell, good to see you."

"Andy," he replied with a nod.

They shook hands, and when the banker was introduced to Vivi she could feel his appreciative glance.

"As in Stansfield?" the man asked.

"Yes," she replied warily.

Andy whistled. "Every banker in town is buzzing about your dad. Any word from him?"

"I'm sure he'll return soon and deal with the . . . situation."

"Actually, I believe you. Your father is like a cat. He always manages to land on his feet and has a whole slew of lives."

"What do you mean by that?"

Andy looked at her closely, then at Max, and suddenly seemed to realize he shouldn't have said a word. "Nothing, really, but I'm sure he'll make this mess go away," he offered, then forced open the front door.

Thoughts, concerns, and confusion fled when the smell nearly knocked all three of them to their knees.

"Sorry about that." Andy cleared his throat. "You know how estate property can get. When I heard we needed to liquidate the house for a client, I came over to take a look. I should have warned you. It's a mess. The owner had cats that the Humane Society finally picked up. The woman was put in a nursing home for the last six months before passing."

"It definitely has that old-person, neglected feel," Max observed with a cough.

"The woman wasn't all that old. But she had cancer and no family to look after her—or the house. She never married, apparently, but from what they tell me, she lived with a man who everyone assumed was her husband. Quite the neighborhood surprise, I hear, when they found out he wasn't. The guy died about a year ago."

"Who does it belong to now?" Max inquired.

"The nursing home. The owner used the property as collateral against admission."

"Looking like this, no one is going to get much in a sale," Max surmised. "And we both know this isn't the sort of thing for MBL Holdings."

Andy only smiled. "I realize that, Maxwell, but I was hoping you'd do it for me as a favor."

Max studied his friend.

"We go back a long time," Andy continued, clearly not

caring that he was taking advantage. "You and me, two kids from the old neighborhood who made good."

For a second Vivi was sure she saw a certain vulnerability that flashed in Max's eyes before it was gone.

Then Andy turned to Vivi. "In fact, we didn't live far from the old Stansfield plant. It was a sad day when your dad closed it." He looked at Max. "Come on, say yes. Besides, there's something I want you to see."

The men disappeared down a long hall, but Vivi didn't follow. She stood in the living room, staring at the faded curtains, the putrid shag carpeting, and all the stuff. The place was crammed with old newspapers and magazines, furniture in varying states of disrepair, and even small car parts.

It was truly horrid, but . . .

Excitement started to brew with what-ifs, only they were good what-ifs. That's when it hit her.

She practically raced down the hall to find the men to tell them her idea. She knew it could work.

The house was silent except for the sound of her shoes pounding against the matted carpet as she wove her way through the tiny cluttered space.

"Max," she started enthusiastically when she found them in a bedroom at the front of the house.

But words trailed off at the look on his face.

That darkness she had seen before was combined with confusion.

"Max, what is it?"

The banker looked decidedly uncomfortable. "I thought you'd want to know before I let anyone else inside."

Vivi drew closer, having to step over a huge pile of yellowed newspapers.

Max still didn't say a word, only stared at an old box. Unable to imagine what was in there, Vivi scooted in beside him. She stepped on a glossy magazine and slipped, but before she could cry out or fall, Max reached out and steadied her. But he never looked away from the box.

Then she saw. Glancing inside the beaten and worn cardboard, she found a jumble of old photographs mixed with yellowed pictures cut out of newspapers and magazines. All of them were of Max and his family.

"I don't understand," Vivi said, glancing up at Max. "Who did all of this?"

Without so much as a glance her way, he said, "My father."

"Your father?"

Max didn't expand. He turned to Andy. "Sell the place, burn it. I don't give a damn. But don't bring it up to me ever again."

He slammed out of the house, and even when Vivi ran after him he didn't stop.

She and Andy watched his Mercedes speed down the hill toward Mesa Street. She knew he was upset, and she could imagine how hard it would be to learn that the man who had abandoned him and his siblings had been living so close by and keeping track of them without a word.

She also knew that Max would regret leaving all of this behind for others to see. Which dovetailed nicely into her plan.

The banker shoved his hands in his pockets. "Shit."

"Andy," she said, "I have a deal for you."

He looked at her curiously.

"This house is awful."

"Agreed."

"And Max said it won't bring much looking like it does."

"No question."

"So why don't you let me go through and . . . let's say, get it ready to sell." That wouldn't take a license.

"Meaning?"

"I clean the place out, decide what needs to be thrown away, decide what should go to Goodwill, put everything in order for an estate sale. Underneath all the grime, there are a few decent antiques."

"How do you know?"

She pointed to herself. "Do you doubt that Vivi Stansfield knows everything there is to know about anything that has value?"

Andy conceded with a smile.

"Good. Then once I'm finished, you will have a property that any realtor will be happy to take on. I guarantee it."

"What's in it for you?"

She didn't so much as blink. "A one-thousand-dollar fee for the work—"

"One thousand dollars!"

"Plus a percentage of everything in the house that sells. A small price to pay for the increase you'll gain in value. When I was looking at real estate, I learned a thing or two about values. My guess is you can get twenty thousand more out of this when I finish with it."

He crossed his arms and studied her.

"I can do it, Andy. And if I'm guessing correctly, the bank isn't doing this out of the goodness of its heart, and will earn a percentage of the eventual sale."

A slow smile spread on his lips. "All right."

It was all she could do not to leap up and clap her hands.

"I'll agree," he continued, "if you convince Max to accept the listing once you're done."

Her excitement took a nosedive. "Max has no interest in this place. We both saw that. Why push it when there are plenty of real estate companies out there?"

"MBL is the top firm in town. The bank wants him. What can I say?" His smile broadened. "If you can get him to agree, you can fix this disaster up to your heart's content, then handle the estate sale." He locked the front door behind them, the bright November sun shining a deep burnished gold. He gave her his card. "Let me know."

Number 15 Pinehurst Drive smelled of baked bread and succulent roast. One of Vivi's famous Texas pecan pies sat out on the counter, along with an assortment of other goodies she thought might make Max's mouth water. If she couldn't get him to see reason through intellectual debate, she would try bribing him with food.

The minute she heard his car pull up, she ripped off her apron and smoothed her clothes.

"Max," she called out grandly when he walked in the door.

He stopped in his tracks. "What's happened now?"

Vivi laughed. "Nothing's happened."

"You look different."

Lila and Nicki walked into the kitchen.

"It's the clothes," Lila explained.

Nicki leaned over the counter to grab a piece of celery stuffed with crab salad. "And her shoes."

Max looked Vivi up and down, as did the girls. An unaccustomed blush rushed to her cheeks. "What?"

"Like Max said, you look different," Lila offered.

Vivi wore a pair of wool trousers and a sweater set—one step deeper into the world of boring. She cut off the thought. One step deeper into the world of respectability, she corrected herself.

With Velda paid off and each of her payments made for the month, Vivi had decided that if she was going to be a professional, she had to look the part. Short skirts or even her new khakis wouldn't do. She had gone to the department store and found the outfit on sale.

Max set his briefcase down on the built-in kitchen desk. "Come on, let's have it. Something has to be wrong."

Instead of getting mad, she swallowed back a retort for the good of her cause, then told them to wash up for dinner.

"I'm going out," Max stated.

"You can't go out!"

"I always go out."

"Yes, and . . . and . . . it is so unfair to the girls."

"Not that again."

"I don't mind," Nicki offered.

"Neither do I," Lila added.

"Of course you mind. Come on, Max. Please join us. I made all your favorites."

"How do you know what my favorites are?"

"Actually, I don't. But I can imagine what a big, strapping, handsome, extremely intelligent—"

"Vivienne," he warned.

"—man like you would like. Meat and potatoes." She turned to the girls. "He looks like a meat and potatoes kind of guy, doesn't he?" She turned back. "Plus home-made bread and fresh baked pie?"

A grin got the better of him, and ten minutes later the four of them sat around the dining room table.

"Wow," Lila said. "Great dinner."

"None of that fancy cra—crud you usually make," Nicki said.

Vivi blotted her lips. "Why doesn't everyone share a little about their day?"

Lila leaned forward. "Have you forgotten what happened the last time we caught up over dinner?"

This wasn't going as Vivi planned. But at least Max was in the house.

"So, is everyone ready for your big Thanksgiving ski trip?" she asked.

Nicki said she'd be ready, Lila said she had been ready since Friday, and Max picked up the newspaper and turned to the business section.

Earlier in the week he had asked if she wanted to go on the Landry family outing to Ruidoso for the Thanksgiving holiday. She desperately wanted to go, but how pathetic was that, she thought, if she had to tag along instead of having plans of her own?

Rather than focus on having to spend time by herself, she decided it was best to think of it as having some quality private time. The prospect terrified her. It was hard enough filling the regular weekends. What was she going to do with herself between Wednesday and Sunday?

Now she had her answer. That is, if she could convince Max about the wisdom of her plan.

As usual, with their homework finished, the girls didn't hang around after dinner. They went to the den and watched television. Max, thankfully, went to his office. Vivi took her time washing the dishes and cleaning up.

Finally it was time for the girls to get ready for bed, and forty-five minutes after that, she heard Lila call out good night. Vivi waited one more second, then went to find Max.

She drew a deep breath, knocked, and entered.

He looked up from a document he was reading. At the sight of her, he leaned back in his chair and smiled.

"I take it I'm finally going to find out what all that pie and prime rib was about."

"Now, Max, why is it so hard to believe that I simply wanted to make a special meal for three people I care about?"

"Because everything you served was normal. There wasn't a single oddball appetizer or unique slice of pie."

Vivi bit her lower lip. "Well, I did have the urge to shape the bread into a volcano and put the gravy inside."

Max's appreciative laughter rumbled through the room. "But you held back."

She looked at him shyly through lowered lashes. "You might not believe it, but I really have changed."

For a moment, he studied her. "I guess you have," he conceded softly.

An unfamiliar moment of ease passed between them. Something shifted, a palpable change settling in, though she wasn't sure she understood it. Max tilted his head. "So tell me, really, what's on your mind?"

She realized that she could sit there all night, just sit and enjoy talking to him as if her world was in order, no bills to pay, no missing father. This must be what it was like for most people, regular people who sat after dinner and shared each other's company. It was nice, peaceful. And for a second she didn't want to ruin the moment.

But that was ridiculous. They weren't Ozzie and Harriet. They weren't even a family.

"I want you to accept the listing on the University house."

That wiped any hint of ease right off his too-handsome face. "No, Vivienne." He snatched up the document he had been reading.

"Max, please—"

"I said no. I want nothing to do with it."

"Look, I understand how hard it would be to walk in there and see all those pictures. I'd be furious if I found out someone was keeping track of me like that." She hesitated. "It's completely understandable that you're angry at him—"

With tight control, he slapped the document down. "You don't know the half of it. He was a bastard. My mother was already weak from long hours working at the plant, having so many kids, and trying to take care of us all. But that didn't faze my father. He knocked her up again, then packed his bags and walked out on Thanksgiving Day."

"He left her pregnant?"

"And sick."

Her mind spun. Belatedly she realized she was in over her head. What did she know about long years of responsibilities? She was having a hard enough time dealing with them now—as an adult. But she couldn't stop herself. Something deeper than intellect, something in her gut, told her to keep pushing—for him as much as for herself. "I know that had to be hard on you—"

"Forget me. I was eighteen when my father left, nineteen when my mother died. But the others were just kids. Hell, he never even laid eyes on Lila."

His anger and suppressed pain shimmered through the room. She slipped between him and the desk and sat on the edge, her palms flat on either side of her as she leaned forward. "Don't you see, you have issues you need to work through. Sadness, hurt—"

His fingers curled around the armrests of his leather chair.

She hesitated, feeling a different sort of emotion for this man starting to creep in on her. It wasn't the heat of desire, or the loud beat of wanting. It was something deeper than a simple need to fix his family.

"You gave up a lot to step into your father's shoes. And I know how it must slay you to think he was only a few miles away and never let you know."

"I said, this isn't about me."

"Of course it is. It's about how incredibly caring you are. You dropped everything for your brothers and sisters." She smiled at him with all the unsettling emotion she felt for him. "Deep down I knew it the minute you gave me a job despite the fact that I didn't know the first thing about taking care of children."

His chest rose and fell, and he looked as vulnerable as she had ever seen him.

"Clearly you're a stronger man than your father ever was."

"If I wanted therapy," he managed to say, "I'd pay a professional."

"He shouldn't have run out on you, Max. He shouldn't have done a lot of things. But what you need now is closure. Accept the listing, and close up the house. Close up the past."

He exhaled, suddenly appearing relieved, and he stood. With amazing swiftness he regained his footing and tapped her on the nose. "Ah, yes, the real reason for all this. How could I forget? The listing."

"That isn't why." She tipped her head. "At least not the whole reason."

When she glanced up, their gazes locked, she sitting on his desk, he standing inches from her. The world around them seemed to tick like a grandfather clock in an empty hall. His control was barely held but still there. He studied her, and she knew he was deciding what to do.

Granted, if he accepted the listing, it would help her, but that truly wasn't the entire reason she wanted him to say yes. She hadn't understood until now how completely he had not dealt with his father's abandonment. That had to affect the way he kept himself separate from feeling. It had to be the reason he refused to relinquish an ounce of control.

"You aren't going to let this go, are you?"

"No," she said.

Max hung his head. "If I agree, I still can't let you sell it without a license."

She had actually looked into getting a license, but it took money for an application fee and a minimum of three months of full-time classes. She couldn't afford either.

"I understand, and completely respect your decision."

He raised a suspicious eyebrow.

"Really. Besides, I've come up with a great alternate plan. If you accept the listing, your banker friend has agreed to pay me to get the house ready to sell."

Max slanted her a look. "What are you talking about?"

"The place needs work, a little pampering." She smiled and held her hands out on either side. "Who better than me to pamper?"

After a startled second, he laughed out loud. Encouraged, she lurched ahead.

"This is a chance for me to really do something, Max. A way for me to make some money so that I can start seriously paying off these debts."

"You have a job here."

"A job that, no offense, we both know isn't doing a whole lot to dig me out of the hole I'm in. You said so yourself. At best, I'm treading water. And once you and the girls leave for Thanksgiving, I have Wednesday through Sunday with nothing to do."

"You said you were spending the holiday with friends."

Oh, that. "Sure. Of course. No question I have zillions of friends." She had too much pride to admit she didn't have any. Determination spurred her on. "But I'll still have plenty of time to deal with the house. Please, Max, say yes."

He stared at her long and hard, that reluctant smile pulling at his lips. "Who are you, Vivienne Stansfield?"

"Is that a yes or a no?" she persisted.

"All right. Yes," he agreed. "I should have known I'd give in to you on this too. I'll take the listing. And you can make your money fixing up the house. But promise that you'll clean out every trace of my father and get rid of it."

Vivi threw her arms around him without thinking. "Thank you! You won't regret it!"

Instantly she felt the way heat flared through him. For one fleeting second he ran his hand down her spine, pressing their bodies close. He groaned, burying his face in her hair. But just as quickly, he set her away.

She could see it in his eyes. Tonight he wasn't giving an inch. Not to her. Not to any sort of feeling. His control had always been formidable. But this was something more, something deeper.

"Is there anything else?" he asked.

Vivi stood back and wrinkled her nose. "Well, there is the whole Lesson Two possibility."

His gaze suddenly burned. Slowly her heart went still as he reached out and cupped her cheek. The touch was like fire, instant and hot. As if it were the most natural thing to do, she closed her eyes and tilted her face so he could kiss her.

"Thank you," he said, tiny puffs of air brushing against her skin.

Thank you? And no kiss?

Her eyes popped open, and he smiled down at her.

"Thank you for what?" she demanded.

He chuckled. "For being a pain in the ass."

"Excuse me?"

"Okay, if you don't like it said that way, how about thank you for making me open my eyes."

"Oh." She waved the words away. "No problem." Then she leaned into him again.

But still he didn't kiss her. "Good night, Vivienne."

She made a frustrated strangling noise. "What about Lesson Two?"

"That was the lesson."

"Thanking me?"

"Let's just say that this time the lesson was for me."

• • •

The deal was done, the arrangements made. Vivi was thrilled about her new project. By Wednesday morning at nine, with Max agreeing to pick the girls up from a half day of school before they headed for the mountains, Vivi was at the University house, ready to get started.

Dressed in a pair of sweatpants and an old shirt she had taken from a pile of Max's castoffs, she opened the windows despite the cold, then went from room to room, stepping over piles of junk and awful smelling who-knew-what, determining what needed to be done.

Once she had a plan, she gathered newspapers, magazines, broken dishes, empty perfume bottles. Anything that couldn't be sold went into the trash. By noon it seemed she had barely scratched the surface. But by three she started to see a change. By four she managed to drag mattresses out into the alleyway that ran alongside the house. Broken wooden chairs, bent bed frames, and splintered picture frames soon followed.

By the time she got back to Max's house, it was late, and a red light flashed on the message machine. Dusty and stiff, she pressed Play.

"Vivienne?"

Max's voice, deep and confident, ran down her spine like the warm soapy bath she longed for.

He paused as if he wasn't sure why he was calling. *"Just checking in. Wanted to make sure you were doing all right."* Another pause. *"I called your cell, but you didn't answer."*

She hadn't heard?

She dug her cell phone out of her purse and sure enough found that she had two messages. The first was from Max. The second was from her father.

"Hello, princess. Umm, I heard about the article in the paper. You believe in your old man, don't you? Sure you do. So don't pay any attention to it. I'll explain when I get back. Well, okay. I better go. Hang in there, baby."

Then he was gone.

She stared at the phone, trying hard to keep her mind a safe blank. She was tired, felt vulnerable, making it harder to hold emotion back. She didn't want to think about her father—about whether he had lied or not. Tomorrow was Thanksgiving. Yet another holiday.

She wondered how Max and the girls were doing. She had heard the snow was great. She hated to admit how much she missed them.

Was that how it would always be for her? Holidays without family? Nothing to celebrate because she was alone?

And then she got mad. Her. Vivienne Stansfield, who had worked a lifetime to never get mad. She felt a low, burning fury at her father.

For the next two days, she worked obsessively. She refused to think. She ripped up old carpet, revealing hardwood floors. She scrubbed and cleaned, polished and waxed, until finally she could tag and itemize the furniture and china for the sale.

At the end of Friday, her mood hadn't improved. But that couldn't override the awe she experienced at the transformation she had made with this small, unloved house. She had made a difference. A *project* that had really worked! And she knew that on Monday, after she dropped the girls off at school, she'd be able to begin the estate sale to rival all estate sales.

But when she started to leave for the day, she couldn't

help but look over the yard. Stretching her sore back, she knew one more thing had to be done. And she couldn't afford to hire someone to do it.

Early the next morning, tired and aching in every inch of her body, Vivi returned to University, dressed in more of Max's castoffs, her hair pulled up out of the way. Cut and scraped, she was beyond caring about anything but success. She felt numb as she kneeled in the weeds and tangle of wild grasses to clear the mess by hand. This wasn't part of the job, but she understood the yard lining the walkway would set the tone for people coming into the sale. So she pulled and yanked until the gardener from next door came over and showed her how to run a small sprinkler section by section, making it easier.

Within minutes she turned into a muddy mess, but it saved fingers that were already bleeding. No one seeing her now would think she was pampered.

The sun had gone down by the time she picked out the last weed. She would have been proud if she'd had a single ounce of energy left to experience anything besides sheer exhaustion and pain.

As she drove along Mesa, every muscle screamed. It was all she could do to turn into the driveway, pull out of the car the very last box she had taken from the little house, then make her way inside.

She tucked the tattered cardboard box under the kitchen desk. Despite what he said, she felt certain that at some point Max would want to know that his father had cared. She just needed to wait for the right time to show him.

Shedding her shoes in the laundry room, she washed her hands, grimaced at the sting, then mindlessly pulled out something to eat. When she finally sat at the table, she told herself she would rest for just a second.

Laying her head down, the world grew soft. Pain receded and she gave in. Words echoed softly in her head, kind words, like a caress.

And then there was Max. Striding into her mind like the knight she had tried to convince herself he wasn't.

She sensed his smile, felt his voice whispering down her spine.

"Vivienne."

Her full name, in that intimate tone he used when she knew he wanted her.

She sighed in her dream, her body reaching toward him.

"Vivienne, wake up."

The words drifted through her, and she felt his strong hands pulling back her hair. How kind he was in her dreams. How gentle and unintimidating.

"Vivienne."

She felt the word against her cheek. Then she felt something more. In a nearly drunken haze, Vivienne opened her eyes just as Max reached out and swept her up in his strong arms. Solid and very real, not the man in her dreams.

"Max," she whispered through her sleep-filled mind. "Is it really you?"

He smiled, those full lips pulling into a crooked grin. "Yes, it's me."

"Where are the girls?"

"They're coming back with Pat tomorrow."

"Oh," she breathed, feeling his arms around her, holding her secure. "Why are you back early?" She tried to focus, tried to smile. "For another lesson?"

He looked at her long and hard, the wealth of emotion that he kept so close to his soul burning in his eyes. Then he cradled her to his chest as he headed for the stairs, and she would have sworn he whispered, "Because I couldn't stay away."

Chapter Twenty-two

Moonlight spilled through the skylights, painting the white walls in silver. Vivi held on to Max, half awake, half asleep, her head cradled against his chest, her defenses spent.

She curled close, refusing to let concern about where he was taking her surface as he took the stairs. When he walked into her bedroom and kicked the door shut behind them, she only sighed and curled closer.

He set her down on her feet, and it was all she could do to stand, aches and pains stabbing through her. She groaned.

"Shhh," he whispered against her temple, then he reached down and started undoing the buttons of the oversized shirt.

"What are you doing?" she asked, her mind not wanting to let go of that delicious state between sleep and awake—and those words. *"I couldn't stay away."*

"I'm getting you out of these clothes. What were you doing today? Rolling around in the mud?" He looked down at her, his gaze intense. "Again?"

She thought of the day in the rain, and a smile cracked on her lips. But even that hurt, and she remembered she had worked outside for hours in the desert winter sun.

"I think I'm sunburned," she explained.

He started to pull the shirt free. She told herself to undress on her own. But his careful ministrations felt deliriously wonderful, and in seconds her eyes fluttered closed and she stood on the carpet, wearing only a tank top and panties.

When the room grew silent, she finally, reluctantly, opened her eyes.

Max stood looking at her, a mix of appreciation and humor on his face. "What are you wearing?"

Looking down, she studied herself, then glanced back at him, offering a sheepish smile. "My Wonder Woman Underoos."

"Aren't those for girls?"

"They were on sale at Target, and I figured I needed all the inspiration I could get."

Max smiled, running his finger along the soft edge of the red camisole. "That house was a mess. You shouldn't feel bad if you couldn't fix it—not everything is fixable, Vivienne."

The words kicked at the exhaustion, and she thought of her family. "Maybe not everything. But a lot of things can be. Just wait until you see the house. Wonder Woman worked wonders." She added a whip of snapping fingers in the air. "We're talking clean." But the simple movement zapped her of every remaining ounce of energy, making her knees go weak.

Before she knew it, he had swept her up again and carried her into the bathroom. "That house might be clean, but you aren't."

He set her on the velvet chaise, then started the water.

"Now what are you doing?" she squeaked.

He answered by taking each of her hands. "These have got to hurt."

She looked down at the scrapes and cracks, her nose wrinkling. "They've felt better."

Max pulled her up. Then he started to lift the Wonder Woman tank top.

"I can do that." But when she tried to tug it free, her muscles screamed in protest.

With quick efficiency, he undressed her completely.

In some deep recess of her mind she knew she should be mortified or outraged—or even a little indignant. But she couldn't muster up more than a "Can you help me into the tub?"

He did, but not before he found her Extra Bubbly Champagne bubbles and poured plenty in. When she finally sank into the warm water, she sighed.

She lay back until the bubbles lapped at her chin. "Good thinking to clean me up before our next lesson," she said, her eyes closed, her brain doing its best to string words together in what she hoped were coherent sentences.

He didn't respond other than to take a washcloth, lather it with soap, and start a slow, methodical cleansing of her body. Yet again she searched around in her tired body for one ounce of energy to do it herself.

Instead she only breathed deeply at his ministrations. It was half a cleaning, half a kneading of muscles she never knew she had. Every inch of her ached, followed by every inch sighing in pleasure as Max washed the pains away.

When he told her to sit up, she did, curling her arms around her knees as he ran the cloth over her back, down her spine to her hips. Something welled up in her at the touch, deeper than awareness, stronger than need and longing. She felt the stinging bite of tears tighten in her throat at the realization that no one had ever touched her with such care. Not her mother, not her father, not anyone in the boarding schools she had grown up in.

How had she lived without this?

"So, you can't live without me," she murmured into her knees, wanting to change the direction of her thoughts.

His hand stilled for a fraction of a second before he laughed softly and continued on. "Apparently."

"As much as I'm flattered, I think there's another reason you're here."

"Really? What would that be?"

"You hate this holiday."

"What are you talking about?"

"It only makes sense. You said your dad left on Thanksgiving, and your mom died a year later."

"You remember that?"

"I told you, I have a mind like a steel trap."

He chuckled for a second, then he sighed. "She died a few days before Thanksgiving—like she had finally accepted he wasn't coming home and she gave up."

"I'm sorry."

He wrung out the washcloth. "The kids were in shock. I remember that. All of them sitting in a row on this old vinyl couch we had in this tiny room. Pat holding Lila, who was barely six months old. It was like they couldn't get their minds around what had happened. Like they didn't know what death meant." He set the cloth aside. "Hell, I hardly understood. But I was too damn busy to think. I had a funeral to plan, a hospital breathing down my neck, wanting to know when I'd pay the bill. And then Thanksgiving Day. Mom gone. The first taste of being on our own." He shook his head. "I thought I'd make everything seem as normal as possible. But the turkey was still pink inside, and the rolls about caught the place on fire."

"So the minute you had enough money you started taking them to Ruidoso to ski."

"Yeah. I guess that's the easy way out."

"Not easy, Max. Never easy. Just easier than having a *family* dinner that does little more than remind you that your mother and father are gone."

She turned her head to look at him. He stared at her for what seemed like an eternity. "What is this between us?" he asked, confusion lining his strong features.

"I'm not sure anymore," she answered, her candor surprising her. "I just know that I'm not ready for it to end."

He laughed out loud, like a release, as if that was something that he could handle.

"You might drive me crazy, but you always make me smile."

She rolled her eyes with as much energy as she could muster. "Go on with the flattery."

Instead he whipped out a soft-bristled manicure brush. "Let me have a look at those hands."

She hardly recognized this dominating man as once again that ease she experienced only with him settled between them. Moved by his care, she reveled in it, amazed that pulling weeds could do such damage. He sat on the floor next to the tub, his shirt tossed aside, his button-fly jeans hanging low on his hips as he took her fingers one by one and brushed them clean.

All too soon he finished, making her stand as the water drained away. Then he took the handheld faucet and rinsed her. When he was done, she marshaled her strength and started to get out. But he was ready for her, wrapping her in the largest velour terry towel she had ever seen. Then he swept her back into his arms.

The moon drifted through the sky as Max dried her, then returned her to the chaise, where he brushed out her hair with mesmerizing strokes. This massive man, who was filled with a primal arrogance and sensuality, cared for her without the slightest concern for his own vulnerability. He thought only of her. And just when she was sure he would leave, or kiss her, he kneeled before her on the floor. She looked into his eyes, uncertain what she felt.

Fear?

Unease over someone else's selfless act of caring for her?

Or was it that she couldn't allow herself to believe that anything this good could be real?

In the dimly lit room, as the silver moon slipped through the nighttime sky, she was afraid to truly look at the feelings that churned inside her.

She knew he wanted her. But he also had told her that he didn't understand that desire. It had never mattered before, because she hadn't wanted him either—at least she hadn't wanted anything more than a mindless way to satisfy what she had told herself was only a physical attraction.

For reasons she didn't understand, this man made her forget. He had the ability to set her precarious world aside—make her feel as if she could survive when all the rules she had grown up with had been tossed aside, her paddles lost, her boat drifting free in waters she didn't know how to navigate.

But, looking at him now, she had the bone-chilling thought that perhaps she felt more. That what she didn't want to end was something deeper. Perhaps she wanted more from this man than escape and safe passage through white waters.

She turned away from the thought, because if she was honest with herself, she didn't want to want more than sex from him. Not now, when she was building a new life for herself. An independent life. She was proving that she didn't need anyone to take care of her. She was building a normal life. But she couldn't be complete until she had filled the emptiness inside her. She had to be whole on her own first, before she could be whole with someone else.

Her confusion must have shown.

"What's wrong?" he asked.

"Nothing."

She started to push away, but he held her there, coming up to sit beside her.

"What is going through that head of yours?" he persisted.

"Just thinking."

"You do a lot of that."

"Amazing, isn't it? Most people think I don't have a brain in my head."

"I think you let people believe that."

Vivi scoffed, working up indignation. "Don't tell me we're back to the *Oprah* self-help sessions?"

"No, but you constantly prove how different you are from the person you pretend to be. You told me you had *zillions*—your word, not mine—of people to spend time with over the holiday. Instead, I find that you worked day and night at that house."

She shrugged, not liking the direction of this conversation. "Holidays are for family. I didn't want to intrude on all those zillions."

"Ah, family. But yours isn't here."

She tried not to care. "No."

"I'm beginning to wonder if your parents are ever around."

She hated the tightness she felt in her chest. "Don't look so aghast. It's not that big of a deal." How many times had she told herself that? "There are more people than you can count who don't even have parents to spend any time with. Heck, look at you."

She saw him tense and she felt bad. "I wasn't trying to be mean. I'm just pointing out that I at least have parents. So there's no need to feel sorry for me."

"Then I commend you. Not everyone would be so understanding."

"It's just the way it is." No doubt it was the long days of fatigue that made her susceptible, but her mind drifted back to the early years. "When I was really young, my parents were crazy about each other. I was more the third wheel than the daughter. Then, as I got older, I could see the cracks starting to settle between them, and next thing I knew they were traveling all over, but separately."

"Leaving you at home?"

"With friends, or at school. I didn't live here a lot of the time. And it's not so uncommon for girls in boarding school to spend a holiday or two there."

"It sounds like you spent most there."

"Yeah, well." The thought trailed off, then she laughed. "I remember thinking that if I could just be perfect enough, then my mom and dad would see how good

I was and what a great family we could be, and everything would be okay."

"So you became the perfect princess."

She looked him in the eyes. "Not the perfect princess.
I wanted to be the perfect daughter. My father wanted
me to be the princess."

His face darkened. But he didn't say anything. He
stood, then surprised her when he pulled her up into his
arms, cradling her, nothing covering her but the thick
towel.

"Ah, the lesson?" she managed, thankful to change the
subject.

He held her close for a second, his lips against her hair
without really kissing her. She felt the shift in him, as if
his long-held control had eased another notch. Then he
looked at her, and she realized in that moment that he
saw her differently.

His lips quirked, and his dark eyes seemed to lighten.
"Yes, now for the lesson," he said.

"Good." Safer ground. Sex and none of those emotions rushing through him as if he felt more for her than
she could afford for him to feel. "Yes, good," she added
with a firm nod. "Some real live sex. Let's get it on."

Max grimaced.

"Not the sex talk you had in mind?" she inquired. "All
right. How about . . ." She considered. "Maxwell, you
fine specimen of a man—"

He nearly dropped her.

"Hey!"

Muttering about patience being tried, he carried her
into the bedroom. But when she thought he'd peel the
towel away, he went to her chest of drawers, not returning until he had a long flannel nightgown.

"Stand up," he commanded.

She stood, not happily, until her towel fluttered to the floor and Max's impatience evaporated, his gaze like a heated caress. He looked at her with sheer, undiluted awareness.

A blush crawled up her body to her face, but she didn't cover herself. She stood before him, and he drank her in.

"You are beautiful," he said, his voice fierce. His gaze ran over her as he took a step closer, just close enough so that he could reach out and touch her.

"Your nipples are like cherries that I want in my mouth."

Instantly, she felt them pull into taut peaks even before he gently squeezed the buds between his thumb and forefinger.

Her breath winged out of her, but he didn't take her in his arms. He reached out with both hands, his palms just barely drifting over her nipples until she wanted to demand that he do more.

He didn't read her mind, or if he did, he didn't comply. He pulled back, leaving her yearning.

"Your arms are beautiful, and your hands, even now, are elegant. I dream of you going down on me, pulling me into your mouth."

He took her hand and pressed it to the unmistakable ridge of his hardness. "Do you feel that?" he asked, his voice raw.

"Yes."

"Do you feel how much I want to be inside you?"

She could only murmur, her eyes fluttering closed until his fingertips grazed down the center between her ribs. Lower and lower, until he nudged her feet apart with his own.

Sensation coursed through her when his fingers trailed lower, parting the curls between her thighs.

"You're wet," he stated with an arrogance she had come to recognize.

He found her clitoris. "Do you feel that?" he asked.

She couldn't breathe, much less talk. Then she sucked in a breath when his finger began working magic. Slowly he pressed her back toward the bed. With insistence, he laid her down on the mattress. Not letting her move when her eyes opened wide, he gathered her knees and opened her to him.

"Max?" she asked, her voice shaking.

"Hush, Vivienne." He kneeled between her thighs.

"I was thinking more about sex, not . . . this."

"There is more to sex than intercourse."

"Okay, so I was a little generic—"

He parted her gently.

"—ah, in my wording."

When his mouth came down on her, his tongue like fire where his finger had been seconds before, she forgot about protests.

Her hands curled into the bedspread as his lips closed around the sensation-filled nub, her hips lifting up to him. His palm came up and flattened on her belly, then slid higher, caressing her and gentling her at the same time.

Every muscle in her legs was taut, straining, and he whispered against her to relax. "Open for me," he commanded.

Shaking, she spread her feet for him, barely, but enough that he took her more deeply and she gasped.

Her body burned and sought, reaching for that pleasure he had shown her before, but never with such slick, fiery need. Rocking her head from side to side, she wanted more of this, of him, her mind aware of nothing but the desire to find release.

"That's it," he murmured. "Let go, Vivienne."

Then he reached up and took the taut bud of her breast between his thumb and forefinger, sucking her core one last time, making her cry out as her body shattered.

Vivi arched off the bed for the intensity of her body's reaction, sensation pulsing through her in waves. He cupped her mound as she orgasmed, murmuring sweet words as he came over her, stretching alongside and pulling her into his arms. He held her tight as her body quivered with the echo of passion, leaving her spent.

"Max" was all she could say when finally her body began to calm, and he brushed his lips against hers one final time.

After long minutes, she looked up at him, his blue eyes shimmering like hot coals in the silver light. "You keep doing that," she whispered, not certain what she felt.

"Doing what?" he asked, his confident grin pulling at the corner of his mouth.

"Making me feel," she finally said. "Over and over again you make me feel until I think I'll die."

"A little bit of heaven," he said, kissing her again, then rolling away.

"Where are you going?" she asked before she could stop herself.

He tugged the covers from underneath her, then instructed her to put on the thick nightgown. He helped her get into it when her limbs couldn't manage on their own. Then he tucked her in, pulling the blankets and comforter around her.

She wanted to stay awake. There were so many things she wanted to talk about. But her eyes wouldn't stay open. He leaned over to kiss her on the forehead, then smiled. She sensed more than saw a change in him, that shift from earlier shifting even more.

She tried to focus her mind, tried to understand what it was. But it took too much effort, and she couldn't bring herself to leave this blissful place.

"Thank you," she said softly, burrowing deep into the pillows.

For a moment he seemed surprised. Then he chuckled. "You're welcome."

He headed for the door, and just as she curled up on her side, her mind floating, she said, "Next time it will be my turn to give the lesson."

Chapter Twenty-three

Two weeks later, the West Texas December cold finally wrapped around the city in a relentless grip. Max was standing in his bedroom when the front door banged open. He thought how surprised the girls and Vivienne would be that he had come home early from work.

Since the day Max had carried Vivienne upstairs to the bath, his mind had been filled with thoughts of her, his body taut like a drum, his hands itching to touch her again.

But it was more than sexual. God help him, she had the ability to make him smile. She made him happy.

There was no question that he wanted to lose himself in her in a way that he had fought against since the second she walked into his office. She did something to him, always had, twisting his thoughts and emotions until he hardly recognized himself.

But the wanting went to a place that had made him begin to wonder if it had to do with how she saw him. Really saw him. No matter what he said or tried to portray, she always saw the truth. She understood him in a way that no one in his life ever had. She didn't care about his power any more than she had cared that he was a poor boy from the wrong side of town when she walked toward him on the stage.

For weeks now he had concentrated on the memory of her turning away from him, again and again. He had consistently refused to think about the fact that again and again she had reached out to him. Something had drawn her to him from the beginning.

But now that she was in his home, he had no choice but to see beyond her carefully constructed facade. He was forced to admit that she wasn't the spoiled princess he had always felt safe in believing she was. She worked hard, wanted no one's pity, and seemed to live for helping other people. She wanted nothing from him in return—at least nothing emotional. All she wanted was a flight from reality through uncommitted sex. The minute any emotion swelled around them, that was when she pushed him away. As if she couldn't afford intimacy. As if the night he had come home and found her asleep at the kitchen table, she had revealed too much, had felt too much.

Which brought him to his current dilemma.

Vivienne had jumped through hoops to avoid him since that night. The minute he showed up, she ducked away with some task or another that she had to do for the girls. When he pulled into the drive, she hopped in her car and was gone.

He had given her time to adjust. But his patience had run dry.

Max left the room and went to find Vivienne. He wanted to see her, wanted to feel that foolish schoolboy smile she always brought out of him.

He found her in the kitchen. He stopped in the doorway as she talked and laughed with Lila, while

Nicki stood to the side, eating a Fruit Roll-Up, interested but pretending to be cool. None of them saw him.

The change in Nicki was amazing. With the black makeup gone, she was truly beautiful. And now she wore colorful shirts with her jeans. Lila seemed happier as well. She had even forgotten to send him her usual week's end memo because she'd been invited to another girl's birthday party. Granted, the following day Lila had apologized with an extra long memo, in which she had praised Vivi's "dedicated plan" for befriending the junior high set. Lila felt certain that in May, around the time of her birthday, *hint hint*, she would probably be in a position to have her own party because she felt certain she'd have several friends by then. She had added she would get back to him with details in the new year.

Then there was Vivienne herself. A sizzle of pure pleasure washed over him at the sight. She wore her uniform of khakis and white shirt, but as if she couldn't help herself, she had sewn a lavish pink-sequined V on the collar.

"So tomorrow's the last day of the estate sale," Lila said from her place at the kitchen counter stool. "How much money have you made so far?"

Vivienne paused as she straightened the clutter on the countertop, then smiled and walked over to the kitchen desk, straightened a bit more, before pulling out an old box, the top popping open when she hugged it tight, excitement brightening her features.

"I've sold nearly five thousand dollars worth of stuff!" she enthused. "And I get ten percent."

Nicki didn't say anything but looked grudgingly impressed.

"That's five hundred dollars!" Lila gasped.

"I know," Vivienne said. "Can you believe it? We'll have to go out and celebrate. Maybe tomorrow tonight!"

Nicki wrinkled her nose and looked back and forth between Lila and Vivienne. "I can't."

"Why?" Lila asked.

Nicki hesitated, then burst out, "I have a date!"

"A date?" Vivienne and Lila squealed.

"A date?" Max demanded, coming into the room.

All eyes went wide, and Max noticed that Vivienne glanced nervously at the box in her arms.

"What are you doing home so early?" she asked, while his sisters stood like deer caught in headlights. "You're supposed to be at work."

Max ignored her and focused on Nicki. "What is this about a date?" he demanded. "You know you aren't allowed to go out with boys."

Nicki found her tongue and banged the roll-up down in her fist. "I'm in high school now."

"True, but you're barely fourteen," he countered.

"You are so unfair!"

"And you are too young to date."

Nicki stamped her foot, then froze, and Max was certain she was rethinking her approach. His jaw went tight.

"It's not a date date," she offered, the belligerence magically gone, her tone suddenly cajoling. "It's just a bunch of kids getting together."

"Will boys be there?"

She bit her lower lip and looked at him through lowered lashes. "Would you believe me if I said no?"

Max groaned inwardly at the thought that Nicki had gone from in-your-face belligerence to trying her hand at pretty-girl manipulation, and he knew exactly where Nicki had learned the tactic. He shot an accusatory glare at Vivienne, who popped back up as if she hadn't been trying to stash the box back underneath the desk.

What the hell was in that box?

"Excuse me, Nicki," Lila interrupted. "But you've already mentioned the word *date*, and if you add *no boys*, Max might mentally go places you really don't want him to go."

Nicki was confused, but Max and Vivienne weren't. Max felt a vein start pounding in his head, a throb that only got worse when Vivienne covered a laugh with a cough.

"How do you know about these things?" he asked incredulously of the eleven-year-old.

"It is the new millennium, Maxwell. And I do watch TV. Homosexuality is everywhere."

"Homosexual!" Nicki burst out. "I am not gay. I have a date with Brandon Bonner!"

Max turned a hard glare on his sister. "So it is a date. A date you are not going on. You are too young. And he's a senior. Case closed. We'll revisit the subject in another five years."

"Five years!"

Thankfully, Pat chose that moment to walk in. Dates and homosexuality. Didn't raising kids ever get easier?

When Pat came over to give Vivienne a hug, Vivienne nearly dropped the box in surprise.

"What's going on?" Pat asked.

Lila cringed. "We've just experienced our first dating dilemma."

"Meaning?"

"That Max said Nicki is too young to date."

"Ah," Pat said with a knowing nod of her head. "I remember those days."

Max grumbled.

Pat laughed. "Just think, Max. Only two more sisters left to deal with."

"And I promise not to give you dating fits," Lila swore.

"Don't make any promises you can't keep," Pat interjected. "Come on, girls, let's go." But then something inside Vivienne's box caught her attention. "Hey, what's this?"

Vivienne slapped her hand on top and nearly sent the whole thing tumbling. "Nothing! Really, nothing."

But Pat helped her regain the box's balance, and she set it on the counter. Vivienne practically tackled the box. But it was too late.

"Pictures?" Pat was confused. "Of us?"

Vivienne cringed, and Max's heart jarred in his chest when he realized what it must be.

Nicki and Lila opened the box the rest of the way and gaped at the photos.

Max stood still as stone.

"Max," Pat asked, puzzled, "what are these?"

Anger leaped through him like a flame. Anger and something else. Pain and betrayal. At Vivienne and at his father. He knew that's what the box was. Those things Max had told Vivienne to burn.

"Why don't I take it for now," Vivienne suggested, "and Max can explain?"

"Explain what?" Pat asked, her fingers clutching the edges of the cardboard.

Max's gaze went from Pat, to Vivienne, to the girls. Then he cursed. He felt his thoughts harden when he realized he had little choice, so he explained about the house, about their father who had been only miles from them all these years, living with a woman, before he had died. How they had found the photos in the house.

"You mean he kept pictures of us but never came to see us?" Nicki breathed.

"Yes," Max responded, his tone clipped.

"How could he do such a thing," Pat spat. "The bastard."

"Pat, I know how you feel," Max said.

He hesitated, looking at Vivienne. She was willing him to lead with caring instead of an iron fist. He saw it, understood it.

His jaw muscles leaped, fury surrounding him. But after one more look at Vivienne, then at his sisters, he knew what he had to do. "At least it shows that he cared."

"Cared, my ass," Pat shot back.

Nicki looked shocked. Lila didn't even notice. She crawled up onto a high stool and started rummaging around in the box.

"Do you think he remembered me, too?" Lila asked hopefully.

Max's heart all but stopped. Their father had left before Lila was born. And his concern solidified when he saw Vivienne's face blanch.

"Of course he remembered you, sweetie," Vivienne said. "Just keep looking."

Without another word, Vivienne silently slipped out of the room as Lila continued to dig, her little face taking on a haunted expression the deeper she went without a single glimpse of herself.

Nicki and Pat started looking, too, and each found photos of themselves, old photos of days long passed.

Lila finally straightened. "There's none of me," she said, her blue eyes troubled.

Pat and Nicki instantly realized what was happening. They stood very still, not knowing what to do.

Max felt powerless. He also felt a slow tick of anger renew its beat. What a fucking mess this was. Lead with caring, and look where it had gotten them. He should have slammed the box shut and thrown it away. He should have said no to Vivienne's damn plan in the first place.

Just when he started to reach for the photographs, Vivienne burst back into the kitchen, another box in her hands. "Here's the other one. It's amazing all the pictures your father kept of you guys. There are tons of them."

Lila held her breath, and Max breathed a sigh of relief that there was more. But when Vivienne whipped open the box, he recognized a stack of photos from the box he stored in her closet. Photos of all the kids, including Lila.

But the eleven-year-old was smart, too smart, and Max felt his chest squeeze hard at the realization that his sister would see through the ploy.

Feeling furious and helpless, he watched Lila take each photo in her hands one by one. She looked at each closely, and then her face crumpled.

Damn it.

And when she made a tiny heartbreaking cry, Max had to force himself not to put his fist into the wall.

Tension sliced through the kitchen as she looked up at him, tears in her eyes. "Oh, Max, he loved me, too."

Silence crashed through his mind as he couldn't seem to move. Then Lila was in his arms, holding on tight. "He loved me, too," she whispered again, her face buried in his side.

Fiercely fighting back foolish tears of his own, he

stroked her hair, and when he glanced up, he could see the emotion in Pat's and Nicki's eyes. Then suddenly all four of them were holding tight. Max could hardly fathom this feeling of love that he rarely acknowledged for his sisters.

He glanced over their heads and found Vivienne standing there, looking relieved and joyous. But strangely sad as well. In that moment he finally understood the shift that had happened inside him.

Vivienne might look at the world from a completely different perspective, but underneath all the outlandishness, she was caring and honest and kind in ways he'd never seen before.

He wanted this woman, yes. And he had come to admit that she made him happy. But he needed her as well. That was what he had been running from. The need.

In that second, standing in this kitchen of this grand house that left him feeling little more than empty, he knew that he wanted her in his life permanently. And he realized he would do whatever it took to make her his own.

The understanding brought a sizzle of shock but of anticipation as well for the years he would have with this woman. And he *would* have her, in his bed and by his side. As his bride.

His mind reeled with all he felt. But the minute she noticed him studying her, she only smiled through the poignant sadness he saw in her eyes. Then she disappeared out of the kitchen before he could pull her close and thank her for this gift.

My Wedding Diary

EAT, DRINK, AND BE MARRIED

clearly I will never

How could I have been so careless? If Lila hadn't accepted that second box as having been her father's, she would have been devastated by being forgotten. And I would have been the cause.

I don't understand what is happening to me. I've been holding the panic at bay, or at least I was. Now I feel it beating inside me. When I saw Max and Pat and Nicki and Lila hug tight, I couldn't deny that I felt horribly lost—and without the possibility of marrying and having a family of my own.

Chapter Twenty-four

Nicki was both excited and terrified as she walked into the crowded Saturday night party with Brandon's arm slung across her shoulders. Music blared from speakers, guys and girls slouched together. There wasn't a parent in sight and most everyone there was smoking cigarettes. One guy she kind of recognized served beer from a keg.

The minute they walked in, the others noticed.

"Boomer!"

"My man!"

"Looking good, Nicki."

A chorus of hellos and ritual handshakes were exchanged between guys who gave her power-pink-short-skirt-clad body appreciative once-overs.

It felt totally great and Nicki told herself not to worry about the beer Brandon accepted. And when he handed one to her, she stared at it for long seconds before she smiled weakly and took it. After the way he had looked at her when she snuck out of Pat's apartment and met him in the parking lot, it would be worth running the risk of getting caught.

Taking a sip, holding back a grimace, she ducked her head and smiled at Brandon Bonner in his jeans, baby-soft flannel shirt, and black boots. She felt giddy and amazed that she was going with him, and that his friends knew her now. She was part of the gang.

At least that's how she felt until Brandon lifted two beers into the air like Rocky and announced that it was time to play. The guys cheered, the girls laughed.

"Play what?" she asked, hardly recognizing the strange little giggle that bubbled out of her after she finished her beer.

"Strip poker," the guys bellowed.

The other girls who were there weren't surprised. But Nicki felt a jab of major anxiety through her beer-induced sense of calm.

Strip poker?

"Oh, I can't play," Nicki said nervously.

Brandon's face clouded. "Don't be like that, Nick," he crooned, pulling her close and kissing her hairline. "It's fun."

Yeah, maybe for everyone else, but she doubted everyone else had stuffed big fake boobs in their bras.

Yikes!

Suddenly Brandon's *"Wow, you are going to be awesome tonight"* took on a whole new meaning. Little did he know how un-awesome things would get if she lost her clothes.

But then she looked up and saw Brandon, so great, so popular, so exactly who she wanted for her boyfriend, and she rationalized that by growing up in a house full of boys, she knew how to play poker, and she wasn't half bad. So when hands were dealt, Nicki found herself sitting next to Brandon at the table.

For the first few rounds, she didn't lose a stitch of clothing. By the fifth hand, she started to relax, sighing over how cool Brandon looked when he shuffled the deck of cards. Then she actually started having fun after another beer and one of the guys got down to tube socks and boxer shorts.

That's when the girls started to lose.

In the next thirty minutes, hand after hand, Nicki lost a scarf, then a belt, a bracelet—if Vivi only knew what was happening to her few remaining frilly clothes—then her outer shirt. Thank God she had on a pink tank top underneath.

Nicki's mind raced as fast as her heart pounded, while she tried to come up with a way out of this situation without looking like an idiot.

Just when she decided being thought an idiot would be way better than being humiliated if anyone got a look at what was inside her bra, she was rescued from both because Brandon grabbed her hand and pulled her away. "Later, guys," he called out.

Relief! She was saved. She nearly threw her arms around Brandon in gratitude.

But before she knew what was happening, they were out the front door, practically racing to the cars parked along the neighborhood street. In a matter of seconds, he had her in the back of his mom's Suburban, which had the seats folded down.

No question she had been psyched about the prospect of her first true kiss. However, rolling around in the back of a Suburban wasn't what she had had in mind.

But this was Brandon, she reminded herself. He liked her, he really did, so surely all she had to do was say, "Brandon, please stop. I'm not ready." And she did.

"Don't worry, baby. I'm not going to hurt you."

Then down they went onto the scratchy car-grade carpeting in the back of the SUV, and she got the French kiss she had been longing for.

Only it wasn't quite what she had expected.

His hands moved like lightning, his tongue practically choking her, and if she could have gotten a word out she would have said, *Excuse me. Gross!*

But the really wet and disgusting French kiss was the least of her worries. Brandon's hands were everywhere, and Nicki had to twist here and there to keep them away from her chest—and Victoria's biggest Secret.

Good God, it was like an athletic event. This was not how she had envisioned her first real date with Brandon. It had never occurred to her that she'd have to fend him off, and belatedly she remembered Vivi's warning that wearing breast enhancers could only cause trouble. Now she knew why.

But enlightenment came too late, and now that Nicki had leaped into the deep end of the pool—and gotten results—she was determined to make it work. She would make Brandon keep his hands to himself, and twist her way out of the car.

"Brandon," she managed to say, pushing at his chest.

But the push and twist only gave him better access. With an expertise that could only mean he had spent many years getting his hand inside bras, he slipped his inside hers.

Nicki gasped. Brandon sighed with great passion, squeezed once, then paused before giving a somewhat hesitant pinch, making him go completely still. After one painfully long second, Brandon let out a strange strangled noise, then jerked his hand free. When he did, one really expensive rubbery fake breast came out as well, flopping onto the folded seat back, then shuddered like it had a life of its own.

"What the fuck is that?" he demanded, rearing up, banging his head on the ceiling.

Nicki couldn't speak, sheer mortification scorching through her.

He looked from it to her, that nipple protruding like a cherry on a hot fudge sundae, his brow furrowed, until she saw comprehension register. His mouth fell open, then suddenly, horribly, he started to laugh. Nicki didn't think she could stop herself from crying as she snatched up the breast and shoved it back in place just in time for the door to whip open.

Steve Bonner stood there, his face creased with fury. "What the hell are you doing in here?"

Nicki sat curled against the side of the car, her purse clutched to her chest. Belatedly, she realized she must have looked traumatized. Of course she was, but for reasons she wasn't interested in sharing with Steve.

But the younger Bonner didn't wait for an explanation. As soon as Nicki crawled out, he jerked Brandon from the car so fast that the older boy didn't know what hit him.

"Hey, man, watch it." Then Brandon laughed some more.

Laughter stopped, however, when Steve banged him up against the side of the Suburban.

"Hey, Steve, I said watch it." This time the older Bonner wasn't laughing.

Steve got in his face. "I say make me."

The two brothers were virtually the same height, but Steve was clearly the stronger of the two from working out with the varsity football team. "Keep your fucking hands off Nicki. She's a kid."

"What do you care about her? Hell, you should see what's in that shirt of hers."

"I don't give a rat's ass what's in there. And if you so much as breathe a word of what went on, you'll answer to me."

For half a second, Nicki didn't think Brandon would listen, and she had a fleeting, completely mortifying thought of what her life would be like at Coronado High if the fake boob incident got around.

But then Brandon glanced between her and Steve. With a belligerent shrug, he pushed Steve away. "Like I care."

Then Brandon sauntered away.

Nicki watched him go. "I am so embarrassed," she said to Steve.

"My brother can be an ass. You aren't the first freshman he's lured out to this car. When I saw he took my mom's Suburban, I knew what he had in mind." He looked at her with the same sort of exacting gaze that Max frequently skewered her with.

She looked down at her shoes. "I thought it was a real date. I thought he liked me."

"My brother doesn't like anyone. But he liked what he saw in the new you."

"What did he see?" she had to ask.

He shoved his hands in his pockets and for the first time looked a tad uncomfortable. "The whole stuffed bra thing."

"You knew!"

"I figured it out."

"But I had never worn anything but baggy shirts before this."

Steve smiled. "Even in all those crappy clothes you used to wear, you were cute, but flat. And I doubt any girl can grow that fast."

She prayed the ground would open up and swallow her. But when the pavement stayed firm and unmoving, she ducked her head and started walking.

"Hey, where are you going?" he called after her.

"Home."

With a few bold strides he caught up to her. "You're going to walk?"

God, she hadn't thought. She was miles from Pat's apartment, and she sure couldn't call and ask for a ride.

They heard the front door of the house open up, and the sound of hard rock filtered out to them.

"Steve! Where are you?"

Nicki didn't think it possible to feel any worse but was proven wrong when she caught sight of Natalie Vincenze coming their way. Sensing her distress, Steve called out, "Wait for me inside, Nat. I'll be there in a sec."

Natalie huffed, but returned to the house.

"You can't walk home, Nicki."

"Don't worry about me. I'll . . . call my sister. You go ahead."

"I'm not leaving you out here alone. Here, use my cell, then wait on the porch."

Nicki panicked, not knowing whom to call. Then it hit her. She dialed Vivi's cell phone number, and the minute Vivi answered Nicki started talking.

"Hey, it's me, Nicki. I'm at a friend's house—"

Nicki smiled at Steve while Vivi screeched and guessed that she had gone on the date after all.

"I really appreciate your coming to pick me up," Nicki said as if nothing was wrong. She gave the address. Signed off. Then promised Steve that she wouldn't leave the lighted front porch until her ride got there.

Just when she thought Steve would leave, he said, "I'll make sure Brandon doesn't talk." Then he smiled at her, a really great smile. "We all do stupid stuff sometimes, Nick. Don't worry about it."

For a second she almost thought he was going to stay outside with her. But then he shrugged. "I better go find Natalie."

A surprising jab of disappointment raced through her, and for the first time she realized how cute he was. Cute and nice, and he didn't care if she was stacked or not.

He left her on the porch, and with every second that ticked by, her stomach churned. She felt embarrassed and a kind of weird sad, and mad. Really mad at the realization of what she had done. She had gone off the deep end to try to win some moronic boy.

She couldn't believe she had chased after Brandon. But having a boyfriend, being a part of something besides a family that was so big that hardly anyone noticed her, had been wonderful. But none of that had been true.

Suddenly it seemed like it was all Vivi's fault. Vivi and her stupid clothes, and Vivi who was like a stupid Barbie doll that men ogled. And when the rattletrap Olds pulled up, Nicki leaped in, slamming the door hard.

"I don't want to talk about it," she stated bluntly. "You are so not my mom, so this is none of your business."

But Nicki forgot all about questions or sneaking out when she remembered she was wearing Vivi's clothes.

Vivi stared at her long and hard across the darkened car, though Nicki couldn't tell if Vivi was mad or what. Feeling awkward and hating life so bad that she wanted to hit something or cry, Nicki slumped down in the seat. Suddenly the whole night got to her. Brandon and his hands everywhere. That fake breast flopping on the seat. In that second she felt overwhelmed and she hated everything and everyone. Most of all she hated Vivienne Stansfield.

"What?" Nicki demanded. "So I wore your clothes. It's not like I ruined them or anything. And it's not like you have anything really good left anymore. I mean, really, what did you do with everything? Sell stuff to pay your bills?" she scoffed, this strange fury riddling her. Crossing her arms, she sat back with an angry huff.

Vivi turned and looked out the window, staring out into the dark night. They sat there for a second. Then without a word Vivi put the car in gear and drove, gripping the steering wheel real tight, the streetlights lighting the way like a line of birthday candles in the dark.

Finally, when they rolled over the train tracks at Country Club Road and then headed up Mesa, Nicki couldn't take it any more.

"So yell or something."

Vivi's grip got tighter, but she didn't yell. "Nicki, tell me you didn't buy breast enhancers."

"What if I did?" Nicki sank lower, as if she could make her chest disappear.

Vivi pulled in a deep breath, then sighed. "You wanted that boy to ask you out so badly that you'd resort to stuffing your bra?"

Nicki jerked up in her seat. "Oh, I'm not pretty enough for a guy like him, is that what you're saying?"

"This has nothing to do with pretty. You're fourteen. Seniors don't go out with freshmen unless they want something."

"What would you know?" she shot back as they pulled into Pat's parking lot. "I bet no guy has asked you out for any other reason besides wanting sex."

Vivi looked a little like she'd been punched, but Nicki was too frustrated and sad and mad to care.

"You're right," Vivi said. "Guys don't take me out because of my mind, I admit that. They ask me out because they think I'm rich, or because they think I make good arm candy. Plenty of reasons that have nothing to do with the real me. But the reason men take me out or don't take me out has nothing to do with you. You, Nicki Landry, are wonderful and sweet and beautiful all on your own."

Nicki sucked in a breath.

"And I won't let you use harsh words to push me away just because you're scared and lashing out."

Nicki leaped from the car.

"Hey, Nicki?"

Nicki hesitated, though she told herself not to.

"You're a terrific kid. And there are plenty of guys out there who will think you're the greatest. I promise."

Nicki's throat tightened. She didn't want this. She didn't need this, not from a Barbie doll nanny. But still her eyes burned.

Before she could embarrass herself and cry, she banged the car door shut, then raced toward the apartment, aware the entire time that Vivi didn't leave until she had crawled back through the window.

My Wedding Diary

RISKY BUSINESS

Nicki is angry—at me, at the world. I want to show her that no matter how hard she pushes, I'll still be there. But is it the fear of loving that scares her? And if she's unwilling to let herself love or be loved, can anyone break through that wall?

I wish I didn't understand so well how sometimes a person can't afford to risk her heart to anyone.

Chapter Twenty-five

Vivi paced the empty house on University. She had come back after returning Nicki to Pat's apartment, determined to finish up the last few details before morning. The winter moon was high and one single naked bulb burned, casting the room in faint silver and gold. She felt caged and confined. Nicki's hatred still stung.

But that wasn't what mattered. Only Nicki mattered, and how Vivi should handle the situation. Should she tell Max about his sister's clandestine activities? Or should she first give the girl a chance to tell Max herself?

And didn't all kids sneak out at one time or another? If she told Max, would he be too hard on the teenager?

Could she find a way to deal with Nicki, find a means of both showing the teen she was loved *and* bridging the gap between brother and sister?

He had made strides in opening up with the girls, but would this event, which Vivi felt certain Nicki had learned from, undo the progress they had made?

Vivi made a noise deep in her chest, trying to decide.

Like a girl plucking petals off a flower, she went back and forth. Tell him, don't tell him.

But the question got more immediate a few seconds later when Max himself pulled up to the little house.

All too soon she was faced with decisions, and as much as she didn't want to admit it, she knew this was about more than Nicki sneaking out. It was about this precarious world Vivi had been trying to build for herself. She had been trying to live a regular life and shed her old facade completely.

But was it ever truly possible to erase who she had always been? Had she been kidding herself these last few weeks with the new, improved Vivi?

She didn't have answers, about Nicki or herself. But she couldn't put off facing Max.

Standing as still and as calm as she could manage, Vivi stared at the door. He didn't knock. He simply pushed inside, stopping at the sight of her.

He stood there for a second before a smile pulled at his lips. "Hello, honey," he said, his blue eyes glittering with pleasure. "I'm home."

For half a second a sense of fluttering relief washed through her, and she wanted to laugh. But she pushed the feeling away. "Funny," she stated.

Closing the door behind him, he tossed his keys on the windowsill. "What? No cartwheels that I'm here? Not even a kiss hello?"

"Sorry, hello." Though she didn't dare kiss him. "I was just leaving." Did she really have to face him now? Why not wait until morning, when she could look at everything with a clear eye?

She reached for her purse and keys, but Max stopped her. His smile evaporated in the dimly lit room, and she felt a surge of concern.

"What do you keep running from, Vivienne?"

He looked as serious as she had ever seen him.

"I knew I'd find you here, and we need to talk," he said.

"Talk?" She grimaced. "What about?"

"You've been avoiding me."

Ah, that. Yet another topic Vivi didn't want to discuss. She wasn't interested in admitting that things had changed between them, had become more intense.

She had always been deeply attracted to him. But the night he gave her a bath, she had let down her guard. Since then, whenever she closed her eyes, it was as if she was an outsider looking on, watching as the washcloth slid down her spine. And every minute of it had been simply to care for her, all to rinse the dirt and the aches and the pain away. He had wanted nothing more than to cherish her.

Now every time she saw him she felt awkward. She could deal with the whole no-strings-attached sex thing. But the idea of touching and caring left her off balance.

"I have not been avoiding you," she lied, her scoff echoing against the empty walls. "Now that I'm a working woman and all, I'm busy."

His expression slowly turned heated, his blue eyes intense. "I've missed you," he said, his voice rumbling through the room as he took a step closer.

Her heart lurched, but she ruthlessly squelched it. "Missed me? You can't miss me. I'm . . . I'm the nanny, remember? You don't miss the nanny."

"Why not?"

"Because." Panic started to rise. "Besides, I have more important things on my mind."

Max's gaze bored into her. "Tell me what's wrong and I'll fix it."

Her mouth fell open. "Haven't you understood anything about what I am trying to do in my life? I'm the one who is going to fix it. Remember?"

He didn't look all that contrite. Instead he looked extra arrogant and really, really sexy, before he began taking in what she'd done to the house.

"It certainly doesn't look like your problem is here. You've made an amazing change in the place." He nodded. "My hat goes off to you. I hope Andy paid you well."

That got a reluctant smile out of her. "Yeah, he did. With a bonus too."

Max raised a brow. "Really? Andy is as tightfisted with money as anyone I know. You must have impressed him."

At the time she had thought so. But now she wasn't so sure. All she had done was her job. Had he given her a bonus because of the work she had done, or because she was Vivi Stansfield—with or without money attached to her name?

It was ridiculous—she knew it. But it was hard to trust in anything just then. Herself or what she believed others thought of her.

After her run-in with Nicki, thoughts and doubts and questions ran through her head, all of which she didn't know how to answer. Was she being silly or was she being realistic?

Max surprised her when he came up behind her and pulled her close. Like she had no will of her own, her eyes closed at the feel of his fingers on her body. As always when he touched her, she felt the sharp edges of worry and panic fade from her mind.

When he turned her around to face him, taking her fingers, tracing the delicate fan of bones in the back of her hand, she told herself to push away. But how could it be so wrong to let herself forget for just a while? She'd been working hard, relentlessly making everything pull together. She had dealt with Max's house, cleaned up this place, gotten the girls everywhere they needed to be. And in that second, she wanted to savor what she had believed was a true success. She wanted to erase any doubts that had surfaced.

"You're cold," he whispered.

She was, and when he pulled her inside the warmth of his shearling jacket, she went willingly, Nicki and caring and practical thoughts melting like ice against sun and stones.

The coat nearly swallowed her as she molded her body to his. She could feel his heart, feel its reassuring beat. He kissed the top of her head, his hands running down her spine to her hips. Her fingers curled into his shirtfront when he cupped her, lifting her up to her toes. And he kissed her. Long and leisurely, as if they had all the time in the world.

"You like that, don't you?" he stated with the confidence of a man who knew how to pleasure a woman.

"I hate it," she responded, leaning closer.

Max chuckled, lifting her with ease, curling her legs around his waist. "I know you do," he whispered.

Then his mouth captured hers, a kiss that quickly turned into a demand.

He took the few steps to the wall, pressing her against it as their lips slanted together. They held on tight, clutching each other, touching and tasting.

"I've been dreaming of this," he groaned against her. "Night after night."

The words became a ragged oath as his lips skimmed

down to her neck. He nipped her skin, sucking until he let her down to stand on her own feet. The minute he stepped away she felt cold, though not for long. He ripped off his coat and laid it on the floor. In seconds, he guided her down onto the thick shearling and leather, before his powerful body came over hers, his expression austere, intense. Commanding.

"I want to make love to you," he said.

A shiver of anticipation ran through her and she wrapped her arms around his neck. She relished the feel of his lips on her, his hand coming to her breast.

His thumb grazed her nipple, bringing it to a tight bud beneath the sweater. "And you want to make love to me," he added with a primal arrogance.

Her mind soared and she felt yearning pulse through her. She also felt power mix with anticipation, and she looked him boldly in the eye.

"I take it we're moving on to Lesson Three?" she said with a crooked smile.

But she didn't get a smile in response. His beautifully etched face darkened, his gaze growing intense.

"No, Vivienne. No more lessons. This is real."

Her heart slammed against her chest. "Come on, Max, don't be so serious."

But that only made his expression darken even more, his large hands brushing her hair from her face.

"I am serious. No more games. No more pretend. I want you, Vivienne."

It was the gravity of his tone that seeped into her mind.

"I want to take care of you," he added into the silence, his eyes boring into hers. "I want you to belong to me."

He hesitated for one long second as her world turned upside down, then added, "I want to belong to you."

Thoughts froze in her head, her heart seeming to go still in her chest. She couldn't think, couldn't breathe. "What?"

"We are meant to be together. This"—he gestured to their bodies twined together—"you and me, is about more than lessons and forgetting. It's time we both faced it."

With those words, her mind broke free. "No!" She jerked away, pushing so fiercely, so suddenly, that surprise gained her release. When he rolled off her, she leaped up from the floor, her thoughts wild and raging.

"Vivienne—"

"No! I don't want to hear any more. This is craziness."

Max got to his feet. "It's not crazy, it's the truth, and you know it."

She gaped at him. "People don't *belong* to each other."

"You know what I mean."

"No! I don't have the foggiest idea what you mean. How can you go from hating that you want me—which, thank you very much, you have made abundantly clear—to now wanting to . . . to . . . belong to me!"

She started to pace, acutely aware that Max stood very still.

"True," he said, "I've resisted my attraction to you—"

"But now you've decided to go with it?"

She heard the sarcasm, knew she resorted to it when she felt panicked or trapped.

He took a step toward her, but she warded him off with her hand. "No!"

"Vivienne, I hated the loss of control you made me feel." His features took on a strength and power that went beyond the ruthless control he always maintained. "But I've realized that the only thing that is weak is if I refuse to admit that I love you."

Air rushed into her lungs. He loved her? This dominating man loved her?

Fiercely, she slapped her hands over her ears, tears burning. "No, no, no! No love!" She found her purse and rummaged frantically around in it until she located her keys. She could feel Max behind her, staring at her in shock.

"This was never about love," she stated. "This was about sex, and fun, and a way to forget until I could find my way out of the mess I was in."

"I realize it might have started out that way—"

"Might?"

"But you can't get around the fact that things have changed."

She pivoted and looked him in the eye. "Maybe you can't get around it, but I can. Love me if you have to, but I'm not interested in loving you back."

Yanking on her coat, she started for the door. But Max caught her arm, forcing her to look at him. "You can't just walk out and expect this to go away."

She closed her eyes, wondering how she had come to this point. "Why can't we just forget this happened?" she whispered desperately. Her gaze flickered to his face, and she offered him a feebly hopeful smile. "We'll ignore the L word. Pretend that everything is back to normal—you and me at each other's throats. It'll be great."

He didn't smile. His expression was grim. "Why can't you accept what's happened between us?"

She nearly resorted to some flip remark, but she swallowed it back. Emotion welled up, and burst inside her. The tears slipped over, streaking down her cheeks. "Because I'm not so good in the love department."

Now he looked mad. "Stop joking for just one second," he ground out.

"I'm not!" She turned away. "Everyone I have ever loved leaves me."

"Like who?"

She blinked. "Who?"

"Hell, have there been more than Grady?"

She whirled back to him, relishing the anger that surged up. "No, there wasn't anyone before Grady. And Grady isn't the point. He never was the point. I could afford to marry Grady because I didn't love him."

She cut herself off. She couldn't believe she had admitted it to him—and to herself.

"What are you talking about, Vivienne?"

But she was in too deep to stop now. "I'm different from everyone. I don't fit in."

"Vivienne—"

"Look at me! Remember all those zillions of friends I told you about? I made them up. I don't have any friends. What normal person doesn't have friends?"

"That doesn't make you bad. That makes you lonely."

"I don't know how to open up. I don't know how to love people back." She hesitated, then plunged ahead. "I never loved Grady, and that way he couldn't break my heart. Bruise my pride? Sure. But I can live with a bit of battered self-esteem. That was safe. He was safe."

She could tell Max didn't understand, and suddenly she wanted him to. "Don't you see, you aren't safe. You want and need and claim. Just like my father. You want those tangible signs of success—the house, the car, the perfect princess. Just like my father. And my father breaks my heart over and over again. I'm not interested in falling in love, especially with a man who's just like him."

"I am not your father," Max stated coldly. "I think that's just an excuse because you're afraid of a serious, mature relationship."

She stared at him, her chest aching, her mind confused and scared. Was he right? she wondered. Was she afraid?

Shaking the thought away, she focused. She wasn't afraid. She had survived years of dealing with people and their varied forms of loving her. She knew the ropes, understood what it meant. Loving on their terms. And she wasn't going to do it again with this man who would demand more than she knew how to give.

"Fine. Think what you want, Max. But the fact is I don't love you."

She felt his anger leap up and burn through the room, his jaw tight, his hands fisted at his sides as he stared at her. The fine hairs on her arms rose when she saw the wildness in his blue eyes. A streak of terror reared, but she held it at bay. She was not afraid of his fierceness.

"No matter what you want to believe," she continued ruthlessly, "the only interest I have in you is sex. And I've never given you any reason to believe otherwise."

She saw the wildness turn to a warrior's fury, and her heart swelled into her throat. But she didn't run like she wanted to, or say another word of explanation or apology. She took her purse with as much calm as she could muster, then turned on her heel and strode out of the house.

Chapter Twenty-six

Max listened to the sound of Vivienne's heels moving carefully down the steps, then suddenly hurrying before she slammed herself into the car.

He didn't move as something raced through him. Fury? The need to erase her from his life? He didn't know. The only thing he knew for sure was that this wasn't the end of this conversation.

He pounded out the front door, but Vivienne had already sped down the alleyway and onto the street. Leaping into the Mercedes, he threw it in gear and roared after her into the dark night.

He knew the minute she realized he was behind her. The Olds surged forward until they were careening through the nearly deserted midnight streets, up and down the undulating hills toward the West side. He cursed when she came to Shadow Mountain, her taillights barely lighting up the darkness as she screeched around the corner.

"Hands at ten and two, my ass," he muttered, taking the corner with an expert ease.

Minutes later, she turned right onto Thunderbird, then flew up the long expanse that sliced the mountain, like she was flying into the black, midnight sky. Blood ticked like a time bomb through his veins as he pursued her. Anger pushed him on. Anger and irritation and a strange stinging frustration that this woman made everything so difficult. So complicated. And when she wheeled into his driveway, stopping in the circle rather than heading to the garage out back, Max slammed to a halt behind her.

They both emerged into the quiet darkness, enraged.

"You're a maniac!" he bellowed, his voice echoing in the night.

"You're one to talk!" she bellowed back. "You were chasing me!"

"I was following you—a big difference. And I was only driving like that to keep up. Hell, you could have been killed."

"Ha! Not in this baby," she shot back, banging the Olds's trunk.

Max bit back a curse. "All I wanted to do was talk to you like an adult—"

"Ah, but of course I'm not an adult. Is that what you're going to say? Not mature enough? Not boring enough for you?"

Aggravation ticked through him. "Boring and mature aren't interchangeable adjectives."

"They are in you!"

She stormed into the house. Max counted to ten, then noticed the neighbor peering out the window.

"What are you looking at?" he demanded.

Mrs. White's eyes went wide before she leaped back, the curtain fluttering closed.

Max cursed at himself, muttering, "She's turning me into a lunatic."

But that didn't stop him from charging into the house. "Vivienne!"

Her name shattered like glass through the foyer, and when he slammed the door shut he saw her on the stairs. She stood there with her hands on her hips.

"I'm done talking," she said defiantly.

"Too bad. I'm not."

He felt a ruthless determination sizzle through him. And it didn't fade at the alarm he saw come into her eyes. Her defiance evaporated. She whirled around and fled. But he caught her before she made it to the top.

In one leap, he grabbed her ankle. She caught herself on the banister.

"We are not done, Vivienne," Max said with feral precision.

Her breathing was harsh. "You know, Max, this has gotten out of hand."

He could tell she fought for calm. She even managed some sort of a smile.

"We're adults," she added, "and believe it or not, I do have the ability to be mature—ultra-mature even. And ultra-mature people would go to sleep, then rethink this whole situation in the morning. So just let go of my leg like a good Neanderthal, and I'll head upstairs to bed. I'm really exhausted, and it's late."

"Liar," he ground out.

Her head tilted and he saw wryness surge in her eyes. "Maybe it's not late to you," she offered, her smile tight, "but I'm more the in-bed-at-ten type."

"I'm not talking about the time, and you know it."

"That's right." She slapped her palm against her forehead. "I forgot. I'm a mind reader."

He felt the growl rumble deep in his chest. Exhaling,

Max held her relentlessly, until she couldn't do anything but sit down on the stairs, her ankle still in his hand. He studied her, could see a wealth of emotion racing across her face like clouds in a stormy sky, her pulse fluttering in her neck.

"I understand that this is hard for you," he began, willing himself to find the calm he was used to.

Her brow furrowed, as if she wasn't sure what to make of this new tone. She opened her mouth and no doubt would have made some smart quip, but he pressed his fingers to her lips.

"Hear me out. Just this once, don't protect yourself with sarcasm and humor."

Breath rushed out of her lungs, and she looked truly vulnerable, as if he had stripped her of an arsenal she depended on.

"I'm not trying to hurt you, Vivienne." He was going to force a conversation if it killed him. "I am not like your father. I won't leave you, and I would never hurt you. But I don't believe for a second that all you want from me is sex. Whether you want to face it or not, there is more going on between us than that."

It was as if a shade slipped down over her eyes, the pale gray going dark.

Unable to help himself, he pulled her closer, forcing her down a step, as if he was reeling her in with his patience and care. "Yes, you want sex. I understand that. You're twenty-six and have never had a decent, caring relationship with a man. You think losing yourself for a few minutes in orgasm and holding close is all there is. I think it's all you know how to deal with. The rest, anything deeper, scares you."

She tried to jerk away, but he only pulled her down another step.

"Stop," she pleaded.

"Not until you hear me out."

Another step closer.

"You want more, Vivienne. I can see it in your eyes, and I can see it in everything you do when you let your defenses down and you aren't so busy keeping everyone at arm's length."

He saw her throat work, saw that she was holding back the very emotion he was talking about.

"Let go, Vivienne. Let yourself admit that you want more, that you need more."

He pulled her to where he stood braced against the banister, his body looming over hers. Unable to help himself, he let go of her ankle and leaned down to kiss the delicate bone above each of her eyes. He felt her body tremble at the touch.

"No," she pleaded.

"I fill you, Vivienne. I fill your soul, just as tonight I am going to fill your body. I am going to spread your legs and make you come as I show you that we are meant to be together."

Her eyes shone with tears. He wanted to be gentle, wanted to prove to her that he meant what he said. She stared up at him, and he was certain that he saw a flicker of belief—or hope. But the minute he pulled back, she leaped up and ran.

So that's the way it would be. She would fight him. She refused to believe. She would play games to make him think she was willing to listen, then run.

Max was tired of games, and with a fighter's roar he charged after her.

She fled up the remaining stairs and had nearly made it to her bedroom when he caught her. His weight crashed her against the wall, his chest to her back, her cheek pressed to the fine paisley paper, her arms spread like a criminal being frisked.

"You will hear me out," he demanded, his breathing harsh, the smell of her perfume mixing with his driving lust.

She tried to push away, but her bottom only managed to cradle his cock. Instantly he hardened. Like a warrior needing possession, he pressed against her. He knew the moment she understood her mistake.

"Do you feel that?" he demanded. "Do you feel how much I want you?"

She held herself very still. He only pressed into her again. Holding her captive with his body, he reached around and cupped her sex with his hand. With infinite care, he captured her to him.

Her breath shuddered and he could feel the fire light inside her.

"You want me, too," he whispered gently.

He turned her to face him. "Yes, there is desire and sex and lust between us. But it's more. You're drawn to me," he stated, his voice ragged. "Just as I'm drawn to you."

Tears spilled down her cheeks. She was caught, lost and drowning in his love—he could feel it. But he had to believe that his love was also her anchor. Because he had come to admit that she was that and more to him.

He realized in some deep recess of his mind that he tasted tears—his or hers, he was no longer certain. He felt the burn in his eyes, the tightness in his chest. "I love you, Vivienne, as I have never loved anyone in my life. Stop pushing me away."

Her cry turned aching, and with force, she broke free. But instead of running, she threw her arms around his neck, and their mouths slanted together in hunger.

"I hate you," she cried into him.

"I love you," he told her fiercely, his hands trailing down her body to cup her hips, then lift her up.

"You're arrogant," she accused, kissing his eyelids.

"You're beautiful."

He kissed her neck, her head falling back. Ripping her white shirt free, he dipped his mouth to her breasts.

"You think you know what's best for everyone," she stated, her voice a rasp of sound.

"I only know that we're meant to be together."

He wrapped her legs around his waist as they crashed into her room, the door banging back on its hinges as Max carried her inside, their lips ravenous, exploring, never parting. They lurched and stumbled their way to her bed. He laid her down, looking so tiny and delicate against the thick comforters as he stood before her, ripping at his clothes impatiently, discarding them on the floor.

He saw her take him in, saw the awe and a little fear. He was big, he knew that, and he'd have to be careful. But he wanted her, needed her. And he would make love to her tonight.

Silvery winter light drifted in through the windows as he summoned the barely held patience he needed to peel her clothes away, carefully, reverently, piece by piece, before he came down on top of her, skin to skin.

Sliding his thigh between hers, he captured her hands above her head. He felt the intensity and the madness of a need he was willing to give in to.

He saw a matching intensity in her eyes, but a wariness as well. The walls she had built around herself were precarious and crumbling, but they were still there.

"Let me into your life," he said, as he bent his head to her breast.

He laved first one nipple, then the next, her back arching. "Yes," he murmured. "I love your passion."

She whimpered and moved against him, his thigh riding higher until he could feel the tight curls at her sex brush against his leg. Her body twisted as he kissed a path down her nakedness. He kissed and licked, biting, and when he let go of her hands, her fingers curled into the bedspread.

Somehow a wildness let loose, as if she had given in completely. Suddenly, she sought and demanded. She let him cherish her body, but then she'd had enough. She jerked free, coming up, then pushing him down on the mattress. With an abandon he had only guessed at, she learned his body, kissing as he had, licking and biting, taking his nipple in her mouth, his own back arching, his hands fisting in the covers.

His body screamed for release, but he forced control. Forced himself to let her do as she wanted.

She straddled his body, then reached down and cupped him, gently pushing him high. Every muscle and tendon in his body strained against release. Her palms slid up the hard length of him to his abdomen, then higher, the hot sweet lips of her sex gliding along his shaft, touching his swollen head. In seconds, knowing that if he didn't sink inside her he'd spill himself like a schoolboy, he whipped her over, coming down between her thighs.

She looked up at him as he reared over her, and only then he saw her tears mixing with the wildness.

His heart went still. He wanted to close his eyes and lose himself. But he held himself back. "What is it, Vivienne? Am I wrong? Do you truly not want this?"

The words choked him. But if he was mistaken . . .

His breath caught, making him feel weak and vulnerable as he hadn't since he was ten years old and staring at Vivienne, even then wanting so badly to touch her, to hold her, to keep her forever, that he thought he might break.

With shaking hands, she touched his lips. "Can you really love me just for me?"

The words shuddered through him. "I'll love you forever, Vivienne. I always have."

He thought he saw a flash of darkness flare in her eyes, but then she pulled him to her. "Then show me, Max."

The words whispered along every nerve ending. He wanted to thrust hard and deep, but he knew he had to prepare her. Despite her insistence that she was experienced, he understood that she was innocent of true lovemaking.

Moving beside her, he forced her to lie flat. "Shhh," he murmured when she tried to curl close. He gentled her with his palm, sliding his hand low until he parted the soft folds, finding the tight nub, circling. Then he slipped his finger deep, ensuring that she was wet and ready for him.

Her mouth fell open when he widened her knees, pulling them up, slipping his forearm between her thighs, caressing her with the calloused tips of two fingers. Her body seemed to hum with desire.

"Max?" she whispered, looking at him, not understanding the intensity of her body's need.

"I won't hurt you, sweetheart."

He could see that she trusted him, letting him touch her as he would, until she couldn't take it any more.

"I want you inside me," she gasped.

And he was lost.

He came over her, sinking deep with a primal thrust and a soul-shattering roar. She was tight, and she cried out. His heart thundered and his body throbbed with the need to pound hard. But he had to go slow.

He started to pull away so he could ease their bodies together more slowly. She looked at him as if he had betrayed her.

"Don't treat me like I'm fragile. I won't break."

Like a china doll behind glass.

In some recess of his mind he understood. And when she frantically moved against him, words were lost as he groaned and he forgot.

Their bodies came together with spiraling intensity. It seemed she tried to melt into him, seeking and wanting, admitting the need he had confronted her with.

They held each other, sensation shivering through them as he thrust inside her, his back arching, her hands clutching his arms. He couldn't look away from her, and their gazes locked until her eyes fluttered closed, her lips parting, and he could feel her body shatter. Then, only then, did he bury his face in her hair and find his release.

He clutched her to him, his body on fire with sensation, each of them panting. Seconds ticked by before their breathing started to settle.

Afterward, they lay together without saying a word. They remained that way until their hearts settled, then Max lifted up on his elbow.

He didn't say a word, just looked at her, and she clearly grew uncomfortable. A shyness that he wouldn't have guessed at surfaced, and she turned her head away from him.

"No," he whispered. "Don't turn away from me ever again. We are together forever." He kissed her brow. "I'll never hurt you, Vivienne. Trust me."

Then he pulled her into his arms and felt the moment she relaxed against him and was asleep.

My Wedding Diary

THE DAY YOU HAVE BEEN WAITING FOR

I love Max! There, I admit it! And he loves me!

It hardly seems possible that he just came into my life two months ago, when I feel like I've known him forever. But because of that, it makes it easier, makes it feel safe to give him my heart.

Chapter Twenty-seven

The following morning, Vivi stood in the drive of Number 15 Pinehurst, after returning from the grocery store, a carefree, girlish smile pulling at her lips. She huddled against the cold in an oversized, navy blue bulky sweater she had found in Max's drawer and had put on over leftover burgundy leggings and a pair of Keds.

She hugged the bag of groceries tight as she looked at the house, the perfect architecture, the perfect lot, on the perfect street. Despite its undeniable beauty, the perfection had always bothered her. But for the first time she noticed the imperfect initials carved into a square of cement between the drive and the front walk. All eight of the Landry children had signed the cement, including Max, his initials looming over the others'. So like the man.

She felt giddy at the thought that he loved her. Her. Vivi Stansfield. And he loved her just . . . well . . . because he did! Not because she was Jennings Stansfield's daughter. Not because she would look great on his arm.

Without a worry for who saw her, she did a little dance as she hurried into the house, wanting to escape the December cold.

That morning, Max had kissed her awake. For one glittering space of time her world had consisted of nothing more than Max. She hated that he'd had to make a quick day trip to Ruidoso to view a parcel of land. But he promised he'd be back that evening for the family dinner he had arranged.

Now, hours later, the feeling of joy and happiness was still there, only mitigated by the old habit—the very bad habit—of being afraid to believe he could really care for her. And that made her mad. She refused to be someone who couldn't let go of the past. So what if her father had wanted a daughter to parade around, a showpiece for the press? Last night Max had said that he truly loved her.

She would dive in headfirst, refusing to let her fear of being vulnerable to someone hold her back. She would open her heart to Max.

Using her key, Vivi entered the quiet house. Pat must not have dropped the girls off yet. She headed for the kitchen, but a noise stopped her.

Max!

Setting the groceries down, thrilled he had already returned, she headed for his office.

The faint sound of voices drifted toward her as she made her way down the hall, then she froze when she came to the door. Nicki pranced around wearing Vivi's tiara and reading aloud from Vivi's wedding diary.

"Nicki, don't," Lila pleaded, crying. "Vivi's going to be home any minute."

"So what?"

"She'll get mad."

"Like I care. I hope she does, and then maybe she'd finally get the message that she's not wanted here. Look at this. She says I'm angry and afraid."

"But I like her."

"Too bad."

"Max likes her, too."

That stopped Nicki and she snorted. "Look at this one," she said, turning the page. "*I love Max! And he loves me!* Yeah, right. She makes him crazy but I bet he wants to screw her."

"Nicki!" Lila gaped.

"Don't be a baby. Just look at all these pictures he has of her. You know Max. Vivi's just one more notch in his belt, a conquest—just like the awards, the money, this house. Mark my words, the minute he screws her, he'll move on. He never dates any woman for long."

Confused, her stomach churning, Vivi tried to understand. She saw an old accordion file sitting on the floor, and just beyond, she could make out old newsprint spread out on the floor. At first she thought they were the photographs and newspaper pictures she had found at their father's house.

Forgetting the girls, Vivi stepped into the room. She ignored the gasps. She didn't glance at either Nicki or Lila as she made her way across the thick, hand-knotted rug.

"Don't look!" Lila cried out, racing to her.

But it was too late. Vivi stared down at the floor, taking in newspaper photos laid out like a child's game of Concentration. A lifetime of photos with captions.

Princess in Pink.

Daddy's Girl Shops at Opening of Alice's Treasure Trove.

But the two that snagged her attention were of the photo of her cutting the ceremonial ribbon at her father's new plant. Then of her, again, dancing with her father at the debutante ball. Each with the same caption, like an echo of who the world thought she was.

A Texan King with His Pampered Princess.

Vivi turned to the girls. "Where did you get these?" she asked, the sound of blood pounding in her ears.

Nicki looked half-scared, half-belligerent. It was Lila who answered. "They're Max's. I guess he's been collecting them for a long time. It's a total compliment though, don't you think?"

Vivi felt as if she couldn't take a deep enough breath as she remembered the day she had walked into his office at MBL Holdings. She had thought for a moment that he had recognized her. Then it was gone. What had he said?

"No, we've never met."

Vivi gave a small strangled sound. No, they hadn't met. But he had known who she was. He had actively pursued her. He had taken her to see that first house, then had met her at the second. Max Landry, one of the most important men in town, had dropped everything to take her to see some insignificant property.

Like she were drifting through water, she reached down and picked up the article on the Stansfield plant opening with its faded photo of her helping her father cut the ribbon, the jewels in her tiara catching the sun.

Yes, Max wanted her—but he had wanted the princess all along.

"I would never hurt you."

She ripped the clipping in half. "Liar," she whispered into the room.

She thought Max had been drawn to her—just her— as if he had seen something inside her, seen something deeper than what the newspaper photos had shown of her over a lifetime. She had believed he saw beneath the facade. But he hadn't seen anything deeper.

She felt used and manipulated. And in that second the intensity she had felt for Max since the second she saw him shifted to something different, something darker, more complicated. She had let down her guard, had fallen for him. He had made her believe.

"Vivi," Lila said, her tiny voice choked. "Please don't be mad."

Nicki still said nothing, though every ounce of belligerence had fled. The girl snapped the diary shut, then pulled the tiara from her head, her long dark hair catching before fluttering like wings when it finally tugged free.

Carefully, she set the book and crown on the desk.

Vivi stared at her father's gift that she reluctantly cherished and the diary filled with her hopes, fears, and dreams. But they were empty dreams, as was clearly represented by the fact that she had continued to write in a book called *My Wedding Diary* even after her engagement was broken.

Without looking at either of the girls, Vivi took the tiara and diary and headed upstairs to her bedroom. Lila hurried after her. Even Nicki followed, then hovered in the doorway.

With deliberate actions, Vivi pulled out her clothes, and stuffed them in green trash bags, because she had sold all her luggage.

"Vivi! What are you doing?" Lila asked.

Vivi took everything that was important, everything that she would need. She'd send for the rest. The last thing she included was the damned tiara and diary, as if she could do nothing else.

After she had what she needed, she pulled her cell phone out of her purse, then dialed.

"Pat, this is Vivi. I need you to come and pick up the girls."

"But—"

Vivi hung up. For a second she closed her eyes against the sound of Lila's sobs. In some recess of her mind, Vivi knew she was running—running from Max, from these girls' emotions that she didn't know how to handle, and from herself.

Or was she running to something? Running to the self that she had just begun to find before she opened her heart and admitted that she loved Max?

Her eyes popped open, and she tried to pull those thoughts to the surface, to make sense of them. She walked into the bathroom, shut the door, and leaned back against it. But then her cell phone rang. Without thinking, she answered.

"Vivi? Is that you, love?"

"Mother?" she breathed.

"Vivi! My poor broken dove, I've heard what a mess your father has made of things."

"Mother" was all she could say, her heart surging and breaking all at once.

"Yes, dear, I'm here, at the Camino Real hotel. You must come right away."

And when Pat showed up, frantic and not understanding, Vivi loaded her things in the dark green Olds and rumbled off beneath the icy gray sky.

Max paced back and forth in the kitchen. "I don't understand," he said.

Lila and Nicki sat at the table, not saying a word.

It was late, and he had hurried back from Ruidoso for dinner with the family. And to see Vivienne.

He picked up the cordless phone and dialed her cell number. But she didn't answer. After her voice mail came on, he spoke. "Vivienne, where are you? What happened?" He glanced at the girls, then walked out of the kitchen and into the laundry room and closed the door. With a sigh, he leaned back against the dryer. "Talk to me, Vivienne. Call me. Please."

After a long second, he pressed the OFF button. He stared at the wall, then noticed a dry board with multi-colored pens. It was a schedule, he realized, color coordinated for the types of clothes she needed to wash on what day. There were piles already ready—whites in a white basket, colors in a pink basket, and towels piled in another made of green woven plastic. She had taken the laundry room and turned it into an organized machine. Just like the house. Lists everywhere, making sure she didn't fall down on the job.

He nearly smiled, then he remembered she was gone.

Something must have happened for her to leave. And he damn well wasn't going to sit around hoping to find out what it was. He would find her.

Banging out of the house, he drove to every place he could think she might have conceivably gone, including the property on University. A burn started low, threatening to consume him, as he all but tore the town apart looking for her. But there was no sign.

After long, sleepless hours, the next day was no better. His brothers and sisters had come and gone from the house last night. First thing in the morning, he left without eating or reading the paper, and didn't even say a word to the girls. He drove to Andy's office at the bank.

"Yes, Max, I've talked to her, but really, I don't know where she is."

Before Max knew it he had the man pinned back in his fine leather chair.

"Max," Andy gasped. "I swear, she called but she wouldn't leave a number."

He knew then that she was safe, that she hadn't been hurt or lay somewhere wounded. But she didn't want to be found. What did he feel? Upset? Fury?

A simple slow-burning rage.

Christmas was right around the corner. What a fool to have believed that he would enjoy this holiday with Vivienne. When he pulled into the drive he saw Pat's car. She stood in the kitchen with the girls.

"Did you find her?" she asked Max the minute he walked in the door.

"No." His jaw ticked.

"What did you do to her?" she demanded. "Why did she run out of here like that?"

Before he could answer, Chris came in from the side drive. "Is she back?"

"No," Pat stated.

Chris banged his hands together to warm them. "What the hell did you do, Max?"

"Why does everyone assume I did something?" he shot back. "I didn't do anything."

But was that true? he wondered. Had he pushed her too far by making her admit that she needed him? When faced with something she didn't want to deal with, had she run? That was what worried him the most—that she had run away from him. But why?

"We know you, Max, and we've seen how demanding you are," Pat explained. "Of everyone, including Vivi."

Max scowled. "I don't believe it."

Chris agreed with Pat. Then Nicki burst out in tears. "She's gone because I ran her off!"

The room went silent. Max's brow furrowed. "What are you talking about?"

"It's my fault."

Lila started to whimper.

"Will someone tell me what happened?" Max demanded.

It was Lila who spoke up. "She . . . found all the pictures and stuff you have of her."

A moment passed before understanding came clear. A chill slid down his spine, and he felt all eyes on him. "What pictures?" he asked carefully.

"The ones in your brown file. Those old newspaper articles and photos you keep in your office."

He felt as if someone had put a left hook into his gut. "She *found* those?"

Lila cringed. Nicki started to cry more.

"I did it on purpose," Nicki suddenly blurted. "I was mad at her—even though all she wanted to do was help. We were in your office and she walked in." She squeezed her eyes closed. "I was making fun of her."

Max stood perfectly still as Nicki hurtled on, words spilling out of her as she told him about going to the party despite his command that she couldn't go. She told him about the fake breasts, about Brandon in the back of the car, and about Vivi coming to get her. The horrible things Nicki had said.

"One minute I would like her, then the next I just hated her so much," she whispered. "It was like everyone thought she was so great, and I couldn't do anything right."

Max banged his fist on the counter. "Why the hell were you going through my things?"

But just as suddenly he stopped himself. He remembered the photos his father had kept of him. He had felt violated. As if someone had been looking over his shoulder all those years without him even knowing it.

That was exactly what he had done to Vivienne, only worse because he hadn't even known her. He stood there furious at Nicki when he should be furious only at himself. All Nicki wanted was a way to find herself, to have him see her, just as Vivienne had said. And if she had to get in trouble to do it, so be it.

With his mind reeling with brutal understanding, he leaned forward and took Nicki's arms. He felt sick when she flinched. "Nick, I'm sorry. You and I are going to talk about you sneaking out and about all you've been dealing with. Just as soon as I find Vivienne."

Nicki's lower lip trembled. "But you don't know where she is."

Chris flipped open the newspaper. "I think I do. I saw something this morning." He paged through, then whistled. "Here it is."

Then he started to read, each word making Max's brain chill.

" 'Jennings Stansfield Returns to His Kingdom,' " Chris read the headline. " 'The errant Jennings Stansfield has returned to town, staying in style at the Camino Real after he was evicted from his former residence. Isabelle Stansfield has returned as well, but don't expect the former husband and wife to reconcile. Jennings is sporting a new woman on his arm—the very wealthy and very young Maybelle Masters, the coffee heiress from Boca Raton, Florida.' "

Chris looked up. "You've got to be kidding me!" he said, before continuing. " 'Could Ms. Masters be responsible for the sudden relief of Jennings's debts? And is it possible that El Paso will see a Christmas bride after all—with Jennings at the altar and his precious daughter waiting in the wings another year?' " The younger Landry shook his head. "Vivi must be devastated. What do you think, Max?"

But when Chris glanced up, Max was gone, the only sound coming from the front door slamming, then the Mercedes screeching down the drive.

Chapter Twenty-eight

The stormy sky threatened as Max wheeled up to the hotel. In some recess of his mind he realized it was going to snow. But he only leaped out, tossed the keys to the valet, and headed inside without waiting for a ticket.

At the front desk it was all he could do not to grab the clerk by the lapels and drag him across the counter when he said he had no Jennings Stansfield listed.

"Though I do have an Isabelle Stansfield," the man squeaked.

"Give me the room number."

"Oh, no, sir, I couldn't do that. Though I can ring her."

Which would no doubt get him nowhere. But he didn't see much of a choice. If he had to, he'd sit in the lobby as long as it took for Vivienne to come downstairs, because he was certain this was where she had fled.

The clerk picked up the phone and dialed. "Ah, yes, I have a Mr.—" The clerk looked expectantly across the counter.

"Landry."

"A Mr. Landry." He paused. "Yes . . . yes." He glanced at Max. "Of course, I understand."

He hung up the phone, his expression grim. "She'll see you. Room 1112."

Relief shot through Max. He hurried to the bank of elevators, then was expelled into the long carpeted hall on the eleventh floor. He had to force himself to knock instead of pound on the door.

An older woman answered, her gray hair pulled up in a loose bun, her face gently lined and tan, her clothes like gauze, flowing about her like drapery in the wind.

"So you are Maxwell," Isabelle said grandly, taking his hand and pulling him into the room.

Once inside, he saw that she had a suite. His mind cemented as he wondered what the hell was going on.

"I see you've noticed the room." She floated past him, leading the way. "I imagine you are wondering why, if I can afford this, my daughter was working in your home as a domestic."

Max looked at her hard. "She was the nanny."

"Of course, of course. I'm sure there's a big difference. Regardless, Vivi shouldn't have been put in the position of getting any sort of job. It's her father's fault. Really, how was I supposed to know any of this was going on when I was halfway around the world? India's beautiful this time of year—that is if India ever can be considered beautiful, given the poverty. But what better place to find one's true spiritual core?"

"I take it you have money, then," he said without hesitation.

"Not exactly. I am dependent on alimony, since I was the only woman Jennings married who wasn't wealthy. But back then, he had money of his own and could afford to marry for love." She sighed dramatically. "We were a love match. But then the money ran out, and, well, somehow the love ran dry. Jennings has been replenishing his bank account with rich wives ever since. I really don't know what they see in him."

Max could hardly believe what he was hearing. "Does Vivienne know this?"

"Vivienne. You call her Vivienne. How powerful you sound. No wonder you give her such fits." She smiled at him. "She told me about the two of you."

He wanted to ask what she said, but held back. He would ask Vivienne what she felt, not her mother.

"Does Vivienne know about her father's financial situation?"

"She knows now, poor child. It's always distressing to have the wool pulled away from one's eyes. She actually believed in the man, believed he was an outrageous Texas king like the newspapers make him out to be. I tried to explain that she should think of this as yet another adventure in life. She seems only to think of it as having lived a lie." The woman waved the words away. "Her father isn't a bad man. Just a dreamer who found money in rich women. He could have been a whole lot worse. He has always found a way to pay for the things he wanted Vivi to have. And she's led a wonderful life. Skiing in the Alps, schooling in France."

"What about spending time with family?"

He saw the woman flinch. And suddenly the show was gone. Isabelle looked abashed.

"I love my daughter, I do. But not every woman is meant to give up her whole life to be a dutiful mother."

"You should have figured that out before you had a child."

Isabelle's chin rose, but then an inside door opened, and Max expected Vivienne to appear. Instead, he recognized Jennings Stansfield.

"Max Landry." The man's voice boomed through the room. He was larger than life, a misguided hero from a comic book story.

Max glanced back and forth between the two.

Isabelle rolled her eyes. "Don't look like that. The new, soon-to-be Mrs. Jennings Stansfield is in that room—and paying for all of this, I might add."

What kind of a family is this?

"She's a pretty thing," Jennings boasted. "Pretty—"

"And not terribly smart. Talk about stereotypes," Isabelle scoffed. "But who am I to complain?"

Jennings lit a cigar. "Sorry that my daughter has been such an imposition, Landry. I hated leaving her in the lurch that way."

Isabelle snorted. "You only hate that you didn't snag your newest wife sooner to save yourself the embarrassment. You're losing your touch, Jennings." She skewered her ex with a glare. "This time, however, Vivi will not forgive you."

But Jennings laughed confidently. "Of course my little princess will forgive me."

The memory of that debutante ball surfaced in Max's mind. He saw her beauty. He remembered the dance. And the newspaper photographs.

But then another image reared up. Of Jennings leaving, the night still young, and Vivienne standing at the window, thinking she was alone, pressing her hand to the glass.

"*Daddy*," he had heard her whisper.

Max understood that she had spent a lifetime forgiving this man in hopes that one day he would stay. She had learned the hard way that her mother never would. She had needed her father to be there—she had needed him to love her as more than an accessory.

But what Max realized now was that this man, perhaps even this family, had nothing to give other than the show. Love like a Hollywood facade. Nothing behind the fake front.

No wonder Vivienne didn't know how to love. Or how to trust that anyone she cared about wouldn't hurt her.

Max wanted to wring the man's neck. But he also cursed himself for not looking beyond his own insecurities and for not seeing Vivienne for who she truly was.

"Where is Vivienne?" he demanded.

"She doesn't want to see you," Jennings said.

Isabelle studied her ex-husband. After a second, she turned to Max. "I might not have been the ideal mother," she said, "but I can help her now." She wrote out an address. "This is where you'll find her."

The sky split open and it started to snow, a whirling, intense desert storm that would be gone by morning. When Max saw the old building on Texas Avenue, he didn't know what to think. What could Vivienne be doing in a place like this?

The stretch of road was commercial, hosting small businesses of a clearly unsuccessful sort. There was a paint store with a peeling veneer, and a bakery with hand stenciling on the glass that had faded years ago. It was like stepping back in time to the days before strip shopping centers or malls. MBL Holdings wouldn't touch a place like this.

Pulling over to the curb, he parked and went to the door. When he turned the knob, it was unlocked, a tiny overhead bell ringing when he pushed inside.

The place was old, tattered, and colder inside than it was outside. But there was evidence of someone cleaning it up. The smell of turpentine and soap stung his nose. Someone had been scrubbing, fixing the place, which assured him that Vivienne was indeed there.

"Just a minute," he heard her call out.

Holding a bucket of paint, she emerged from the back part of the building, dressed in coveralls and a heavy coat, wearing mittens with the fingers cut out, her hair pulled up in a ponytail. At the sight of him she stopped in her tracks. He was certain that her eyes went wide first with surprise and joy. Then they darkened, the flip sarcasm coming up like walls around her.

He had never been so glad to see anyone in his life. His heart opened up, the tight vise that had clamped around his chest since he found her gone easing just a bit. As always when he was near her, he felt desire shimmer through him.

"What are you doing here?" she demanded.

"Nicki told me about finding the diary."

Just that, and he was sure something flashed in her eyes. Not anger, but embarrassment.

"Ah, the infamous wedding diary, kept by a woman who isn't getting married. Did you read it, too?"

"No, and I never would. Nicki feels terrible."

Vivienne didn't look as if she believed him.

"She told me everything," he explained. "She told me she went to the party with the Bonner boy when she wasn't supposed to, then about how you picked her up. She also told me about how badly she acted toward you.

Thank you for being there for her." He hesitated. "And thank you for helping me see that I have to be there for her, too," he added truthfully, unable to keep the intense emotion he felt from his voice.

At the sound of it, her hard stance wavered, but she held firm. Barely. He was sure.

"I'm glad it all worked out."

She walked past him to a tarp she had laid out on the floor and set the bucket down. Then poured paint into a roller pan like a pro.

"Pink?" he asked.

"Do you have a problem with that?"

He realized he didn't. Vivienne was Vivienne, in all her enthusiasm and jangling bracelets. More than that, she was the woman he loved. "If anyone can pull off a pink room, you can."

She slanted him a suspicious gaze. "I'm doing the ceiling sky blue," she added defiantly. "With fluffy white clouds. The perfect setting for my new business."

"Business?" he asked.

She studied him for another endless second, then she pointed to a tiny box sitting on the floor. Leaning down, he opened it up.

"My first business card," she stated proudly, defiantly.

The minute he pulled a card from the box, his brows slammed together. " 'Pampered Princess,' " he read, glancing from it to her, unable to hide his confusion. "You're making a business out of being a pampered princess?"

Vivienne arched a brow. "Read the whole thing."

He did, silently, his heart clenching in his chest as understanding came. Then he smiled.

Be a . . .
Pampered Princess
Let someone else do the dirty work for you.
*Estate Sales, Party Planning, Errands, Home
Organization*
Vivienne Stansfield   915-555-8378

Her perfect chin rose. "Andy has already hired me to
do two more houses for the bank. The job on University
really did impress him. If it hadn't, he wouldn't have
hired me for more."

"Of course he was impressed. You did a great job.
Congratulations, Vivienne. You should have your debt
paid off in short order."

"I've already paid everything off."

He should have realized. Her father had returned to
town with money. He must have cleared up the debts and
her name while he was at it. Andy had said he thought
the man would land on his feet.

Max started to say something about that and her
family, but stopped abruptly when he saw a small satin
box discarded in a pile to be thrown out. He took the
steps to the pile and retrieved the box. It was empty.
Turning back, he met her gaze. "You sold your tiara?"

"I did."

"But you loved it."

"No, I didn't. I loved what I thought it meant. And it
was actually worth quite a lot of money. Selling it was
easy."

He saw in her eyes that she didn't mean it. But he saw
as well that she was proud of what she had done.

"You're amazing," he said quietly.

He wasn't sure what she expected, but he could tell it wasn't the smile he felt pull on his lips.

"What's wrong with you?" she asked, her expression growing suspicious. "Are you sick? Dying? Did you come to tell me you've lost your mind?"

"I did that a long time ago. I was crazy the minute I didn't take you in my arms in that damned stone weather tower and tell you that I loved you. That I have loved you for as long as I could remember."

Her chin rose defiantly. "Why didn't you tell me that you knew all about me?"

He set the box aside and crossed the room, stopping in front of her. Even with paint streaks on her cheek she was still beautiful, but now it was in a wild, unruly sort of way. He wanted to pull her close, hold on tight, and make her love him in return. But he wouldn't do that. He made himself keep his hands at his sides, not take her in his arms. This time he wouldn't force her to admit anything.

"I'm sorry that I didn't, Vivienne. I should have told you. But I didn't know how to tell you that I had wanted you for as long as I could remember—how to tell you that I had needed you since that first day I saw you."

"What are you talking about?"

He hesitated. He had never been much for talking. It was action that got results—commanding, demanding, making things happen. But with Vivienne, it was the commands and the demands that continually got in the way. So he knew that if he was ever going to make things right between them, he had to open up, be vulnerable as he had made her be the night they made love. He had to tell her everything.

"Do you remember when you were six years old and

you cut the ribbon at the opening ceremony of your father's plant? I was there that day, and the second I saw you, for reasons I can't explain, I wanted you to see me." He shoved his hands in his pockets. "I'm sure you don't remember, but you walked over to me and reached out—like you really saw me. It was amazing. But just before our fingers touched, your father pulled you away. Then he made you give me money."

Her eyes narrowed, the pale gray intensifying, and he could see her mind swirling back in time.

She tilted her head, her eyes narrowed. "I do remember."

"From then on you represented my greatest dream—and my greatest anguish. You were what I wanted and what I couldn't have. Standing in that crowd, I realized that I had to become someone different from the little boy who needed a dollar shoved in his hands."

"I'm so sorry," she whispered.

"No. Don't be. The truth is, who would I be today if that hadn't happened?"

"You were shaped by your responsibility to your family, Max, not by me."

"Sure, but you planted the seed for me to be more than just a poor kid who lived on a dirt road. It was you, and even your father, who started the change. We all need to find a way to recognize who we really are before we can realize the potential of who we can become."

"That's what you said to me."

"Yes, and I said it because I know firsthand that it's true." His blood thundered through his veins. He needed her to understand. "That day was the first time I realized I was poor—and that there was a different world out there. I worked hard to become more than I had been every day after that. But just when I started college, the first person in my family ever to go, my plans got torn apart when my father left. When my mother died, I had to quit altogether and face the reality of taking care of seven brothers and sisters."

"Which you did and succeeded anyway."

"Yes!" It was all he could do not to touch her, hold her. "But I succeeded because every picture of you I saw or article I read that had you in it motivated me. It was a strange, unsettling mix of dreams and torture that pushed and pulled me through year after year when what I really wanted to do was run. There were days when I wanted to leave the kids so badly that I could taste it. But I stayed, because I knew if I ran at nineteen or twenty or even twenty-one, I'd spend the rest of my life running . . . and I'd prove that I really wasn't more than the poor kid who could never touch someone like you."

Vivienne didn't move, just stared at him.

Max raked his hand through his hair. "I didn't run, but deep down I resented it. I was defiant and angry and I cut myself off from my family emotionally. I supported them and made the tough decisions, but I didn't have anything left inside to give them. In my mind, I had succeeded despite my father, despite your turning away from me.

"The day you walked into my office, I felt like someone had punched me in the gut. I wanted to reach out, but just as badly I wanted to erase every last bit of the little boy who needed you to see him. I realize now I was afraid that despite my success, despite the house and awards, that somehow I'd always be the grimy street kid who had to claw his way through the mud to succeed and you'd always be the pampered princess who'd always pull away from me. But despite the different ways we were raised, I realize now that we are very much the same. Our worlds aren't as different as I thought."

She looked at him as if he had lost his mind, but he had to forge ahead.

"We both grew up too fast, neither of us fitting into the world we lived in. I was alone despite all my brothers and sisters, just like you were alone in your world of privilege."

The urge to touch her had become overwhelming. Only sheer ironclad control kept his hands to himself. She had to come to him. She had to reach out. Not because of his pride. But because he understood that he couldn't force her to love him.

"I realize I should have told you that I had known you forever. But you have to understand that it was you who got me through the years of wanting to run. Just seeing you, reading about you, reminded me of the goal. Yes, you reminded me of the kind of prize I could have if I became a strong, important man—the kind of man, whether moneyed or not, who would gut it out and take care of those kids. Like or not, it was the tease of you that made me want to be a man that I can be proud of today.

"But what I've learned since you walked into my office is that the reality of you is far different from any photograph. You're a fighter, a survivor. You don't have a pampered bone in your body. Instead of whining and taking money from me or anyone else, you pushed up your sleeves and did what you had to do."

His control was barely held. He wanted to pull the ponytail holder from her hair and peel their clothes away until he could sink his body into hers, finding the peace he had never known until her.

But still she stood apart from him, her expression hard and set. His heart pounded with the thought that maybe this would be one battle he could never win, that she would always turn away from him.

Habits died hard, and he nearly stopped right then, his pride surging up. But he quashed it.

"The minute you took the job as the girls' nanny I saw that you weren't a pampered princess. You were never the shallow person I wanted to believe you were. I love you. And I have since I was ten years old. Can you forgive me for taking so long to admit it?"

He was almost certain he saw her wall crumbling.

"I love everything about you," he added relentlessly.

Her delicate brow furrowed. "Everything? No matter what I wear?"

He smiled and nearly touched her cheek. "I love you, Vivienne. I love everything about you, including your blue sky ceilings, your jangle of bracelets . . . and the incredible enthusiasm you have for other people and the unique passion for life that burns through every inch of you." He saw a flicker of something that told him to keep going. "If you can love me just a fraction of how much I love you, I promise it will be enough."

She looked at him, her pearl white teeth sinking into her lower lip. "Even if I wear my Girl Scout Honor T-shirt?"

"Especially if you wear your Girl Scout Honor T-shirt."

She dropped the unused paintbrush onto the paper, her lip beginning to tremble with a fragile smile. "I mean really, what are the chances that either one of us will ever change a whole lot? I'm not sure I can see you not giving commands. And truth to tell, I really am more sequins and feathered mules than khakis and respectable shoes."

Unable to help himself, he took a step closer until they stood just inches apart. "I can live with that. Can you? Can you accept me for who I am?"

Her eyes went wide with understanding—each of them had to accept the other. Then she was in his arms, holding on tight.

"Yes, I can," she whispered. "Oh, Max, I love you."

A tide of relief swept through him, and he laughed as he swung her around. "Then say you'll marry me. Say you'll be my bride."

Epilogue

The room was dark except for the single flicker of a flashlight, casting a tiny face in an eerie glow.

"Shhhh, let me finish," Lila whispered, her voice hushed, as each of the eight seventh-grade girls in their sleeping bags huddled closer. "The storm got worse, with snow and wind coming through an old vent as she sat alone."

Jennie Harland, the most popular girl at Morehead Middle School, shivered in her girl-power nightshirt. Cheerleader Tiffany Sewell pulled her sleeping bag up to her chin, then leaned closer to Missy Crandall, who wasn't all that popular but was really smart and had become an important part of Lila's new circle of friends. No one could deny that Lila's twelfth birthday was an unmitigated success.

But none of that mattered just then.

"What happened next?" Jennie wanted to know, her pretty face scrunched up in anticipation.

"Just then the door burst open, bringing the hero in with a gust of swirling white snow."

The girls squealed their delight.

"How did he find her?" Tiffany breathed.

354 Linda Francis Lee

"He was given her diary. A good thing, as it turned out. Which led him to her."

"What did they do then?"

"He swept her up in his arms and carried her out of the old building like a knight in shining armor."

"Ahhhh," the girls sighed.

"But that's not all." Lila leaned forward dramatically. "He brought her home to his hacienda and set her in front of the fire."

Each of the girls turned dreamy.

"Then he kneeled before her, taking her hands in his."

Jennie sat up straight. "And he kissed her!"

Tiffany came up on her knees. "He pulled her down onto a bearskin rug and had his way with her!"

"No way!" Missy stated, pushing her glasses up on her nose, much as Lila did. "I bet he opened his shirt and placed her ice-cold hands against his chest to warm them."

The adolescents got wide-eyed and nearly swooned.

"Actually," Lila interjected in her no-nonsense voice, "he proposed."

Instantly the girls sighed.

Lila enjoyed the attention as much as she was enjoying her new friends. Without warning, the difficulties of junior high had become less difficult. Even Nicki had a new friend, one she had yet to tell Max about, but that would come. And the sisters knew that Vivi would pave the way, since the new friend was none other than Steve Bonner. While he wasn't a freshman, he was a completely respectable sophomore, and if she had to, Lila was fully prepared to inform Max that he should feel lucky that Nicki had switched brothers.

"Hurry, hurry, tell us how he proposed," Jennie said.

Vivi stood out of sight, her robe wrapped close around her against the springtime chill. She sighed, much like the girls did, as she leaned her head against the door-jamb, remembering.

She felt the instant Max stood behind her, felt his heat. He smelled like wild summer grasses—and joy. He was her hero, and her love.

Pulling her back against him, her whispered in her ear. "What are you doing out of bed?"

"Just checking on the girls."

"Is Lila telling ghost stories?"

Vivi smiled. "No, she's telling the *romantic* story of how Maximilian and Viviandi got married. She calls it 'The Wedding Diaries.'"

Max chuckled, the sound warm and deep against her skin. "Has she mentioned yet Viviandi's wicked step-mother fighting at the reception with her flaky mother?"

"My mother is not flaky."

"I would never call your mother flaky. I'm referring to the fair Viviandi's mother. Especially when I can say much worse about *your* parents, since they left shortly after the first toast at the reception."

"They're traveling."

"They're always traveling."

"True," she said with a shrug.

He kissed her hair.

The girls suddenly sighed again and Max chuckled. "They must have gotten to the part where Maximilian swept Viviandi up in his arms and carried her to bed and made love to her all night long."

"I hope not," she scoffed in a whisper. "They're only twelve."

She could feel his heated smile, and when he lifted her in his arms, she protested. "I want to hear the rest."

"Not to worry," he offered, carrying her upstairs, laying her in the bed they had shared since their wedding night. "I just happen to know how it ends."

Max came over her, supporting his weight on his elbows, his strong palms cradling her face.

"All right," she said, with a grin. "What comes next?"

"As the story goes"—he kissed the delicate skin above her eyes—"the gallant, extremely good looking Maximilian kneeled before the kind of wenchy Vivi—"

"I am not a wench."

"—knowing that he couldn't live another day without her at his side."

A shiver raced through her. "Despite her smart mouth?"

"Because of her wonderful mouth." He leaned down and brushed his lips against hers. But when she would have melted into him, the tale forgotten, he pulled back and chuckled. "Don't you want to hear the end?" he teased.

Vivi giggled, much like the girls downstairs. "Yes, yes, tell me what he said."

"I've waited a lifetime for you, and I won't let you go again."

Vivi's smile turned into a swooning sigh.

"And even if it takes the rest of my life, I will do whatever it takes to make you my bride."

Vivi felt tears burn in her eyes, half-joyful, half-embarrassed. The story had become something of a legend in the short time she had been Max's wife. He had indeed made her his bride, marrying her on Christmas

Eve, just as she had always dreamed, in a surprise ceremony that had moved her as nothing had in her life.

"I love you," she whispered. She bit her lip. "I love you because you're good and kind. And I love you because you accept me despite my silly dreams."

Every ounce of humor fled, his face growing dark. "It wasn't a silly dream, Vivienne. And I was a fool to have thought it was—I realized that the minute I found you in that rundown office building while your parents stayed at the Camino Real."

She felt confused. "What are you talking about? What did you realize?"

"That your dream of marrying at Christmas had nothing to do with being spoiled. You wanted to marry at Christmas so that for the rest of your life you didn't have to spend the holiday alone."

A piercing happiness filled her, and she felt amazed again and again at how this man understood her, this man who she had been certain was everything she didn't want.

Suddenly he leaped up from the bed like an excited kid.

"What are you doing?" she asked.

"I have a surprise."

He looked young and carefree as he pulled out a box. Her breath caught when he came back to her, and she sat up on the bed.

Reverently she pulled off the top and found a beautifully tooled leather-bound book.

"What is this? *The Baby Diaries*?"

His smile crooked at one corner, his hand running up her calf beneath her long flannel gown. "I thought it was time you had something else to write about."

"But I thought that after raising your brothers and sisters, you weren't ready for children."

Suddenly the diary was tossed aside and he had her on her back, his strong body arching over hers. "I wasn't ready for a lot of things until I met you."

He kissed her then, and Vivi held on tight, relishing the feel of him.

"You know," she whispered, "they say it takes courage to find a happy ending."

Max laughed out loud. "Then with you around, we're guaranteed to find one."

And when he kissed her again, she knew she had already found her happy ending—in this man, and in whatever else the future tossed their way.

My Baby Diary

I never believed it was possible that I could feel so much love for any one person.

He has dark hair and amazing blue eyes, and his name is Max. Max Junior to be exact, and we call him MJ.

Sometimes I can hardly believe that I became a bride and mother after I had stopped believing it would ever happen. But dreams do came true, and now I have two men in my life whose worlds seem to stop when they turn around and see me.